Dear Reader,

Writing this book brought back many memories of my childhood. My family lived about forty miles inland in Maine, and one of my mother's favorite outings was to drive to the coast with no particular destination in mind. We ended up seeing beautiful beaches and harbors, old forts, lighthouses, and much more. We peeked in at art galleries, walked out on tide flats, and haunted antique shops.

One thing that stands out in my mind is that on each trip, some point would come when my mother would say, "I smell the sea." She was right, of course—the salt water and ocean breeze carry a distinctive fragrance, and it meets you as you approach the shore. Of course, in those days, we Mainers didn't have air-conditioned cars, and in summer we drove everywhere with the windows of our station wagon open, so I expect we caught the scent earlier than some of those wealthy "summer people" did in their fancy cars.

Traveling with Margaret to Port Clyde for the Art Fair was a special journey for me in the writing of *Hopes and Dreams*. Of course, I had to send the friends to the lighthouse there. I hope you enjoy the journey as much as they do.

Blessings,
Susan Page Davis

HOPES AND DREAMS

MIRACLES *of*
MARBLE COVE

HOPES AND DREAMS

SUSAN PAGE DAVIS

Guideposts
New York

Miracles of Marble Cove is a trademark of Guideposts.

Published by Guideposts Books & Inspirational Media
110 William Street
New York, NY 10038
Guideposts.org

Acknowledgments

Every attempt has been made to credit the sources of copyrighted material used in this book. If any such acknowledgment has been inadvertently omitted or miscredited, receipt of such information would be appreciated.

"From the Guideposts Archive" originally appeared as "Mysterious Ways" by Carolinda Jankel in *Guideposts* magazine. Copyright ©2009 by Guideposts. All rights reserved.

Cover and interior design by Müllerhaus
Cover photo by Jeremy Charles Photography & IStock
Typeset by Aptara, Inc.

Printed and bound in the United States of America
10 9 8 7 6 5 4

CHAPTER ONE

Margaret Hoskins awoke suddenly, sucking in a breath and sitting bolt upright in bed. The room was dark, with a faint glow from the streetlight at the end of Newport Avenue defining the window, and the numbers on the bedside clock reassuringly normal.

Allan rolled toward her. "What is it?"

"Nothing. A dream. Go back to sleep."

Allan took her at her word and settled into his pillow once more. Margaret lay down but stared at the blue 3:05 on the clock. What on earth was her cousin Buddy doing in her dreams? She hadn't seen Buddy for nearly a year—since the family reunion that had included a rather awkward meeting. She and Buddy had reconnected after a long estrangement, but they hadn't stayed in touch since. And now he had wormed his way into her dreams somehow, along with the surf and Marble Cove. Was this about her latent memories of the time she'd nearly drowned and Buddy had come to her rescue?

She tried to remember other details of the dream, but it fragmented and evaporated. The only other thing that hovered in her mind was the sound of bells. That seemed very odd. Buddy and water didn't have anything to do with bells.

With a sigh, she rolled over toward the wall. No sense letting this trouble her. Allan's soft breathing told her that he'd slipped easily back into sleep, but it didn't come so quickly for her. This would be another long day at the gallery, and she couldn't afford to lose an hour or two. She had no idea what Buddy was up to these days, and fretting over the dream wouldn't help him.

Father, give me rest, she prayed silently. As she relaxed, she added, *And keep Your hand on Buddy.*

She awoke again at 6:30 AM. Allan was dressing, and she threw back the coverlet.

"Sleep well?" he asked.

"Yes. I just had a few wakeful moments after that dream."

"What was it about?" He grabbed his shoes and sat down on the edge of the bed.

"*Hmm,* it's misty now. Buddy, I think. And … and bells. I was swimming. That's about all I can remember."

Allan frowned. "Well, don't let it bother you."

"I won't." Margaret headed for the bathroom. When she came out, Allan had left the bedroom. No doubt he was in the kitchen fixing breakfast. Margaret wriggled into her swimsuit and pulled on her cover-up and sandals. As she passed her daughter's door, she heard Adelaide stirring.

Allan looked up as she entered the kitchen. "You're going swimming?"

"Thought I would. I won't be long."

He nodded. Margaret loved to swim, and early mornings were one of the few times she could get to the beach these days. Usually few people came out at this hour, and she loved the solitude as well as the soothing water.

"Be careful," Allan called as she opened the back door.

She turned and threw him a smile. "I will." He was thinking about Buddy and her dream, Margaret could tell. Worrying just a little bit that she might have trouble in the ocean cove again. She'd had a close call that one time when the undertow seized her. But a man had appeared and hauled her to safety. Only much later had she learned that her rescuer was her cousin Buddy. Now every time his name came up, she thought of how close she had come to drowning.

But she would be safe today. She knew the vagaries of the tides and currents on the beach near Orlean Point Light. With her towel hanging over her shoulder, she hurried down the sidewalk past her friend Diane's house and onto the boardwalk that led down to the sand.

She saw only one figure, far down the shore, walking in the direction of the lighthouse. After dropping her sandals and cover-up on the dry beach above the sheet of wet, packed sand closer to the surf, she approached the waterline. Waves persistently kneaded the shore, then retreated. This morning they seemed gentle, with little foam showing when they broke.

The water was cool, but not bad. With the morning sun now well above the horizon, Margaret didn't mind. It was probably as warm today as it would get this season. Some of the "summer people" thought the Maine coastal waters were too cold for swimming, but she found their temperature bracing. And August was the best month for swimming here.

Wading out until she was waist-deep, she splashed a little water on her arms. A wave licked higher, soaking her to her chest, and she plunged forward, into the welcoming liquid. She swam under the surface for several yards, relishing the water resisting her strokes and kicks. She loved pushing against it, using it to propel her through a different environment.

She surfaced and shook the hair from her eyes. Taking her bearings from the lighthouse, she swam out from the beach, stroking powerfully against the calm water of the cove. She loved swimming and the fact that it kept her body strong, even though she was past sixty years old. On that bright morning, she felt as free as a harbor seal—content and in control of her life. Swimming was so much better than sleeping. In slumber, she couldn't control her dreams, but here she could control her body and her thoughts.

Margaret liked where she'd come in the past year or two. She'd successfully launched her new business, the Shearwater Gallery, and her painting was better than ever before—selling better too. She had strong supporters in her friends, and her family was also doing well. God had blessed her richly.

She rolled over onto her back for a minute and floated, gazing up into the sky. Herring gulls circled between her and the puffy clouds. The waves nudged her almost imperceptibly shoreward, and she let them carry her. There was nowhere she would rather be right now than in the water off Marble Cove.

Rolling onto her stomach, she fixed her gaze on the lighthouse once more and struck out for shore. The tide was going in, and it wasn't hard to land close to where she'd left her cover-up and towel. While she was swimming, a sprinkling of summer residents had arrived to enjoy the beach. She waded out of the mild surf and across a few yards of damp sand, and a golden retriever/Lab mix ran down the beach toward her, yipping with joy.

"Hello, Rocky!" Margaret looked past the dog and smiled at Rocky's owner—her friend, Diane Spencer, who was strolling toward her carrying her sandals. Though she was fifty-five years old, Diane kept a trim figure and looked youthful in jeans and a gauzy cotton top.

Diane waved. "Good morning!"

"Hi there." Margaret toweled her short gray hair and drew on her striped cover-up.

Diane walked over and waited while Margaret slipped on her sandals and picked up her towel. "Have a good swim?"

"Excellent."

Diane smiled ruefully. "I wish you'd take someone with you, but I guess worrying about you won't do any good."

"I have a great respect for the water," Margaret said. "I don't go in alone unless I'm sure nothing's out of whack. And besides, there are plenty of people here today." She gestured toward the others now strolling the beach and relaxing in the sand. She and Diane set out walking. They passed a couple of moms who sat on a quilt talking and watching their children splash in the waves.

Neither of them spoke of the day she nearly drowned, but Margaret knew Diane was thinking of it.

"So," she said. "It's been a good summer."

"You talk as if it's over," Diane replied.

"Well, you know, it's so short here in Maine, and we're into August now. We have to savor each day."

"I do, and I know you do too." Diane looked back and gave a sharp whistle. Rocky bounded past them and turned to face them, yipping. She smiled. "It's such a relief having my second book finished!"

"I'm so proud of you."

"Well, look at *you*. Last summer you didn't know if the Shearwater would survive the season."

"That's right," Margaret said. "I feel as though it's a well-established business now, and my painting is going pretty well, if I do say so."

"You *should* say so. It's the truth."

They ambled along and climbed the boardwalk leading up to Newport Avenue, where they lived next door to each other.

"You know," Margaret said, "there's only one thing that's kind of nagging at me. Oh, not everything is perfect, of course, but there's one loose end that I don't like to think about."

"You surprise me," Diane said. "Anything I can help you with?"

"I don't think so. It's Buddy."

"Your cousin?"

Margaret nodded. Diane knew the story of how Buddy had plagued Margaret since childhood and the difficulty she'd had forgiving him. But then Margaret had learned that Buddy was the mysterious rescuer who had pulled her from the water.

"I haven't kept in touch with him since the family reunion. I should have."

"What made you think of him today?"

Margaret smiled wryly. Diane had the instincts of a psychologist. "I dreamed about him last night."

"Really? Good or bad?"

"Neither. But I was in the water, and Buddy was there."

"Were you scared?"

"I don't know. I was a little shaken when I woke up."

"And you started thinking about how you haven't been in touch with him."

"Yes, I guess that about sums it up. That and the bells."

"Bells?"

Margaret nodded uneasily. "I'm not sure where that came from. It didn't seem to fit with the dream."

Diane was silent for a moment. "Do you want an ongoing relationship with Buddy? Or is this just guilt for being angry with him for so long?"

"I'm not sure. But I feel that we should be closer now. I mean, he saved my life that day, and what happened turned his life around. He stopped drinking, and he really had changed the last time I saw him."

"Why don't you call him?" Diane asked softly. "Just reach out and see if he wants to stay in touch. And if you get bad vibes, you can end the call pretty quickly. That might be a prudent way to test the waters."

"Yes, I suppose you're right. Sort of making an overture from a safe distance."

"Exactly."

"I should do that." As they approached Diane's snug cottage, Margaret looked across the street.

"Hey, there's a vehicle in front of the Simpsons' house. I wonder if someone's renting it."

Diane followed her gaze. The house directly across from Margaret's—nestled between the Bauers' Craftsman bungalow and Mrs. Peabody's lavender Victorian—did indeed have a vehicle parked in its driveway. Diane had never met the owners, as they lived elsewhere, but they sometimes rented the house to summer people.

"That would liven up our street."

"You never know. It could just be Mr. Simpson doing some work on the house."

Diane squinted at the SUV. "Could be. I don't know what he drives."

Margaret stopped with her in front of Diane's gate. Rocky waited patiently beside them, panting gently. "I hope this good weather holds. If there are renters, they're probably here for the beach and the Lobster Festival."

"I didn't go to that last year," Diane said. "Did you?"

"Oh, we always go for the food." Margaret chuckled. "It brings a lot of tourists in. In fact, it may be our biggest weekend of the year businesswise, except for Memorial Day. Kind of a last hurrah of summer. I go for the lobster and the corn on the cob and—well, all of it."

"Sounds like a calorie fest." Diane rubbed her stomach. "You're making me hungry!"

Rocky woofed, and both women laughed.

"Rocky's hungry too," Margaret said.

"I'd better get him inside. I'll see you." Diane headed up her walk, and Rocky pranced beside her. Margaret headed for home, smiling.

★ ★ ★

Margaret and Diane met on Saturday with their friends, Shelley Bauer and Beverly Wheeland, for coffee at the Cove.

"Have you got a new neighbor, Shelley?" Diane asked as they settled in at a corner table. "I saw an SUV there yesterday, and it's still in the yard this morning."

"Yes, I think so," Shelley said. "I saw a woman carrying some luggage in yesterday. I haven't met her yet, and I'm not sure if she's alone. I sort of hoped someone with kids would rent the place this summer."

"We'll have to look for an opportunity to meet her," Diane said.

"So, what about the treasure?" The mystery they'd been investigating obviously occupied more of Shelley's mind than the new tenant did, and she didn't hesitate to swing the conversation around to it. After cracking a cipher in an antique prayer book and discovering yet another old key and a map in the mysterious box Frances Bauer had handed down to Shelley, the friends were even more confused and frustrated than ever.

But they were hopeful too.

"You've got to admit, all the evidence we've uncovered points to there being a real treasure," Diane said, looking around at the others expectantly.

"Yes, there definitely *was* one," Beverly said slowly. "As to whether it's still out there or not, I'm not a hundred percent convinced. After all, Jeremiah Thorpe lived in Marble Cove and pastored Old First over two hundred years ago. I mean, really, it's a wonder we've found any real clues about his treasure."

Margaret smiled at her. "You are our voice of reason, Beverly."

Beverly chuckled. "Do you think it's time to talk things over frankly with Reverend Locke?"

The other women eyed each other, as though each one waited for someone else to speak.

At last Margaret said, "I suppose you're right, Beverly. He's tied in to this somehow, and we need to know how."

"And I want to know who that woman was that he was with so often," Shelley said.

Diane nodded. "I don't think he's keeping it a secret. After all, he was seen with her in town. If he didn't want anyone to know about her, he'd have been more discreet."

"I guess you're right." Shelley sounded disappointed.

Margaret sipped her coffee as she thought about the clues they had unearthed. Everything pointed to a lost treasure connected to Old First, the church where Silas Locke was the minister. She came to a decision and set down her cup.

"All right, here's what I think: We should call Reverend Locke and make an appointment to speak with him about all this."

Diane nodded slowly. "That makes sense. We could all go together."

Beverly's smile held a tinge of relief—she was the only one of the four who considered Old First her home church.

"That sounds like a good idea." Margaret pulled out her phone. "How about it? Shall we call now and make it official?"

"So long as you do it." Diane smiled impishly. "I'm on his bad side."

"Yeah," Shelley said with shudder. "I don't want to be the one to call him either."

"Oh, you two." Margaret shook her head, but she smiled as she chided them. "Beverly, are you all right with that, or would you rather make the call?"

"No, I think I'll defer to the eldest on this one."

"Ha." Margaret didn't mind the gentle jab—Beverly was more outspoken now that she knew them all better, but she was still reserved, and it was gratifying to see her feel comfortable enough to tease a little. Margaret had saved the minister's number in her phone, and she pulled it up on the screen. "Here goes."

After she punched Send, they all waited in silence.

"Hello?"

Margaret smiled and tried to put pleasantness into her voice as well. "Hello, Reverend Locke. This is Margaret Hoskins."

"Hello, Margaret. How may I help you?"

"As you know, some friends and I have been looking into Old First's history and trying to learn about Jeremiah Thorpe. We wondered if we could meet with you and discuss what we've found so far. You might be able to add to the data we've accumulated." Margaret glanced at the other women. Diane nodded approvingly.

"Well . . . I'm not sure how I can help. What exactly are the four of you hoping to do?"

"I assure you, our intentions are honorable," Margaret chuckled. "Our hope has always been to locate Thorpe's fabled treasure and use it to help restore the church. I'm not sure how that would work out since last month's fire and all, but we haven't given up the quest."

"I see. Well, I suppose I could see you on Tuesday evening."

"Tuesday evening is fine," Margaret said, glancing at the other three. All nodded, with varying degrees of enthusiasm.

"All right then. Can you come to my house? Say, six thirty?"

"Yes, certainly. And thank you very much." She closed her phone. "Well, you heard. We'll go over at six thirty, Tuesday."

They sat in silence for a moment. Margaret wondered what they had put in motion. They'd been looking for clues about the colonial minister and his rumored bounty for months, but none of the hints they had found seemed to lead them any closer to finding it. Were they in for another disappointment, or would they learn something that would lead them to the treasure they had sought for so long?

CHAPTER TWO

I'm feeling rather daring," Allan said the next day as he drove the family home from the morning service at Our Savior's Sanctuary.

"What, Daddy?" Adelaide asked eagerly from the backseat.

Allan looked in the rearview mirror and smiled at her. Margaret waited to see what he would say.

"Well, you both know I like to cook."

"Yes," Margaret said, "and I'm very thankful." Allan had done most of the cooking in the Hoskins house since they were married.

"You cook good," Adelaide said.

"Yes, he does. Very well," Margaret added. She didn't fuss over Adelaide's speech, but she tried to gently encourage good grammar. While she constantly struggled with being overprotective, she didn't want anything to hold her daughter back—not her Down syndrome, or anything as avoidable as sloppy grammar.

Allan grinned. "I thought I might enter the cook-off at the Lobster Festival this year."

"What will you cook?" Adelaide asked.

"I'm not sure yet. There's the pie contest, but they also have categories for baked beans and seafood dishes. I was thinking of entering that one—the seafood."

"You'd do well in any of those," Margaret said. "You're making me hungry just talking about it."

"Do we get to eat it?" Adelaide asked.

Allan laughed. "Maybe. I think they use the baked beans at the big cookout. Remember last year, we got baked beans and corn on the cob with our lobster?"

"*Mmm,*" Adelaide said.

"Well, you'll have to practice your recipes." Margaret swiveled to give Adelaide a meaningful look. "I'm sure we'll get to try his practice batches."

"Do the pies, Daddy," Adelaide said.

Peace surrounded Margaret. These were the moments she cherished. She'd had many adventures and successes in the past year; it was time Allan did something just for the fun of it. She smiled at him. "I think it's a marvelous idea. Let me know if I can do anything to help you."

"I want to help," Adelaide said.

"Help with my cooking?" Allan asked.

"With the festival."

"Oh." He darted a glance at Margaret.

"What would you like to do to help out, honey?" she asked.

Adelaide frowned, puckering her forehead. "Something with kids."

"*Hmm.* I'm sure there's something that would be perfect for you." Adelaide hoped to take a course in child care in the fall, and this might be good preparation.

"Don't they organize games and contests for the children?" Allan asked. "Adelaide used to enter some of those."

Adelaide bounced up and down a little on her seat. "Yeah. I went in the sack race. Remember?"

"I remember," Margaret said, smiling. They had pictures of their daughter taking part in the festivities a couple of summers, when she was about eight to ten years old. Adelaide had loved doing it. "Maybe you could help the people who set up the games."

"Tell you what," Allan said as he turned the car in at their driveway. "I'll make some phone calls tomorrow and find out who is handling that this year. I'll bet they could use some help, and I'll tell them you're available."

"Thanks, Daddy."

They went inside, and after she put away her purse and Bible, Margaret followed Allan to the kitchen. "I'm glad you and Adelaide want to do something at the Lobster Festival. I think you'll both have fun."

Allan grinned and took a head of lettuce and containers of tomatoes and mushrooms from the refrigerator. "Do you want to enter any of the contests?"

"No, I'll have my hands full at the gallery that weekend. We did a pretty brisk business last year, if I remember right. And I ran off over Memorial Day weekend for the art fair. It's your turn now."

"You can have a booth in the art tent."

She shook her head. "I may put up a display there, with a few prints and brochures, but I want to be in the gallery during the day, not over at the field."

Allan set about fixing lunch, and Margaret sat down on a stool and watched him. After a few minutes, he looked over at her with a quizzical smile.

"What is it, Margaret?"

"Oh, nothing really. I've just been thinking about Buddy the past couple of days. Wondering if I should contact him."

"Did your dream the other night bring this on?"

"I don't know, maybe." She clasped her hands and tried to gather her nebulous thoughts. "I just feel as though I should have followed through on our reunion last fall."

"Is there going to be another family reunion this year?"

"I'm not sure. I haven't heard anything from Beth, and I don't blame her. The last one took a lot of work to organize, and some people didn't seem to appreciate it. But I'm not sorry we went. It helped me to understand Buddy better, and I'm glad we got past our differences."

"So am I. But does that mean you should keep in touch?" Allan shrugged. "Don't do it unless you want to. I know he made you very uncomfortable in the past."

"But I forgave him. And I meant it. So...shouldn't I at least call him once in a while?"

"If you *want* to." Allan's face remained sober as he began tearing lettuce into the salad bowl. "I don't want to see you do something that will upset you again. And think about this—he hasn't contacted you either."

"Maybe he's waiting for me to reach out and show him that it's okay."

Allan opened the utensil drawer and selected a paring knife. "Call him then. But not because you ought to. Because you want to."

"I think I will."

"Good. That's settled, then. Want to set the table?"

★ ★ ★

Jeff came by the Wheeland house Monday morning to pick up Beverly. He'd asked her to take a day off from her business so they could spend some time together before he went off on an assignment that would take him farther afield than usual. He would spend two weeks canoeing the Allagash Wilderness Waterway with an outdoor writer, two state senators, and a guide. Beverly seldom took a full day away from home anymore, and spending it with Jeff made it extraspecial.

She met him at the door a little breathless from jogging down the stairs. She'd hesitated over her outfit and chosen tailored jeans, a striped shirt, and a bulky knit cardigan. When she saw Jeff's well-worn khakis and windbreaker, she relaxed.

After driving to the coastal town of Rockland, they strolled at a leisurely pace along the breakwater that jutted out into the harbor. Jeff needed some fresh photos of the lighthouse that sat on a pile of rocks at the end of the stone barrier. His magazine was doing a spread on the midcoast area and wanted some extra shots for ads and future projects. Waves lapped either side of the breakwater, but the sea was gentle today, and no spray to speak of reached the top of the stone walkway.

"I'm glad it's calm today," she said.

He nodded. "Same here—though my pictures might be more dramatic in windy weather."

When they were about half a mile from shore, Beverly turned and looked back. "I didn't realize how far it was out here."

"Another quarter mile," Jeff said. "Are you tired?"

"No, I'm fine. Interesting to see the town from here, isn't it?"

"Yes, it's a different perspective, all right. Almost the same as you'd see from aboard a small boat coming in."

The sea breeze had picked up, and Jeff zipped his windbreaker. Beverly fastened the big wooden buttons on her sweater, glad she'd chosen layers for this outing. They ambled on over the uneven stones. In places, Beverly had to step carefully to avoid cracks and differences in the height of the big slabs of rock. Jeff reached for her hand to steady her. Dozens of tourists passed them coming in from the lighthouse, heading for shore.

When they reached the prominence at the end of the breakwater, Jeff set about taking photos of the square building at the base of the light, and of the harbor, the town, and the skiffs and sailboats putting out from shore. A gust of wind whipped Beverly's hair about her face until she wished she'd tied it back. She managed to corral most of it, give it a twist, and tuck it up beneath her hat.

She sat on a large rock, relaxing and mostly watching Jeff. For a man who was past forty, he was in terrific shape, and several other women took note as well. He scrambled over the rocks in his rubber-soled shoes, searching for just the right angle. He looked up at her once, from below her on the seaward side, and waved. Beverly smiled and languidly returned the wave. How had she come to this place in her life? She was certain that she didn't deserve it. She lifted her sunglasses for a moment and squinted up at the sky. *Thank You, heavenly Father.* She was only now becoming comfortable with God, as she was with Jeff, but today both relationships seemed to fit well.

"Tired of sitting?"

She hadn't noticed that Jeff had climbed up beside her, and she turned toward him. "No, take all the time you want."

He smiled, and Beverly's heart beat a little faster. That smile was only for her.

"Do you mind if I take one of you? Your dad would love it."

She hesitated, then dared to ask, "How about one of us together?"

Jeff's smile spread across his face. "Yes, I think that could be arranged."

They'd sparred over taking her photo on other occasions, but Beverly felt as though she'd gotten past that. She looked awful—her hair was a lost cause—but for once in her life she didn't care. She wanted a memento of this day.

Jeff had no trouble finding a woman among the tourists who was willing to snap the shot for them. He clambered to Beverly's side again. She slid over on the rock, and he perched beside her, sliding his arm around her. The extra warmth felt good, and so did having him close.

"Great, thanks," Jeff said when the tourist indicated she'd got the picture. He retrieved the camera and turned back to Beverly. "Now one just for me?"

Beverly smiled at his gentle tone. "I look terrible, but..."

Beverly inhaled carefully. Part of getting close to Jeff was letting go of her old fears and inhibitions. He'd taught her so much about herself—her new self.

"For me, Beverly?"

"Okay." She took off her hat and shook her hair out. Let it fly where the wind took it.

Jeff focused the camera from below her and then moved in for a closer shot. He was smiling, so it couldn't be too hideous.

He came and sat beside her again. The other people near them had gathered their things and headed back to shore.

"Jeff."

"Yeah?" He sat down close beside her on the rock and looked into her eyes.

"Do you wonder about my name? Why I changed it?"

"Sure. But I hoped you'd tell me when you were ready."

She nodded slowly. Was she ready now? She hadn't used her given name for years—since Will died. Her father had stumbled over "Beverly" at first, but he'd gotten used to it. Not until Jeff arrived in Marble Cove, bringing a sharp slice of memory with him, had she heard the name "Anna" directed at her again. But he'd done very well not to use it after she'd told him she went by Beverly now.

"You don't need to tell me," he said. "Today's been so beautiful. I don't want to talk about anything that will upset you." He reached for her hand.

"I don't think it will upset me now." She smiled and squeezed his strong, warm fingers. "It must seem sort of weird. You knew me as Anna until last fall. Thank you for understanding and not pressing me for an explanation."

He shrugged. "I don't think of you as Anna anymore, honestly. At first, yes, but now you're Beverly. I think your new name fits you, and I'm glad I've gotten to know you again."

She put her hand up to his cheek for a moment. His eyes softened, and peace washed over her.

"I don't really know why I changed it. At least, I didn't know at the time. Now, maybe I do. When Will...I just needed everything to be different, I think. To make a new start. Afterward."

Jeff nodded, frowning as though trying with all his might to understand.

"I didn't want to be me anymore after he died. I wanted a different life. And so...I stopped being Anna. I suppose it was foolish of me."

"No. I don't think so. But why did you choose Beverly?"

"It's my middle name, after an aunt whom I liked very much. So I thought I would use it. That way it wouldn't seem too strange to Father, and people would accept it." She chuckled. "Imagine if I'd decided to call myself Misty or Françoise."

Jeff laughed. "Or Mehitabel."

"Tawny," she said. "Or Delilah."

"I see you could have gone in any one of a thousand directions. I think Beverly was a good choice. It suits you." He looked at her, his deep brown eyes earnest. "You're the same person, but better. You've grown inside. And you *are* Beverly."

"Thank you."

He nodded solemnly. "One more picture?"

She pressed her lips together for a moment. "They're going to be awful, you know. This wind!"

"I think I got some good ones, but I'll tell you what. I'll let you off the hook now if you'll let me take one another time—soon—when we're inside and you can fix your hair any way you want."

Beverly decided it was better to give in than to know he was looking at these wind-tossed ones. She squeezed his hand. "Okay, it's a deal."

He let the camera hang on its strap and held out his other hand. "Ready for the hike back?"

She let him pull her up, and they made their way back over the tumbled rocks to the top of the breakwater. The breeze was stiffer up here, and she was glad they hadn't waited any longer. She let Jeff hold her hand as they ambled shoreward, discussing where they would eat lunch. They settled on a new place that a friend had recommended to Jeff.

"So, what will you be doing while I'm off in the Allagash?" he asked.

"I've got plenty of jobs lined up now. I'm happy to say that I picked up a couple of regular clients in the last week."

"That's great."

"Thanks. I get inquiries almost every day."

"What's your secret?"

She laughed. "I've been networking, and it's paid off. In fact, I'll be going to Portland a week from Friday—don't know if I mentioned that to you."

"I don't think so." Jeff made a face. "The one time you go to my town, and I'll be away."

"Yeah." She chuckled. "That's life."

"So, what are you doing there?"

"I've been asked to lead a seminar on starting a small business."

"Wow." He paused for a moment, and his eyes widened. "I'm impressed. It sounds like something that will be useful for a lot of people."

"I sure hope so. I miss presenting. I used to do that a lot in my old job."

"You'll be terrific," Jeff said. "Are you staying overnight there?"

"Yes, just the one night. I'll be back late Saturday."

"I'll try to call you. I guess your preparations for that will keep you busy most of the time I'm gone."

"Yes, that and the work I've got scheduled for clients."

Jeff looked toward shore. "I'm thinking maybe I should hire a boat and have someone take us out in the harbor after lunch so I could get some shots from offshore."

Beverly shrugged. She felt lazy and content today, with no deadlines urging her home to her desk. Following Jeff on a spontaneous jaunt would bring this day even nearer to perfection. For once, she didn't care about the time or obligations. "If you want. I'm willing."

"You sure? I don't think it's too rough. But I don't want to bore you to death." He hesitated. "We can pick up a magazine or a book for you if you'd like. Then you'd have something to read."

"No need," she said. "I won't be bored. It's been a while since I looked really hard at what's around me. I'm finding today very relaxing."

"I'm glad. And I've got an extra sweatshirt in the car if you're cold." He squeezed her hand. They came to the end of the breakwater and climbed down to the parking lot. "So...seafood?"

"It would be almost a crime to eat anything else, wouldn't it?"

CHAPTER THREE

Diane couldn't help feeling a little nervous on Tuesday evening as she prepared for the meeting with Silas Locke. She felt as though she'd been on the outs with the minister since he learned that she had carried a bundle of Jeremiah Thorpe's letters away from the church. Maybe the reverend didn't see it that way, but guilt always nagged her when she was around him.

"And where would those letters be now if I hadn't?" she asked out loud as she put on her earring. "Probably ashes. So he should be glad I took them." She leaned in closer to the mirror and grimaced as she fumbled with the backing of one of the earrings. "There." She eyed herself critically, unable to think of anything else she could do to improve her appearance without the risk of Locke thinking she had set out to impress him.

She was glad she had returned the letters, and even more thankful that Reverend Locke had kept them at his house after that, so they had escaped the fire in June. But it still smarted a little when she thought about it.

A glint of light swept across the wall, and she turned to glance out the window. Beverly's car was nosing up her driveway.

Diane dashed to get her purse, then paused to pat Rocky on the head. "I won't be long, boy. At least, I don't think so. See you later."

She locked the door and hurried to the car. Beverly was alone. Diane figured she was picked up first because she had no family to deal with at the last minute. She started to open the door, but paused and leaned down to look in at Beverly.

"Shall we put Margaret in front?"

"If you want. I don't think she'd mind either way."

Diane slid into the backseat. Margaret wasn't that old, but Diane's childhood training still dictated that elders get preferential treatment. "So, have you thought any more about running for mayor now that Evelyn Waters has decided to retire?"

Beverly gritted her teeth. After her role in defeating a development proposal in town, someone had suggested she'd make a great replacement for the town's longtime chief executive. "A little, but really, I don't know that I'm the right person for the job."

Beverly backed out of Diane's driveway. Shelley was already bouncing down the Bauers' walkway, so she stopped the car at the edge of the street and waited for Shelley to hop in with Diane.

"Hi! I feel like I'm jumping in the getaway car. Floor it, Beverly."

Beverly laughed. "Sorry, no can do. We have to get Margaret." She turned in at the Hoskins house and put the transmission in park.

A minute later, Margaret emerged from the house and slid in beside Beverly.

"Good evening, ladies."

They all greeted Margaret, and Beverly headed out onto the street.

"How is your writing coming, Diane?" Shelley asked.

"Actually, I've taken a little time off to just unwind. But I need to get back into it. I'll be starting my third book this week. I've done some research and reading, but I haven't begun the writing yet."

"Quite a complicated process," Beverly said. "Is this one going to be set in the same town?"

"Yes," Diane said. "I like my police chief and some of the other characters. I'm starting to feel as though I should look for them when I walk into the Cove."

Her friends laughed.

Shelley leaned forward and asked tentatively, "So what are we going to ask Reverend Locke tonight? Does anyone have a list of questions?"

"I've been thinking about it," Diane said. The truth was, she had thought of little else all day. "I haven't actually written anything down, though. For starters, we need to know what information he has about the treasure."

"Absolutely," Shelley said.

"Yes," Margaret added. "After all, we've shared some of our information with him."

"I think that's reasonable." Beverly eased the car up Newport Avenue and signaled for the turn onto Main Street.

"And I'd like to know who that lady was," Shelley added. "You know—the one he's been hanging out with."

Diane chuckled. "Well, yes, that has us all guessing."

"She probably has nothing to do with the mystery," Beverly said.

"You never know." Margaret's tone was so mysterious and provocative that they all laughed.

"I guess that's right," Shelley said. "You never know."

Beverly turned in at Silas Locke's driveway and stopped the car. She turned off the engine and took the keys from the ignition. No one moved for several seconds.

"Well, we're here," Diane said. "I suppose we'd better get out."

"He'll think we're strange if we don't." Shelley's seat belt buckle clicked, and they all began to stir.

Diane opened her door and climbed out. She dreaded facing the minister again, but at least this time she had three friends backing her up.

"You do the talking, Margaret," Shelley whispered as they moved toward the front steps. "You or Beverly."

Diane didn't take offense, even though she'd interviewed many people in her years as a journalist. After all, among them Beverly was Locke's only parishioner, and Margaret was the oldest and perhaps the most diplomatic. And she hadn't done anything to offend Reverend Locke. Diane was happy to stall a bit and let the others precede her.

Margaret rang the doorbell, and almost at once the minister opened the door. His glance swept over them, and he stepped back, smiling politely.

"Good evening, ladies. Won't you come in?"

As Diane passed him, she managed a nod and something she hoped resembled a smile. He always made her feel just a smidgen inferior with those glasses and close-cropped beard that gave him such an intellectual air. He held the door, and now she wished she'd managed to be in the middle of the pack, as he was right behind her after he had firmly closed it.

"Just go right on into the living room," he called. "Beverly, you know the way."

They all shuffled into the room and fanned out. He still had the green tweed sofa that looked decades old, and the sailing ship prints on the wall. Lots of books—with anyone else, Diane would probably feel a bond, but Reverend Locke still seemed like a stranger. She was surprised when a woman rose from the comfortable-looking leather armchair to greet them. Shelley, beside her, inhaled sharply and shot Diane a sideways glance.

"Hello." The woman's smile included them all. Her short, dark hair had a few gray strands mingled in, and she wore glasses with copper-colored wire frames. She stepped forward and extended her hand to Margaret, who was closest.

"Ladies," Reverend Locke said from immediately behind Diane. She jumped at the closeness of his voice and edged aside, between Shelley and the end of the sofa. "I'd like you to meet my sister, Priscilla Abbott."

They all stared for a moment. Margaret recovered first.

"How very nice to meet you." She gripped Priscilla's hand. "I'm Margaret Hoskins, and these are my dear friends. Beverly Wheeland is a member of Old First." She turned slightly toward Beverly, who stepped forward and shook Priscilla's hand.

"Welcome to Marble Cove, Ms. Abbott."

"Please," the woman said with a warm smile. "Call me Priscilla."

Margaret glanced at Shelley and Diane. "This is Shelley Bauer and Diane Spencer."

When it was her turn, Diane managed to get close enough for a brief handshake.

"We've all taken an interest in preserving Old First, and we've delved into its history a bit," Margaret added.

"How nice," Priscilla murmured.

"Well, please sit down," Reverend Locke said. "Ladies, make yourselves at home. Priscilla was kind enough to make some refreshments and put coffee on." He glanced expectantly at his sister, and she nodded.

"Yes, I'll bring a tray. Does everyone drink coffee?"

A few minutes later, they were all settled in with their mugs and sugar cookies.

"It was very nice of you to do this," Diane said. "I hope we're not interrupting your visit with your brother."

"Oh no, I was glad to have the opportunity to meet you all," Priscilla said. "Silas and I have been trying to learn more about the Thorpe family for quite some time, and he told me you ladies were instrumental in discovering Jeremiah's letters and some other artifacts."

Diane felt her cheeks warm and wished she hadn't spoken. Did the whole world know about her indiscretion?

Silas probably gave his sister an account of the incident that was none too flattering to Diane. In Priscilla's mind, she was probably a first-class thief.

"We've had a lot of fun in this quest," Beverly said, "but our main purpose was to try to help Old First."

"That's right." Margaret smiled at the siblings. "At first we only wanted to help raise the money to repair and renovate the church. But now . . . well, since the fire, it would take a chest full of treasure to restore it properly, I'm sure."

"If we can help do that," Shelley said, "then all of our efforts will be worthwhile."

"It sounds as though you want the same thing we do," Priscilla said.

Beverly leaned toward their host earnestly. "You know, we've all gained from this experience, even if we never find Thorpe's treasure."

"How do you mean?" Reverend Locke's frown was as disheartening as ever. Diane had decided that he just plain thought they were up to no good.

"We're all neighbors," Beverly said. "This mystery—and the puzzle of the lighthouse before it—brought us closer together. I've never had such faithful friends, and I feel certain God brought the four of us together to support each other."

"Well said, Beverly," Margaret told her. "God certainly has blessed us and allowed us to help each other through some rough times." She looked around at the others and smiled. "Now we hope He will let us help Old First."

"I think that's wonderful." Priscilla looked expectantly toward her brother. "I do hope we'll be able to help these ladies in their quest."

"Do you think you can?" Margaret asked. "We've discovered several clues—that is, documents that mention Thorpe's treasure. But we haven't been able to figure out where he hid it. We still need more information."

"I don't know how much we can help with that," Priscilla said, "but we can certainly tell you what we know about our family."

"Your family?" Diane asked.

Silas arched his eyebrows in her direction. "Yes. I suppose you didn't know. On our mother's side, Priscilla and I are direct descendants of Jeremiah Thorpe."

★ ★ ★

Margaret gulped and tried not to stare. No wonder Silas had seemed proprietary about all things relating to Jeremiah Thorpe. She had never considered that he might have a legitimate connection to the colonial preacher. She tried to discern a resemblance, picturing him in a flowing robe. With that beard, she could almost manage it, though his spectacles were far too modern. The fringe of dark hair around his balding head made him look more ecclesiastical, in her opinion.

Diane leaped into the silence, sounding almost gushy. "How wonderful! We must seem like a bunch of buttinskies to you. Have you traced the family history?"

Silas' face was unreadable, but Priscilla smiled. "Our mother worked on it for years, and she passed on her files to me. I understand we have you ladies to thank for saving Jeremiah's letters from the church before the fire."

"They've made very interesting reading," Silas said and raised his cup to his lips.

"I'm glad," Diane said. She opened her mouth as if to say more, but then took a quick sip of coffee too.

Margaret could see that her friend was embarrassed. Diane was probably hoping the whole letter incident would be quickly forgotten and not hashed over again. She decided to shine the spotlight in a slightly different direction.

"You must have a family tree showing your ancestry. That's fascinating. I only know four generations of my family. My husband's aunt did a lot of work on his, though. Allan goes back to William the Conqueror, if you can believe Aunt Myra's work."

Priscilla laughed. "She may be right, but sometimes things get a little gray. But my mother documented every generation of our family back into the 1600s. She's traced a few of her lines back to England and Ireland. Her goal was to get every branch back to the immigrant ancestor."

"Wow," Shelley said. "That must be hard work. I was never very good at history. All those dates..."

"Well, yes, dates are important in genealogy." Priscilla leaned forward in her chair. "I'd be happy to show you the family tree. I brought some of my notebooks with me, with charts in them."

"I'd love to see it," Diane said.

Margaret nodded. "Oh yes, please do."

Priscilla rose and left the room saying, "Be right back."

"Well," Reverend Locke said, "more coffee, anyone?"

They all declined, and Beverly was the next to break the silence.

"Reverend Locke, I have to ask. Have you and your sister been looking for the treasure, as we have?"

He frowned. "I'm not sure there is a treasure, Beverly. But, yes, over the years Priscilla and I have said many times that we wished it were real and that we could locate it. In all honesty, I've been trying to dissuade you from your search because I thought it was pointless and I was worried someone may get hurt in the process. I mean, Jeremiah Thorpe lived over two hundred years ago. How likely is it, really, that any treasure is left around Marble Cove. If we did find it, Old First's restoration wouldn't be in question, I assure you."

"But we feel the same way," Shelley insisted.

He was silent for a moment. "I'm sorry if I've come across as a bit suspicious of you all. But in my mind, Old First and the congregation that meets there—those are Thorpe's legacy, not some hidden treasure. Of course..." He hesitated, then added, "My sister and I have another purpose. We'd like to clear his name as well."

Margaret nodded. The question of what had happened to Jeremiah Thorpe's money weighed on all their minds. Even if they never found it, knowing what happened to it would set their minds at ease.

Priscilla entered the room as the reverend spoke, carrying a three-ring binder. She gave a little laugh. "We'd both like to dispel Jeremiah Thorpe's reputation as the 'Bandit Preacher,' of course. But it's sort of fun having an ancestor with such a mysterious history."

"I'm sure he didn't do anything wrong," Silas muttered.

Priscilla shrugged and addressed the other four women. "I'm afraid my brother takes that part of it more seriously than I do, being a minister and all. Of course, he doesn't like to hear his ancestor maligned, especially when Jeremiah was a man of the cloth, as Silas is. But it could be worse. It's not as if we're descended from Benedict Arnold."

"That's what *you* say," Silas retorted, but the wry smile he gave his sister belied his words.

Priscilla chuckled and opened her notebook on the coffee table. "I have all of this on a computer program, but I keep all my notes and copies of the documentation and correspondence on paper too. I don't want to lose anything." She flipped a few pages. "Here's Jeremiah's generation."

Margaret leaned in with the other women to scan the page. "So his wife's name *was* Evangeline! Augie was right. We thought that's what the letters said, but the handwriting was so hard to decipher. That's lovely."

"Yes, and her story is very tragic," Priscilla said. "She died on board the ship on her way over here from England to join her husband, and poor Jeremiah had to raise their children on his own."

"How sad," Diane said.

"In one of his letters to Evangeline," Priscilla went on, "Jeremiah mentioned a painting of her that he had with him here in Maine and how much it meant to him to have it. He sometimes signed off with Psalm 17:15, which says something like 'I will behold your face in righteousness. When I awake, I shall be satisfied with your likeness.'"

Beverly frowned. "That verse sounds very familiar for some reason."

"Unfortunately, we don't know what happened to the painting," Silas said. "Thorpe remarried some years later and had a second family. The Mauers here in Marble Cove came from that marriage."

The friends listened closely as Priscilla told of her adventures in exploring the family tree.

"Where did you get all this information?" Shelley asked in awe as she gazed at the charts.

"Well, as I said, my mother had done a lot of it before I started, but the state archives in Augusta and the Maine Historical Society in Portland were very helpful. I found a lot on the Locke family in Portland. But the Thorpes were more elusive, especially because there aren't any Thorpes here in Marble Cove anymore, and it's a matter of finding bits and pieces as you go—I'm sure you have seen that when you looked for material on Jeremiah Thorpe."

"Did we ever," Diane said. She looked up at Priscilla. "Thank you so much for sharing this with us."

Silas cleared his throat. "It occurs to me that we stand a better chance of uncovering anything that's still out there if we cooperate. I admit, I was suspicious of the four of you and your motives for a while, but if your intent is truly to help Old First—"

"It is," Beverly said earnestly.

"Definitely," Diane added.

Shelley smiled at him. "That's been our plan all along, Reverend. We knew it would take a lot to restore that gorgeous old building, and we hoped we could help."

Silas still had the same intensity in his gaze, but his features had softened a bit since they'd begun to talk. Now he nodded slowly. "I'm happy to know that. I'm sorry I misjudged you." He paused, then added, "Of course, you all know about the old map that Jeremiah drew in one of his letters."

"Yes," Beverly said softly. "We found that interesting but unproductive."

Silas nodded. "I reached the same conclusion. The treasure doesn't seem to be close to the church. Of course, if it were in the original building when it burned . . . "

"I think the documents we've found rule that out," Diane said. "I mean, we have to put some stock in the later references to it."

"What about the map we just found?" Shelley asked.

"And the key," Beverly said. "The key had to go to something."

"Map? Key?" Silas eyed her keenly.

"We found a key," Beverly said. "Shelley's mother-in-law had it in her attic. She gave Shelley some old things to look through a couple of weeks ago, and we found the key and map in there in an old chest."

Shelley turned to Priscilla. "We thought maybe that old key and the map had something to do with the treasure. The map seemed to have Jeremiah's handwriting on it. I guess it's a long shot, but—well, anything's possible, right?"

"Definitely." Priscilla smiled at her brother. "That's exciting, isn't it, Silas?"

"Well, yes. But my guess is that the map is probably as useless as the one drawn on his letters. His details were not very accurate, or maybe the surrounding area has just changed too much by now. And, of course, if there really is a treasure, it could have been moved more than once. I wouldn't waste any more time following old treasure maps." Silas sighed. "However," he continued thoughtfully, "if the key really went to something he kept his funds in, then it would be pretty conclusive evidence that the fabled stash did exist. But it seems unlikely—"

"But possible," Priscilla said firmly.

"What can we do now?" Margaret asked. "If there's any way to find that treasure and help Old First, we're ready to dive in."

"That's the question," Diane said soberly. "Where should we look?"

★ ★ ★

Margaret awoke the next morning trembling. She'd dreamed again, she was sure of it, but the details were hazy. She'd been in the water—that much she knew. The fear that shook her made her think she'd been struggling—perhaps reliving her panic of the day she nearly drowned. The water had never scared her like that before. It was only in those moments when she'd realized she couldn't beat the pull of the undertow that terror had swept over her.

Allan sat up and peered at her in the gray predawn light.

"Are you all right?"

"Yes. I dreamed again. The same thing, I think. Water. Swimming."

He edged over toward her and put his arms around her. "Maybe you shouldn't swim for a while."

"I'm not afraid to swim. I'm extracareful now. If there's any question, I don't go in. You know that."

"Yes." He held her close for a minute. "I'm sorry. I wish I could make it go away."

Margaret hugged him. "Thanks. It's weird, because I know I'm safe."

"Was Buddy in the dream this time?"

"I...I'm not sure. I think I woke up before I got to that part. That is, if I was dreaming about that day. Maybe I'm just overtired."

"See if you can go back to sleep." Allan pushed back the covers. "I'll go start breakfast and wake you when everything's ready."

"No, I need to get to the gallery early. I'm expecting a new shipment of paintings from Louellen. It's a real honor that she lets me exhibit her work, and I have to be there when the delivery man comes."

"All right." Allan pulled on his robe. "I'll go start the coffee."

Margaret headed for the shower and tried to shake off her uneasiness. She let the warm, soothing water run over her for several minutes. Allan had mentioned Buddy. Was this crazy new dream pattern connected to her cousin? One thing was for certain—she wouldn't let her night visions spoil her pleasure in swimming. If the paintings arrived today, she'd rise early tomorrow and take a dip before going to the gallery.

Chapter Four

The meteorologist said that August 10 would be the hottest day of the year so far, and he wasn't kidding. Shelley had the used air-conditioner unit in the window of the kitchen while she worked all day. Dan had brought it home after he and his boss installed central air-conditioning in a house. The owners had let Dan and Wayne each take one of the portable units they'd previously used. A perk of the new job, Wayne had said, and Shelley was thankful.

She had thought about putting it in the living room, but her baking kept the kitchen so warm anyway that Dan said it only made sense to put the unit in there, and once he put it in, he didn't want to move it. That meant that on really hot days, the kids played in the kitchen and Shelley worked around them. It was awkward, but better than the alternatives she could think of.

She put a box of toys under the small table in the corner, and they used that recess as a playhouse—out of her way for at least part of the time. But today Aiden and Emma were restless.

"Mama, I need another truck," Aiden said.

Shelley turned around to look at him. At the work island, she was packaging cookies to ship, and she needed another fifteen minutes or so for that. If she didn't put the shipping labels on the boxes now, she might mix them up.

"Okay, go get one from your room."

As soon as Aiden left the kitchen, Emma started to howl.

"It's all right, Emma. He'll be right back." Shelley glanced at the clock. Two hours until Dan got home. She needed to think about supper. She had put chili-burger soup in the slow cooker that morning, and she had salad veggies in the refrigerator, but they ought to have biscuits with that. Or corn muffins. She checked the containers where she placed broken or odd-shaped baked goods. There were nearly a dozen cookies, but only two muffins, and they were blueberry crumb. She sighed. Why hadn't she planned a cold meal for tonight?

Emma toddled to the door and leaned against it, jabbering away. Aiden opened it, and she tumbled out toward him, smacking on the floor. She wailed, and Shelley hurried to pick her up and comfort her.

"Oh, I'm sorry, honey." She looked Emma over and kissed her. "You're okay."

"Sorry," Aiden said contritely. The dog scooted into the kitchen before he could close the door.

"It's not your fault," Shelley said. "I should have been watching her. I knew you were coming back. But you know Prize can't come in here when I'm baking."

"I'll get her." Aiden set a small dump truck and a toy tractor on the floor. "Come on, Prize. You can't be in here."

Prize woofed and hopped about, eager to play, but Aiden knew the rules. The law said no dogs in the commercial kitchen. He grabbed the pup's collar.

"You come. Now."

Shelley smiled as she watched him haul Prize to the door and evict her.

"Good," she told him. "It won't be long now. You and Emma go under the table again, and I'll get these boxes ready. Then we'll take a short walk—how about that? And Prize can go with us."

"To the beach?"

"Sure." Shelley calculated just how long they could be gone and still leave her time to throw a batch of cornbread in the oven. A sudden thought came to her, and she opened the upright freezer. "Aha! Breadsticks. Perfect."

She pulled out a package and set them on the counter to thaw. Eight minutes in the oven and the partially precooked breadsticks would be hot and crusty with their supper. Tonight when she made Danish pastries and muffins for the Cove, she would stir up another double batch of breadstick dough too. Having meal-sized portions in the freezer ready to heat was sometimes a lifesaver.

A few minutes later, she grabbed the sunscreen and slathered some on Aiden and Emma.

"Get your hat," she told Aiden as she put a wide-brimmed bonnet on Emma and tied it under her chin.

Soon they were out the door, with Prize yipping and prancing around them. Shelley buckled Emma into the stroller. She'd have to leave it when they reached the sand at the end of the boardwalk, but at least she wouldn't have to carry the little girl that far. As she straightened, movement caught her eye, and she looked toward the Simpsons' house.

The woman she assumed was renting it had come out of the house and walked toward her SUV. She raised a hand and smiled at Shelley. "Hello!"

"Hi!" Shelley really didn't want to get caught up in a conversation right now. That would cut deeply into the limited beach time she and the kids had. She waved back and pushed the stroller resolutely down the driveway and crossed the street to where the beach path began, feeling just a little bit guilty about not being more friendly. She decided that tomorrow morning, before it got too hot, she and the kids would take some pastries over and introduce themselves. And she would wear something besides her ragged cutoffs and a faded Red Sox T-shirt.

A lot of people had chosen to make this a beach day, though with suppertime approaching, families were beginning to pack their things and decamp. Shelley found a spot several yards back from the gentle surf and spread an old quilt. She plopped Emma in the center, knowing she wouldn't stay there long. Aiden was already crouching in the sand, excavating shells and polished pebbles. Prize joined in by digging a hole nearby. She looked expectantly at Aiden every few seconds and yipped.

With a sigh, Shelley pulled her sun visor lower and settled on the quilt with Emma. She knew from experience that she couldn't read or close her eyes with two young children to watch. Too many tempting things surrounded them. Sure enough, Emma had already toddled to the edge of the quilt and was scooping up a handful of sand. Shelley grabbed her before she could put it in her mouth.

"Don't eat," she said sternly. "Yucky." No use trying to keep Emma still. She rose and called to Aiden. "Come on, let's walk a little and see what we find."

She managed to keep Aiden fairly close and walked along the sand with Emma clinging to her hand. They stopped often to examine treasures and stomp on the edge of the waves that licked their toes. Prize stayed near them and didn't get into trouble with any of the sunbathers. But after only thirty minutes, it was time to head home.

"Do we have to?" Aiden moaned as Shelley folded up the quilt.

"Yes. Sorry, honey. Maybe we can come back tomorrow." *And maybe it won't be so hot,* she thought. She carried the quilt and Emma to the stroller. Aiden trailed behind her, carrying a plastic bag of shells and rocks he'd collected.

When they left the beach path for the sidewalk by Diane's house, Shelley saw that Dan was just easing his pickup into their driveway.

It was too hot to push the stroller any faster, but Aiden spotted his daddy and called out when Dan got out of the truck. Dan turned and waved, then sauntered toward them, swinging his lunch box. Aiden met him on the edge of the pavement, and Dan swung him up in his arms.

"Hi, buddy. Been to the beach?"

"Yup, and me and Prize went wading."

Shelley wiped her forehead with her wrist. "It's a little cooler down there, but not much."

"Want me to push?" Dan set Aiden down and handed him the lunch box. He took over the stroller and rolled it toward home.

"Thanks. How was work?" Shelley asked.

"Hot. We had to be up in an attic for about two hours. They had air in the rest of the house, but not up there."

She eyed his damp, stained shirt and wrinkled her nose. "Sorry."

"Can't help it. At least that job's almost done. We start at a new place Monday."

"Maybe it will be cooler," Shelley said.

As Dan stopped before the front steps to unbuckle Emma, he said, "Oh, I asked Wayne and his wife to have supper with us."

"What?" Shelley stared at him, horrified. "Now? Tonight?"

"No, sorry. Didn't mean to shock you. I meant next Friday."

She exhaled and shook her head. "Someday you're going to give me a heart attack. You know that, don't you?"

He laughed and set Emma out on the bottom step. "There you go, little girl. Get on up there."

Emma tripped and fell and began to cry, and Shelley snatched her up into her arms. "That's hot, Dan. She probably burned her hands and knees." She turned Emma's hands palm-up to examine them. Red patches showed on both. "Come on, baby. Let's put some cold water on that."

Dan, Aiden, and Prize all followed her inside.

"Is it bad?" Dan asked. "I didn't mean to hurt her. I just figured she'd like to climb up the steps by herself."

"I know." Shelley sighed and turned the faucet to cold in the old kitchen. She stuck Emma's right hand under the flow for a few seconds, then gave her left hand the same treatment. Emma kept on crying. "It's really not bad."

"Here, let me take her," Dan said. "I'll distract her."

Shelley handed Emma over and dried her hands. "Thanks. You know, it would have been nice if you'd asked me before you invited the Stovers to dinner."

Dan winced and cuddled Emma against his chest. "Sorry. I guess I figured it would be okay, as long as you had a week or two to plan it."

"Well, that's certainly better than an hour or two." Already her mind was racing. What would she serve them? She had never met Wayne's wife. Was she a good hostess? A meticulous housekeeper, like Dan's mother? Maybe she should hire someone to help her clean before the dinner. Shelley cringed at that thought. They were doing a little better financially now, but not to the point where she could hire a housekeeper. Then there was a matter of clothing. Should she dress up fancy to meet the boss's wife? Probably not. But if she went casual and Mrs. Stover showed up in a nice dress...

"Something smells good," Dan said.

"Oh yeah. It should be all ready. Except the breadsticks." Shelley turned on the oven. "Can you give me fifteen minutes?"

"Sure. I need a shower, anyway."

That wasn't quite what Shelley had in mind—she was hoping he'd watch the kids for a bit while she set the table and got the meal ready. Dan just didn't think like a team player sometimes.

She filled a plastic glass with water and handed it to Aiden. "Put that in Prize's water dish." Emma toddled behind Aiden over to the dog dishes. Shelley turned back to the sink to wash her hands. Another thought hit her—the kids. Should she get a sitter for the night of the dinner? Frances would probably watch them if she asked. And what about Prize?

As if on cue, the dog yelped and Emma started to fuss. Shelley whipped around in time to see Emma sit down hard on the floor and Prize nudge Aiden so hard he spilled the water. *Dan, I need you,* she screamed inside, but she could already hear the shower running.

★ ★ ★

Diane felt a little apprehensive as she answered the phone on Friday afternoon. The caller ID told her that her agent was calling, and she didn't have much to report. She'd gotten a little lazy, and she needed to start working seriously on her third book. Not a good time to have a chat with Frieda.

"Hey, Diane, I have some news from your publisher."

Frieda sounded upbeat, but her words didn't match her tone somehow.

"Is everything all right?"

"Well, Jane loves your second book."

Diane exhaled. Jane Veers was her editor in New York, and hearing anything positive from her was a relief, especially after the struggles Diane had experienced in plotting her second mystery novel. Still, she knew somehow what the next word out of Frieda's mouth would be.

"But," her agent continued. There it was, the dreaded killjoy word. "Your publisher isn't as happy."

"Why not?" Diane dared to ask.

"Well, it seems the sales on the first book are pretty flat."

"I was afraid of that. We had those first few reviews, and then nothing. What happens now?"

"I'm not sure. I'll keep you posted on anything I hear from them, but I wanted to give you a heads-up. Diane, it's possible they might not proceed with the third book."

Her stomach felt odd, as though she hadn't eaten in a long, long time. "Okay. So, should I not write it, or what?"

"No, I wouldn't advise that. Go on with the story. If they decide not to publish it, we can shop it elsewhere. I'd say don't give up hope."

"So it still could go forward?"

"It could, and you need to have a manuscript ready if they decide to do that. On the other hand, if they kill this one, you have to realize that this happens all the time in the publishing world. It doesn't mean your books are no good, or that they don't like you, or anything like that. The truth is, times are tough everywhere financially, and publishing houses are being a little conservative right now. They're only putting out books they're sure will make a profit."

"So I'm in the red on the first one?"

"Not necessarily. When we get your first royalty statement, we'll have a better idea."

The whole conversation left Diane feeling adrift. She got up and went to the kitchen. Rocky rose from his bed and padded over to stand beside her as she filled a cup with water and put it in the microwave. She stooped and patted his head.

"A most unsatisfactory conversation, boy." *More like devastating,* she thought. It wasn't that she'd planned on some income beyond the advance the publisher had paid her. Now she had months of her life invested in the mystery series. She would have to tell her friends and her children that she was a failure.

When the microwave beeped, she took out the cup and plopped a chai tea bag in the water. She carried it to the couch and curled up in one corner, cradling the mug in her hands. Rocky settled on the rug beside her and whined plaintively.

"Yeah," Diane said. "That's how I feel."

★ ★ ★

"There's a big article in the paper about Evelyn Waters," Beverly's father said when she brought coffee for the two of them into the library. Mrs. Peabody followed her with a dish of apple slices and a few crackers.

"Here's your snack. Is that because she's stepping down as mayor?" She set down his coffee mug.

"Yes, it gives highlights of her time in office. She'll pass the baton to someone else in November."

"This constitutes a big shakeup in Marble Cove," Mrs. Peabody said as she set the dish on the end table between their chairs.

"What do you mean?" Father asked as he folded up his newspaper.

"Well, Evelyn's been mayor for a long time, and her father held the office before that. If we get someone new in there..." She looked meaningfully toward Beverly.

"An end to the Waters dynasty," Father said.

"How long has Evelyn served?" Beverly sat down in the comfortable chair next to her father's and sipped her coffee.

"Oh, maybe thirty years. At least twenty." Mrs. Peabody shrugged. "Maybe it's time someone other than a Waters was mayor. On the other hand, things have gone pretty smoothly—other than that dustup about the development."

"Yes." Beverly frowned. She could scarcely forget that episode, as she had just spearheaded a campaign against it.

"That Dennis Calder." Her father shook his head.

Beverly still had mixed feelings about the whole thing. She had liked Dennis and considered him a friend until he proposed the real estate deal. It would have brought jobs to

Marble Cove—but at what price? She didn't want to rehash the whole issue, so she decided to change the subject.

"So have you made up your mind about running, Beverly?" Mrs. Peabody cocked her head to one side and surveyed Beverly. "I thought you were considering it. You could do the job."

"Yes, you could," her father said. "The chamber chairperson seemed to think so too, when she mentioned it to you."

"Yes, she did." Beverly well remembered that conversation with Charlotte Vincent. She'd thought about it since Charlotte had made the suggestion, but she really hadn't been able to picture herself taking over Evelyn Waters' office and duties.

"Of course, you have a lot going on already." Her father sipped his coffee but watched her expectantly over the rim of his mug.

"I don't know." Beverly glanced back and forth between them. "I hardly think I'm the one to step forward." However, the idea of having more input on the town's future appealed to her. The mayor's office didn't wield a lot of power, but the person in that position would have her finger on the economic pulse of Marble Cove and be able to initiate civic projects with comparative ease. "What does the mayor do, anyway, besides preside at the Fall Fair and the Christmas Stroll and the Lobster Festival?"

"Lots of things," Mrs. Peabody said. "For one, Evelyn has the tiebreaker vote when the city council makes a decision."

"Really?" That was something to consider. A divided council would need someone who truly had Marble Cove's best interests at heart.

"I wonder if anyone else has taken out papers yet," her father said. He put his mug down on a cork coaster and opened the newspaper again. "*Hmm*, it doesn't give any indication of that, but it says anyone who wants to run would have to file nomination papers by August thirty-first."

"You should look into it, Beverly. I'd vote for you." Mrs. Peabody turned and headed for the kitchen.

"Well!" Beverly stared after her, wondering anew whether she should be taking all this to heart.

Her father lowered the newspaper. "Are you seriously considering this?"

"I've been mulling it over. But I don't know if I'd be able to get enough votes. And I may not even qualify. After all, I've only been a resident of this town for a short time."

"That's true." Father seemed to shelve the topic and reached for his snack dish. "*Hmph*."

"What's the matter?" Beverly asked.

"Fuji apples. She knows I like the tart ones."

"That's my fault. I shopped yesterday, and they didn't have the ones you like best. I did get a few Fujis and a few McIntosh."

"Then why didn't she give me the McIntosh?"

"I don't know. Maybe she plans to make a pie or something." Beverly stood and reached for his dish. "I'll go get you one. Give me that."

"No, no, I'll eat it," he said. "Unless you want it."

She didn't, really, but he looked hopeful. "I'll eat the Fuji. You can work on the crackers while I go get you a McIntosh." As she made her way to the kitchen, she knew she would have to smooth Mrs. Peabody's ruffled feathers over the apple issue. After all, keeping peace between her and Father was much more important than who would run for mayor.

Chapter Five

As Diane left her house Saturday morning to take Rocky for a romp on the beach, he let out a yip and raced down the driveway. He stood at the end, barking. On the other side of the street and up one house, a woman was coming out the driveway with a Jack Russell terrier on a leash.

Diane had made an effort to teach Rocky never to leave her yard unless she was with him, and most of the time he cooperated. She spoke to him, hoping he'd be on good behavior this morning.

The terrier began to bark and pull at his leash, and the woman walking the dog looked their way. Diane smiled and waved. The newcomer waved back and hesitated. Diane decided to take the initiative.

"Come on, Rocky. Let's meet some new friends. But you have to behave." She always took her dog's leash along when they went out, and when they walked through town she kept him on it. On beach runs, it was mostly a "just in case" measure. But meeting a new dog was one of those times when she didn't want to leave anything to chance, so she bent and clipped it to Rocky's collar.

As she'd hoped, the woman had just reached the sidewalk at the end of the rental house's driveway, and Diane stepped quickly forward, with Rocky bouncing eagerly at her side.

"Hello," she called, and the newcomer stopped and waited until she and Rocky were on her side of the street. "I'm Diane Spencer, and this is Rocky. That's a beautiful dog you have."

"Oh, thank you. He's Gallant, and I'm Terri Glazier. Pleased to meet you." She held out her hand, and Diane shook it while the two dogs circled as far as their leashes would allow and sniffed each other. Terri's auburn hair framed her face in an expertly cut style, and she wore discreet makeup. She was probably close to Diane's age, but she obviously took pains to keep up her image. Her oatmeal capris and peach-striped top, with a long necklace of green and peach stones, made Diane feel just a little countrified in her khakis and plaid camp shirt.

"Are you and Gallant headed up to Main Street, or down to the beach?" she asked.

"Oh, the beach sounds good, but I wasn't sure if dogs were allowed."

"They're fine, as long as you clean up after them." Diane laughed and patted her canvas shoulder bag. "In fact, you can let them run free down there if there aren't too many people. Today there may be a lot of families, but in the off season, Rocky and I have the beach to ourselves some mornings."

"Sounds ideal. Lead the way." Terri fell into step with Diane, and the dogs padded along calmly, though Gallant wriggled now and then and tried to stop and sniff something on the edge of the path.

"How long are you here for?" Diane asked.

"For the rest of this month. I take it you live here."

"Yes, that's my house." She waved toward her cottage.

"Right next to the beach."

"Yes. That means all the visitors park here at the end of the street, and everyone walks past my place to get to the path, but I don't mind. And Rocky loves it."

Terri smiled. "It seems like the ideal location, but I suppose that's because I'm an outsider. Do you stay here all winter?"

"Actually, last winter was my first. I moved here last year in the spring. Where are you from?" Diane stepped down onto the sand.

"California."

"Really?" She stopped and stared at Terri. "You drove all the way out here?"

Terri laughed. "No, the SUV's a rental."

"Oh. Are you by yourself? You and Gallant, that is?"

"For now." Terri's face scrunched up for a moment. "I'm hoping my husband will join me next week. He's way too committed to his work. Silly me, I thought I could get him to come for the whole month. Guess I should have known better. I put off coming myself for a week, hoping he'd get with the program. But it was *my* program, not his, and ... well, I'll be happy if he shows up at all."

"I'm sorry." Diane wasn't sure quite what to say, but Terri sounded so unhappy she couldn't leave it at that. "I have some wonderful friends on Newport Avenue, and our little town has a lot to offer. I hope you'll enjoy your stay."

"Thank you." Terri's face cleared and she said brightly, "How about you? Is there a Mr. Spencer?"

"There was. Eric died about three years ago. Heart attack. It was . . . unexpected."

"How awful for you."

"Yeah." Diane shrugged. "I've come to terms with it. God has really blessed me. And I have a couple of grown-up kids, and they come visit now and then. But you know how it is—they have their own lives."

"Oh, do I ever." Terri smiled wryly. "We've got a son who's like that. He comes around at holidays and pops in now and then, but I never know when it will be or how long he'll stay."

Justin and Jessica weren't quite that spontaneous, and Diane was glad, but she didn't say anything. Terri didn't need to get the impression that her kids were perfect.

"At least you see him now and then."

"Yeah." Terri paused and looked down at her cork-soled sandals. "Guess I didn't pick the best footwear for this outing."

Diane laughed. "I just take off my shoes down here. We can leave them anywhere and pick them up when we come back."

Terri looked doubtful. "Are you sure?"

"I do it all the time." Diane shucked her low canvas shoes and set them off the path.

"Okay, I'll trust you on that one." Terri lined up her sandals precisely beside Diane's shoes. "Now what?"

Diane looked down the beach toward the lighthouse. "*Hmm*, there are quite a few people that way. What do you say we go toward the cliff? We can let the dogs loose for a little while, if you think Gallant will stay close to you. If you want to wait until he's gotten used to this place, that's okay."

"I think he'll stay near me and your Rocky," Terri said with a chuckle.

"They do seem to have hit it off." Diane unclipped Rocky's leash, and Terri removed Gallant's. Diane led them along the beach northward, toward the rockier part where nobody swam. The two dogs raced ahead in an erratic path with lots of detours. "So, how did you hit on the name Gallant?"

Terri chuckled. "He's the opposite of my husband. Pays me lots of attention."

Diane wasn't sure how to respond to that.

"So what do you do?" Terri asked. "Do you have a job?"

"No, I . . ." Diane gulped. "That is, I'm self-employed."

"Oh?" Terri's eyes lit with interest.

"I'm a writer."

"Fantastic! What do you write?"

"Mysteries." Terri didn't seem shocked or overawed, so Diane continued, "I'm working on my third book. The first one is out, and the second just went to my editor."

"I'm impressed. And I love mysteries. Is it a series?"

"Yes, cozy mysteries."

"Fun!"

Diane smiled. Terri's enthusiasm suddenly made her feel like writing was worthwhile again. And Frieda was right—if her current publisher decided not to take the third book, they could look for a new market.

Rocky barked, and she looked at him. He and Gallant had found a small tide pool, and Gallant had waded right in, with the water touching his belly. Rocky obviously thought this was bad form and woofed his disapproval.

"This is almost how I found Rocky." Diane hurried toward the dogs. By the time she and Terri arrived, Gallant was out of the tide pool and frolicking between the rocks. Diane sat down on a barnacle-encrusted boulder and recounted to Terri how she'd acquired her dog. "He healed up pretty fast, and no one ever claimed him, even though I advertised."

"He's been a wonderful companion for you, I can tell," Terri said. "He seems like a terrific dog."

"Yes, I've been so thankful for him—he's a real blessing." Diane rose. "I should head back. I really am supposed to do some work today."

"And I want to drive to a grocery store and stock my refrigerator. Where's the best place for that?"

They called to the dogs and ambled back along the shore as Diane gave her the rundown on her options for groceries. The tide was coming in, so they moved a little higher up the beach, and waves swept over the footprints they had left earlier. Soon they were back at the boardwalk.

"Looks like you were right," Terri said with a laugh as she retrieved her sandals. A dozen more pairs of shoes had joined theirs in a sloppy lineup.

They clipped their leashes to the dogs' collars and walked up to the end of Newport Avenue.

"I like to shop locally," Diane said, "but once in a while I go to a bigger town. Let's face it, you can't get everything here. But you can get all the essentials and, to me, that convenience is worth a lot."

"Especially with gas as high as it is this summer," Terri agreed. "I'll give the grocery on Main Street a try."

"Say, can you come in for a second?" Diane asked when they reached her driveway. "I'd like to give you one of my books, if you think you'd enjoy it."

"I'd love it," Terri said.

They went inside, and Rocky hopped about, obviously excited to have another dog in his private territory.

"Calm down," Diane told him.

"Your house is charming." Terri looked about with an appreciative smile.

"Thanks. I had a lot done when I first moved in—mostly painting and other cosmetic stuff."

"It's lovely. The house I have is all right, but it's very 1980s beach house."

"I've never been inside it," Diane said.

"Come over sometime, when you're not too busy. We'll have a cup of tea."

"Thanks." Diane took one of her paperback mysteries from on top of the bookshelf in the living room. "Here you go. I hope it gives you a few hours of enjoyment at least."

"I'm sure it will," Terri said. "*The Lighthouse Goes Dark.* Great title—and I love the cover! Thank you."

She took her leave, and Diane shut the door and turned back to Rocky, who whined and headed for his bed. Diane laughed. "Well, we both made a new friend today, didn't we, boy? I guess I'm a little let down too, now that they're gone." She checked his water bowl and took it to the sink to fill it. "I like Terri, and you obviously like Gallant. I just hope Terri likes my book as much as she thinks she will."

★ ★ ★

Shelley sat on the couch with four cookbooks spread out around her on the cushions, and her laptop set up on the coffee table. Emma and Aiden had played quietly for fifteen minutes with Aiden's toy trucks and a set of large building blocks. But now Emma seemed unhappy. She let out a yelp and jerked away from Aiden, clutching a bright yellow block to her chest.

"Emma, give me that!" Aiden leaned over and tried to pry the block from her tightly curled fingers, which sent Emma into a wail.

"Stop it, Aiden," Shelley said.

"I need that for my warehouse. It's the last yellow one. Make her give it to me, Mama."

The doorbell rang, and Shelley frowned as she shifted her cookbooks and rose. "No. Use a different color. Emma can play with one block if she wants to."

If she weren't so harried, she might sit down with them and try to ease Emma into swapping for some other toy. But someone was at the door, and she still didn't know what she would serve when Mr. and Mrs. Stover came to dinner. She'd hoped Dan would be home all day Saturday, but Wayne had asked him to put in some time today to finish the job they were on. That way they could start a new job on Monday—and it would mean some extra money in Dan's check this week, which they badly needed.

Her friend Allie Fox stood on the front porch with her little boy Bryce.

"Hi." Allie gave a nervous giggle. "We got done sooner than I expected in town. Are you busy baking or anything?"

"Not at the moment. Come on in." Shelley turned to find Aiden right behind her and Emma toddling across the room. "Look, kids. Bryce is here."

"Hey, Bryce!" Aiden grinned and hopped up and down on his toes. "Come help me build a garage."

They tore for the block pile.

Allie surveyed the couch area. "Oh, you *were* busy. You should have said so."

"No, really. I was trying to figure out what to cook when Dan's boss comes to dinner, but I don't have to know today. There's time. I'm just frustrated because Dan sort of sprang it on me."

"Oh?" Allie frowned. "Anything I can do?"

"I don't think so, but thanks. Pardon the toy mess." Shelley hastily stacked the cookbooks. She waved toward the chair. "Have a seat. Sorry it's so dark in here. I'm keeping the drapes shut to keep it cooler. We've got one air-conditioning unit, but it's in the new kitchen. Maybe someday we'll be able to afford another one."

"I know what you mean," Allie said. "I've got one little unit that I think is on its last legs. It barely keeps one room cool, so I have it in the bedroom. The last couple of nights, Bryce has slept in there on an air mattress because it was so hot in his room."

"Well, this heat won't last. Pretty soon we'll be complaining about how cold it is and wishing for summer again, so I guess we should enjoy it."

"That's one reason I wanted to stop by today. We won't stay long, but I thought maybe Monday afternoon we could take the kids to"—Allie glanced at the three youngsters and then lowered her voice—"the B-E-A-C-H."

"Sure," Shelley said. "We go down there a lot of days. In fact, I'll probably take them this afternoon, after their naps. Would you want to come back then?"

"I can't. But we can come after lunch on Monday."

"Perfect."

Allie gave her nervous giggle. "So, sort of scary, meeting the boss's wife?"

"Yeah. I don't have the slightest idea how to act around her. I mean, should we be like friends, or what? Dan and his boss didn't hit it off so well at first. They get along pretty well together now, but I just feel strange about this whole thing."

"I don't blame you. Let me know if...hey, do you want a sitter that night? I could take Aiden and Emma for a few hours."

"Wow, that would be great. I haven't had a chance to ask my mother-in-law yet. I think the kids would love being with you. It would be something different."

"What night is it going to be?"

Shelley wrinkled her forehead. "Let's see, I think it's...*hmm*... Hold on." She walked out to the kitchen and looked at the calendar. "I think it's the twenty-fourth, but I'd better double-check with Dan."

"Sounds fine. All right, I'll see you Monday. I know you're busy." Allie looked toward where the children were playing. "Come on, Bryce. We have to go."

Her son's face screwed up, but he laid down the block he'd been holding and stood. "Bye, Aiden."

"Bye. Come back soon."

For the first time, Shelley was thankful for her helpful friends. Now, if she could just decide what to serve and what to wear for the dinner, she'd be halfway to success.

A stray thought of the renter in the Simpsons' house next door crossed her mind, but she shoved away the pang of guilt. It was too hot to go out visiting. The lady looked rich and very put-together. Shelley wouldn't want to meet her wearing shorts and a tank top, but in this sweltering weather, she'd die in anything heavier. And she hated taking the kids anywhere but the beach except early in the morning or after the sun had started to go down. Maybe tomorrow would be cooler.

★ ★ ★

It was getting so that Diane dreaded Frieda's calls. She hoped her agent couldn't tell how stressful she found their conversations, but sometimes her throat tightened, and she feared she would burst out in tears when she tried to talk. That would be so unprofessional!

"...So they're questioning the wisdom of producing the third book when the sales are disappointing on the first one."

Diane gulped. "But they're still going to print the second one, right?"

"Oh yes, I'm sure they are. Jane told me it's in editing now. But I wanted you to be prepared, Diane. They may want to buy out your contract."

"You mean, like a kill fee?"

"Exactly. You have another payment due when you hand in your third manuscript. If the publisher decides not to produce that book, they may offer you that payment, or part of it, now in lieu of publishing the third book."

"So..." Diane swallowed hard. "What does that mean to me? Do you still think I should I go ahead with writing it, or just wait?"

"As I said before, I think you should proceed with writing," Frieda said. "We don't know yet, and it would be a shame if they decided to go ahead and you hadn't written anything."

"Yeah, I guess so. And you did say that we could take it somewhere else if they don't print it. Is that okay?"

"Let's see what happens," Frieda said. "If this contract doesn't fly, you might want to start a new series with a new publisher, but you could probably adapt the story from your third book. And the contract you have now doesn't forbid you to take the same characters to another publisher if you stop working with this one."

"*Hmm*. Good to know. Okay, I'll keep an open mind." Diane leaned back in her office chair and pried her shoes off with her toes.

"Your stories are good," Frieda said. "You and I both know it. This is just a very bad time economically. You're not the only writer going through this. I know it seems catastrophic to you, but that's because it's your first book series. I really believe you're going places with your books."

"Thanks." Diane sounded like a mouse, squeaking in fear. "And if this company doesn't publish it, we'll find another one that will."

"That's right. And if I can't sell this one, you'll be working on a new proposal that *will* sell. Don't give up now, Diane."

"Okay."

"I want you to stay on track and keep writing, you hear me?"

Diane sat up straighter. "I'll try. Thanks, Frieda."

When they'd signed off, she sat for a minute, staring at the screen saver on her monitor. Could she really write this book with no assurance that anyone would publish it?

That's silly, she told herself. *You wrote the first one before anyone had even looked at your writing. And they loved it. So why do you think you need a contract and a publisher waiting with bated breath to write another one?*

She let out a long, slow breath and closed her eyes. *Lord, I'm scraping bottom here. I know Frieda wanted to buck me up, but I feel lower than Death Valley right now. Please help me to go ahead and do the work anyway. Help me to do it well.* Tears flooded her eyes, and she squeezed them tightly shut. *Please, heavenly Father, help me to make this the best book yet.*

CHAPTER SIX

Diane strolled down the aisle of the pet store, pausing to watch several of the animals. She could have bought Rocky's dog food at a bigger store when she got her groceries, but she loved to come here. She smiled at the gerbils lolling in the wood shavings that made their bedding. Jessica had kept a gerbil when she was a little girl. Those were happy days, with Eric alive and the children at home. In contrast to her present worries, it seemed like the ideal life.

As she moved on to the bird section, her mind went back to her last conversation with her agent. Frieda had a lot of experience in the publishing world and must know what she was talking about. Still, Diane couldn't overcome the depression and feelings of rejection that came each time she thought about the latest news. The commotion the parakeets and lovebirds made chirping around her reached through the gray clouds of her contemplation, and she smiled.

"You pretty things!"

"Hello, Diane," Lee Waters called as he came around the corner at the end of the aisle.

"Hi, Lee. I'm just here for dog food, but I thought I'd say hi to everyone."

He grinned. "They love company. Say, you aren't interested in giving Rocky a playmate, are you? I've got an adorable cockapoo on consignment. His owner died, and he really needs some love."

"Don't tempt me, Lee. One dog is truly all I can handle."

"I understand." He smiled. "I got in a new line of chew toys."

"Oh, I'll have to look at those."

"Great." He glanced at her shopping cart. "Trying a new kind of dog food?"

"No, I—" Diane stared down at the twenty-pound bag she had hefted into her cart. "I guess I wasn't paying close enough attention. You're right, this isn't the brand I usually give Rocky."

"I'll get it for you if you like, and take it up to the checkout," Lee said, stooping to grab the sack.

"Thank you," Diane said. Determined not to brood on the fate of her books, she browsed for a few more minutes and chose a new toy and some canine nail clippers.

At the checkout, Lee rang up her purchases and handed her the receipt. "I don't suppose you'd sign a petition for me?"

"What sort of petition? Animal rights or something?"

"No, it's so I can have my name put on the ballot for the election. They call it a petition, but it's just a collection of signatures from people saying they think I'd be qualified."

Diane eyed him in surprise. "For what?"

"Mayor."

She managed to keep her jaw from dropping. After a moment's reflection, it made sense. "That's right. Your mom is stepping down. So... kind of keeping it in the family?"

He chuckled. "I suppose so. My grandfather was mayor too, for quite some time. If you sign for me, you have to be a registered voter and residing in Marble Cove. You fit that profile, don't you?"

"Well, yes." Diane stared down at the clipboard he'd handed her. It already had a list of nineteen voters, with their names and addresses written in by hand. She noticed Leo Spangler's name among them.

"It doesn't lock you into voting for me when the time comes. It just says that you think I'd be qualified to do the job."

What did she really know about Lee's qualifications? Still, he seemed to be doing a good job running his business. The part-time mayor's post couldn't be too demanding. Diane couldn't see any good reason not to endorse him.

Her earlier conversation with Beverly came to mind, but she hadn't seemed very enthusiastic about running for office, and she hadn't mentioned the matter since. If Beverly was serious about it, she'd have said something. Diane would feel funny if she turned Lee down now.

"Sure, I'll sign it." She bent over the counter and signed her name, then printed it and her address.

"Thanks, Diane. I appreciate it."

"How many signatures do you need?"

"Fifty. Then the town clerk will verify them to make sure they all qualify. She said to get a few extra just in case."

"You'll get them."

"I hope so. I haven't been out canvassing yet, but I seem to be doing okay right here in the store." He picked up the bag of dog food. "Let me put this in your car for you."

★ ★ ★

Shelley lifted the stroller down off the porch and went back inside for Emma.

"Come on, Aiden. No, leave your toys here. We won't be gone that long." She scooped up Emma and went to the counter for the plastic container of baked goods she'd prepared. Aiden and Emma were both spotless for the moment—but she knew that wouldn't last long. She wanted to get this over with fast.

The sky had clouded over and it was still warm, but a little cooler than it had been earlier in the day, with a fresh breeze off the cove. She'd chosen denim capri pants and a sleeveless white blouse for herself and taken time to braid her long hair and apply lip gloss. She might not stack up to the chic renter's standard, but at least she didn't look like a beach bum.

As they reached the end of the driveway, Diane nosed her SUV down Newport Avenue and slowed between her house and Shelley's. She lowered the driver's window and called, "Well, hi! Where are you all headed?"

"We're going to meet the renter at Simpsons'." Shelley held up the plastic container. Diane would understand.

"Oh, you'll like her."

Shelley pushed the stroller out into the street, closer to Diane's vehicle. They were the last two houses on Newport, and the only traffic was people headed to the beach. "You've met her?" she asked in a softer tone.

Diane grinned. "Yes, we walked our dogs together this morning. She's very nice."

Shelley nodded slowly.

Diane seemed to read her mind. "Would you like me to go with you?"

"Would you? I'd really appreciate it. She looks kind of…well, upscale. You might lend me some credibility as a neighbor and sane person."

Diane let out a laugh that was almost a snort. "Hold on five seconds, and I'll be right there. Let me get this thing out of the street."

A minute later, they walked together up the sidewalk on Shelley's side of the street with Diane carrying the food and Shelley pushing the stroller. Aiden trudged behind them.

"Where's Prize?" Diane asked.

"I shut her inside," Shelley said. "I wasn't sure we wanted to have a doggie encounter the first time we humans meet."

Diane smiled. "Probably wise, but Gallant was very well behaved with Rocky this morning."

"He's a really cute dog," Shelley said. "Aiden spotted him out the window this morning and got all excited."

When they reached the rental house, Diane walked up onto the porch and rang the bell while Shelley removed Emma from the stroller.

Terri opened the door with an expectant smile. "Diane! Come right in."

"I brought a few friends," Diane said. "I hope you don't mind, and if you're busy we'll just say hi and skedaddle."

Terri looked past her and smiled at Shelley. "Oh, you're my left-hand neighbor, aren't you?"

"That's right." Shelley straightened with Emma in her arms. "I'm Shelley Bauer."

"And with her are Aiden and Emma," Diane said. "Shelley is a professional baker, and she wanted to bring you this." She placed the container in Terri's hands.

"Oh, thank you! Can I peek?" Terri lifted one corner of the lid and grinned. "*Ooh.* I can tell this is going to be fun. Won't you all come in and help me sample them?"

Aiden plunged eagerly toward the steps, but Shelley held him back. "Those are for you, Terri. We have more at home."

"All right. Would you like to come in for a few minutes?"

"Sure," Diane said, "but only a few. I just came in from a run to town, and I haven't let Rocky out yet."

Shelley was relieved that Diane had a built-in excuse to keep the visit short. She had never been inside the house before, and she found it interesting. The furniture was outdated and a little shabby, and the decorating minimal.

"It's adequate," Terri said as they looked around the living room. "If I owned the place, I'd sure brighten it up fast—like Diane has in her cottage."

"Diane's house is beautiful," Shelley said. One thing that was a lot better here than at her own house—Terri seemed to have an air conditioner in every room, and she had them going full blast. When they left twenty minutes later, Shelley almost hated to step out into the muggy air again.

She blew a strand of damp hair off her forehead as she struggled with Emma's stroller harness.

"Hot enough?" Diane asked with a chuckle.

"I'm not really complaining. This is the coolest day we've had all week."

"Right," Diane said, "but it's still about eighty-eight degrees."

Shelley straightened and grasped the stroller's handlebar. "Come on, Aiden." She looked back at Terri, who was waving from the porch. "Thanks, Terri! I'm sure we'll see you again soon."

"Bye," Diane called. As they reached the sidewalk, she said softly, "There. That wasn't so bad, was it? I think you and the kids made a great impression."

"Really? Even when Emma chewed on her TV remote?"

Diane laughed. "It's part of the toddler charm. I like Terri—and I think she likes you. I *know* she'll have fond thoughts of you when she tastes those muffins."

Chapter Seven

Beverly was expecting Diane when she stopped by the Wheeland house on Sunday afternoon. She'd called earlier to report that the lighthouse brochure they had produced was in need of a second printing.

"Hi!" Beverly let her in at the front door, and Diane held out a stack of loose sheets of paper.

"Here are the proofs. I thought two sets of eyes would be better than one on these."

"Well, we only found one typo in the first batch," Beverly said.

"Yes, but we've added a few things, so I want to go over it all again and make sure the spacing and everything is right. Do you mind?"

"Not a bit."

"Good," Diane said. "I gave the last dozen to the town office Friday, and then I stopped in at the Crow's Nest yesterday and they asked for more, so we need to get the new ones done right away."

"That's fantastic," Beverly said. "Do we have plenty of money to pay for the printing?"

"Yes, if we deduct it from the funds that have come in from selling them."

"That only makes sense." Beverly looked over her shoulder. "I just took Father a cup of coffee. Come on into the living room." She was glad she'd straightened up a little and vacuumed on Saturday. She walked Diane in to join her father, who was reading the latest issue of *American History* magazine.

"Well, my favorite author is here," he said with a sunny smile.

"I'll get us some tea, Diane," Beverly said, "or would you prefer coffee today?"

"Tea sounds good."

When Beverly returned a few minutes later her father was asking, "So, how soon do I get my next book?"

"It's being edited now," Diane said.

"Wonderful. And how's the third one coming?"

Diane grimaced. "Not very well, I'm afraid. I'm just starting it, but I'm not sure it will ever see daylight."

"Really? Why not?"

Beverly set Diane's mug on a coaster near her and took a seat on the sofa as Diane began her explanation. She and her father listened sympathetically to Diane's tale of uncertainty. She sounded insecure—not Diane's usual attitude. In most things she seemed confident, but Beverly had watched her feeling her way slowly into her new career as a novelist for the past year.

"So I still have to write it," Diane concluded, "but I don't know if it will be published."

Father scowled. "What's this 'have to write it' business? I thought you were writing mysteries for the joy of it."

That brought a wry smile from Diane. "You're right—that's how I felt at first. I guess it's become more of a job, and I feel as though I'm about to get the pink slip."

"But you'll be all right if this happens, won't you? Financially, I mean."

"Father," Beverly said gently, hoping her implication was clear—Diane's finances were none of their business.

"Sorry," he said.

Diane reached over and patted his hand. "I'll be fine, thank you. Except for my bruised ego. I'm afraid this has got me very disheartened."

"Of course it has," he said.

"Well, deep down, I know that I need to look past the surface of it. I have a lot to be thankful for, and I really have no business slacking off and feeling all out of sorts about it. I should just keep on working at it and let God take care of the sales."

"That sort of thing is difficult to do," Beverly said.

"Don't I know it. It's just that my feelings keep getting in the way."

"Beverly was telling me the other day that people write book reviews online a lot," Mr. Wheeland said. "Not just pros, but everyday readers. I told her I'd like to post a review of your first book and tell people how much I enjoyed it. Would that help in a small way?"

"That's so sweet of you. I'm sure it would help some. People who look at books online can read any reviews that are posted before they buy the book. Of course, if the reviews are positive, they encourage more sales."

"I'll do it then."

"I'll post it for you," Beverly said.

"Good. That will give me something to work on this evening." Her father sipped his coffee.

"So, Beverly, what have you been up to?" Diane asked. "I know you've got that new client in Brunswick. How's that going?"

"Pretty well. It's a group of summer tourist camp owners, and I'm helping with their mission statement and setting up a budget for them. If all goes well, it could lead to some contract work for the individual owners."

"Sounds good," Diane said. "Didn't you mention a few days ago that you're teaching a seminar too?"

"Yes. It's on Saturday. I have my sessions and my visuals all prepared."

Diane chuckled. "You would. You're so organized. I hope that goes well for you."

"Thanks."

Father raised an eyebrow. "Did she tell you about her other project?"

"What one is that?"

"She's thinking of going into politics."

"What?" Diane turned to Beverly, her eyes wide and her lips parted. "Really? Beverly, I know you mentioned it once, but I hadn't heard any more, so I figured you'd decided not to do it."

"I haven't really decided either way for sure," Beverly said. "Father and Mrs. Peabody are pushing me a little, and even Jeff is encouraging me to run for mayor." She shrugged. "I don't know what to do."

Diane frowned. "I wish I'd known you were still thinking about it."

Beverly and her father exchanged a glance.

"Why do you say that?" Beverly's father asked.

"Lee Waters is running, and he asked me to sign his petition yesterday."

"Oh. Lee is running?" Beverly rolled that over in her mind.

"That doesn't mean you shouldn't," her father said. "You're so knowledgeable on finances and such, I think you'd make a much better mayor than Lee would."

Diane gave her a tentative smile. "I'm so sorry, Beverly. If I'd had any idea you really wanted to run, I'd have told Lee I couldn't sign for him."

"It's all right," she said quickly. "You couldn't have known. And as I said, I haven't made a decision. I admit I'm sort of leaning toward it. But I didn't know Lee wanted the position."

"Well, signing his papers doesn't mean you have to vote for him when the day comes," her father said.

"True, and if it comes to a choice between Lee and Beverly, I'd certainly vote for Beverly," Diane said. "I mean, Lee is a nice guy and all, but I truly believe that Beverly's background makes her more qualified." She turned earnestly to her friend. "And you learned so much about town government while you were opposing the developers last month!"

"That she did," Father almost crowed. "She made them back down too."

Beverly smiled and held up her hand. "All right, you two. At this stage, I'm just considering it. Nothing is concrete yet, so I'd appreciate it if you'd keep that quiet until I decide for sure. And Diane, you mustn't feel bad. I probably would have signed for Lee if I wasn't contemplating doing it myself."

"Well, I think you should go ahead with it. Lee might be competent, but you would certainly be more passionate about the job." Diane raised her mug and sniffed the tea. "*Mmm.* Vanilla?"

"Yes. Do you like it? Because I have—"

"I love it." Diane took a sip.

Beverly relaxed and leaned back in her chair. Diane was such a good friend. And as far as the mayor's race went, maybe she would hold off on that. It might even be a good idea to talk to Lee about it and see how badly he wanted the job. Once she committed to running and submitted the paperwork, there would be no turning back.

"Well," Diane said a moment later, "I guess we'd better look over the booklet so you can get back to work."

"Talking to you is more fun," Beverly said with a smile, "but I suppose you're right." She picked up her stack of papers. "Shall we go up to my office?"

★ ★ ★

Margaret had barely loaded the dishwasher after the family's Sunday night supper when the phone rang.

"I'll get it," she called. Allan and Adelaide had settled down to watch a program together. "Hello?"

"Margaret? This is Beth. Beth Dufour."

"Oh, hi." It had taken Margaret a half second to place her cousin's voice. She hadn't seen Beth for nearly a year, since their last family reunion, but Beth's cheerful face, framed by her short, enhanced blonde hair, brought a pleasant memory.

"Are you hitting me up for this year's reunion?"

"No," Beth said. "Actually, I haven't thought much about it. I'm not sure we'll have one this year."

"That's all right," Margaret said. The family didn't meet every year, but last year's gathering had been so successful in the end—despite a rocky start—that several members had clamored to make it an annual event. But if there was to be no reunion, why was Beth calling her? In the past, she had e-mailed her invitations. Margaret couldn't recall ever talking to her on the phone before.

"I'm calling about Buddy."

Margaret's heart sank. The dark, broody feeling she'd had when she awakened from her troubling dreams settled on her. "What about him? Is something wrong?"

Beth sighed. "I'm afraid so. He's fallen off the wagon."

"I'm sorry to hear that," Margaret said.

"It's a real pity. He'd been sober for several years, and it was great. He was a different man. Last fall we saw each other a couple of times after the reunion, and he was actually fun to do things with. But now..."

"That's too bad, Beth." It really *was* too bad, and Margaret was almost glad she hadn't kept in touch with Buddy, or her disappointment would be worse.

"I was hoping you could help."

Margaret stiffened. "Help? What do you mean? What could I do?" The old Buddy was someone she wanted to stay away from. She'd made peace with her bullying cousin when he was sober and repentant, but if he'd gone back to his old ways, forget it.

"He needs us, Margaret."

"It sounds as though you've kept in much closer contact with him than I have. Don't you think you're in a better position to help him?"

"No. I've tried. When I first realized he'd broken his sober streak, I tried to talk to him, but he wouldn't listen. Yesterday I went to his house, hoping he'd gotten his feet under him, but things were no better." Beth's voice cracked. "He slammed the door in my face."

Margaret let out a long breath. "I'm sorry that happened, Beth, but to be frank, I don't want to be hurt again. We both know Buddy can be extremely cruel when he wants to be, and if he's drunk again, I'll just stay clear, thank you."

"Oh, please don't hang up. Margaret, I really need you. Buddy needs you."

"Why me?"

"I think he'd listen to you. The last time we were together— when he was sober, I mean—he said something about you. How he knew that he'd hurt you deeply, and how much your forgiveness meant to him. I don't think he would consciously throw that away. If he knew that you still cared about him, it might make a difference. He admires you, Margaret. Please."

Margaret sighed and pulled away from the phone for a second. Could she in good conscience refuse to try?

"Look, Beth," she said at last, "I'm not sure. Let's just say I can't promise you anything. But I'll think about it."

"Thank you! Look, I have the number of Buddy's AA sponsor. I talked to him last night, and he wants to help Buddy too. He's not judgmental, but he said that Buddy has to *want* to come back to AA and regain the ground he's lost. If you want to talk to him—"

"I don't," Margaret said quickly.

"Oh." Beth sounded confused and maybe a little hurt. "Well, Greg Hathorn is a potential ally for you—for all of us. Let me give you his number. Just in case you decide to call him. He might give you some insight into Buddy's condition."

"Like I said, I am promising nothing." Even to herself, Margaret sounded a bit testy.

"I know, and I respect that. But just jot down Greg's number—please."

Margaret gritted her teeth and reached for a pen. She doubted she would call Buddy, let alone this Greg person Beth was pushing on her. But if she didn't take the number, Beth would never leave her alone. She pulled a used envelope out of the trash basket.

"All right," she said with the pen poised over the envelope. "I'm ready."

CHAPTER EIGHT

Margaret brooded over the news all evening. She sat down with Allan and Adelaide and watched the tail end of their program, but her mind wasn't on it. Afterward, she settled down with her consignment records from the gallery. She tried to keep her books up-to-date so that she could send checks out promptly to the artists at the end of each month. Overall she was pleased with her sales for the summer, and compared to last year's figures, they looked great. And the Lobster Festival was still ahead of them. That should give her August sales a nice boost.

A fragment of her mind darted to Buddy again. The thought of calling him brought on a heavy dread.

"What are you up to?"

She looked up into Allan's sympathetic eyes.

"Just looking things over and planning for the Lobster Festival. And thinking about..."

"About what?"

She smiled ruefully. Allan read her moods so well.

"Buddy."

He frowned and pulled over a chair. "Did you dream about him again?"

She shook her head. "Not last night, but I may tonight. Beth called me. You know, my cousin, Beth Dufour?"

Allan nodded. "What did she want?"

"Buddy's having troubles." Margaret glanced over her shoulder to make sure Adelaide wasn't within earshot. "He's drinking again."

"Oh no. That's a shame."

"Yeah." They sat in silence for a long moment.

"It's not your fault."

Startled, she glanced up at him again. "I know, but—"

"But you feel like you're to blame. You didn't stay in touch with him, and you still remember all the things he did to you."

Margaret swallowed hard. "I forgave him. But I guess I didn't forget."

"What else did Beth say?"

"She was hoping I could help. Call him or something, I don't know. But she insisted I take the number of Buddy's AA sponsor. Don't ask me what good that will do."

Allan shrugged. "Sounds like she's hoping for a miracle, and she's gathering the people who care about Buddy to carry it out."

Margaret smiled faintly at that. "Well, I *do* care. I mean, he saved my life. And staying sober for all those years was a wonderful accomplishment. I'm just...wary, I guess."

"Yes. Honey, I'm not saying you should do anything. Just consider whether or not you can be an influence on him for good right now. If not, then it would probably be better for you if you let it be. I don't want to see you get hurt again."

"I think I understand him a little better now."

"Maybe, but I'm not sure you should be the one to tackle Buddy's problems."

"You're right," Margaret said.

Allan reached for her hands. "Think about it. I love you, and if you decide to contact Buddy, I'll be there for you. And if not, I'll support your decision."

She nodded slowly. "Thank you. I love you so much. I'd ask you to pray for me, but I know you will be."

"You got that right." Allan leaned forward to kiss her.

"Dad!" Adelaide stood in the kitchen doorway. "You said we'd look at recipes. Come on."

Allan released Margaret's hands and stood. "We're going to find the perfect apple pie recipe for the cook-off."

Margaret smiled. "Good luck. I can't wait to test it for you." She turned back to her records, but her mind was still on Buddy.

★ ★ ★

Diane met Terri at the head of the beach path on Monday morning, with Rocky and Gallant on their leashes. The blistering heat of last week had abated, and Diane was comfortable in her jeans and long-sleeved oxford shirt. Terri wore slim white pants and a red top with white trim, and she'd ditched her sandals in favor of rubber-soled deck shoes. She wore a different pair of sunglasses today—expensive ones, Diane could tell. Her own department store shades did the trick, but she felt a little dowdy next to Terri.

"Not many people out this morning," Terri noted when they reached the sandy shore.

"They'll be out later," Diane said. "Still, it probably won't be as crowded now that the weather's cooled off." Soon summer people would pack up their families and head home in order to get the kids ready for school. August was nearly half over, and summer was waning. Diane was determined to savor each idyllic day remaining.

They turned the dogs loose when they reached the damp, firmer sand. Rocky and Gallant tore off, barking at the gulls that foraged in the surf and stopping every few yards to sniff at something.

Terri stooped to pick up a small green object. "Beach glass. I wonder how long it's been in the water." She held the prize out to Diane.

"Oh, that's a pretty one." Diane held up the small, polished nugget and let the sun glint off it, smoky emerald. "I don't find colored ones too often these days."

"I know—they don't use as much colored glass as they used to, do they? Beer and wine bottles. What else?"

"I don't know. Medicine, maybe, but I think most of that's plastic now." Diane handed the glass back.

Terri pocketed it. "I'll add it to my shells. I'm only going to take home a few to show Jack, but I'm saving several until I see if I find anything better. I got a really spectacular little crab shell yesterday."

"So is Jack not coming?"

Terri frowned and shrugged. "I hope he will, but he called last night, and he's right in the middle of a demanding project. It's taking longer than he expected."

Diane nodded, but she wondered if Jack was making excuses not to join Terri in Maine. Still, Terri sounded less discontent than she had the last time she mentioned Jack.

"I started your book last night." Terri's face brightened. "I really like it! It feels like this place. I mean, it really feels like Maine."

"Thanks." That felt good. Diane had worked hard to bring the feel of coastal New England to the page.

"I could actually smell the salt air." Terri laughed. "Of course, my window was open."

Diane whooped. Suddenly she felt carefree, if only for a short while. Having Terri here was a refreshing distraction, and she felt blessed to have a new friend who was so like her, and yet so different.

"I told Jack about it."

"What? My book?" Diane stopped walking.

"Yes. And that I'm staying kitty-corner to a novelist."

Diane smiled and walked on. She felt as though God had dropped a little blessing on her, the way He had when she'd found Mr. Wheeland's review on a sales page for her book online. His words of praise had soothed her achy heart. And now her new friend was recommending her book to other people. She didn't deserve all of this.

A wave came higher than those before it, lapping her shoes. "Guess we'd better get higher on the beach or take our shoes off." She waved to a group of senior citizens sitting in beach chairs enjoying the sea breeze. Rocky and Gallant came loping up the sand toward them.

"I do hope Jack will come," Terri said. "Some days I think he just plain doesn't want to."

"Is it more than his work?"

"I don't know. I hope not."

Diane nodded, knowing she would pray for the couple, but not yet secure enough in the friendship to feel she should say so.

"How was it with Eric?" Terri asked. "Did you ever have any rough spots?"

"A few. Nothing really scary, though. He was pretty easygoing, and honest to a fault."

"Oh, the type who, if he strayed, would confess to you?"

"Probably." Diane was glad it had never happened, but she was uneasy with the direction the conversation had taken. "I miss him awfully."

"I'll bet. Jack's got the Type-A personality. High-powered, always on the go, getting things done."

"I'm guessing that's a challenge."

"It is," Terri said. "I hoped we could come here and have some time together in a restful, slower place." She chuckled. "I got it for me. Peace and charm." She waved an arm to encompass the beach and all of Marble Cove. "But Jack won't hold still long enough to hear the gulls cry. In the time it takes to watch one wave break on the shore, he's off on another tack."

"I've known some men like that."

"He's a heart attack waiting to happen." Terri stopped and clapped a hand to her mouth. "I'm sorry. I wasn't thinking."

Diane shook her head. "It's all right. I know what you mean. And Eric wasn't like that, but he still had the heart attack."

"So maybe I should quit pigeonholing Jack and concentrate on ... on what?"

"How to love him, maybe?"

Tears glistened in Terri's eyes. "Yeah. I'm not sure I've got that part right. I always seem to do the wrong thing—to want something different from what he wants. And he works with a lot of interesting people ... more interesting than I am, I'm sure."

Diane hesitated and sent up a silent prayer. "Terri, I don't know if you believe in God, but I would be happy to pray for you and Jack, if that's okay with you."

Terri reached for her hand and gave it a squeeze. "Thank you. I guess we need it."

"If there's anything I can do ... Besides prayer, I mean."

Terri smiled and swiped away a tear. "We've only just met, but you've been a wonderful friend."

"Well, I've never met Jack," Diane said, "but even though he seems very different from Eric, relationships can be hard no matter what. It's hard to know if we're doing right by the other person."

"I'm sure you were a wonderful wife. You're a very thoughtful person."

"Thanks. I'm just saying, we all have those days."

"I'm not sure what I can do about it when he's three thousand miles away."

"Maybe just tell him you miss him. And there might be some little thing you do that would show him your long-distance love."

Terri smiled. "Maybe I'll send a copy of your book to his e-reader."

"I'm not sure that gift says 'I love you,' but thanks." Diane shook her head. What *would* a work-obsessed husband think if his wife sent him a murder mystery? "Maybe send him some fresh lobsters. Or, if that's too much, a Maine T-shirt."

Terri laughed. "I went to that Cannery place Saturday— you know, with all the craft and gift shops?"

"Yes, I know it."

"Well, in one shop I saw little cans like pop cans, only they said, 'Canned Maine Air.' Do you suppose it really smells like the sea if you open it?"

"I don't know. It's probably just to look at. They sell a lot of novelty items there." Diane whistled to Rocky, and the dogs romped in their general direction.

"Thanks for getting me thinking," Terri said. "You know, Jack really likes that weird soda pop you have here—Moxie. Maybe I'll ship him some of that."

"If he likes it, that might put him in the mood," Diane said. "Personally, I can't stand the stuff. It's an acquired taste, I guess."

They strolled on along the sand, with the lighthouse gleaming far in the distance.

"I walked down there the other day," Terri said. "The lighthouse seems to be locked up tight. Can you go inside?"

"Not without a special dispensation and a key from the town." Diane told her about the effort she and her friends had made to help raise money to preserve the lighthouse. After a few minutes, she and Terri corralled the dogs and turned back. As usual, she hated to leave the beach, but she knew she'd be back here again soon.

When they reached Newport Avenue, Terri paused at the end of Diane's driveway. "Thank you so much, Diane. And I appreciate what you said about God. You know, I grew up in a home where we went to church every Sunday and said grace at meals. But after I moved to California, I sort of let that slip away. Maybe it's time to revisit my spiritual side." She gave Diane a quick hug and headed across the street with Gallant.

Diane watched her go. *Work in Terri's heart, Father,* she prayed silently, *and show her what You can do.*

★ ★ ★

The waves surged over Margaret's head, smacking her in the face. She opened her mouth to scream for help, and salt water sloshed inside, choking her. She coughed and spat and flailed her arms. Another wave lifted her higher, and she stared about her, looking for something by which to orient herself. In the distance, light flared up. It wasn't steady enough to be the lighthouse. It flickered and jumped and grew into a huge blaze. Something was burning—something large. Another wave buffeted her, and she was thrown beneath the surface. She came up sputtering, trying to keep her head in the open. Another wave came, and she managed to ride it up, up, until she felt she was yards higher than the surface. Again she located the fire and tried to stroke toward it, keeping her head above the brine. Part of a wall exploded in flame. In the glow of the inferno, she noticed a cross. The engulfed building was a church. The cross seemed to shimmer, fixed high above the town. Beside her loomed a dark bulk, closer than the town, something huge in the water. A ship? Possible rescue was at hand. But instead of swimming toward it, she struck out toward the town and the burning church.

Margaret gulped a huge breath and opened her eyes wide. Allan was leaning over her, shaking her.

"Margaret! Wake up! Are you all right?"

"Y-yes." She sat up slowly, feeling groggy and confused. "The church was burning. I . . . " She stared at him helplessly. "I was drowning again."

"I'm so sorry." He gathered her into his arms. *Allan had to be the most comforting man on earth*, Margaret thought. He rubbed her back and held her. "Was Buddy in the dream this time?"

"No, but I couldn't get to shore, and I was afraid I wouldn't make it. Then I saw the cross."

"What cross?"

"On top of the church."

Allan pulled away and frowned at her. "Our church doesn't have a cross on the steeple. Neither does Old First."

"You're right. I think it was just my mixed-up brain. Probably something I thought of last night, and it made its way into the dream as a cross."

"Maybe it was your subconscious mind's way of letting you know it was a church. Symbolic—you know."

"*Hmm*. Maybe. I've been thinking a lot lately about Old First, and the fire there and how badly it needs restoring."

"I expect that's what triggered this," Allan said.

"Perhaps. But there was something else—a ship, I think. Only I didn't try to swim toward the ship. I went toward the fire." She shivered.

"Are you cold?"

"Not really. What time is it?"

Allan leaned his head to one side. "Five twenty."

"I might as well get up," Margaret said.

"This early? You can sleep another hour."

"I doubt I'd fall asleep again." She turned away from him and threw off the covers. "I feel like I want to paint."

She turned on her bedside lamp, and Allan blinked at her.

"All right. I'll make breakfast."

"No, why don't *you* go back to sleep? I'm going over to my studio. I'll come back in a couple of hours and eat with you and Adelaide."

"Are you sure?"

"Yes. I want to do this while I can still remember the dream."

As she spoke, she pulled on jeans and an old shirt she reserved for painting days. Food and a shower could wait. Within five minutes, she was out the door and striding toward the gallery.

As she gained the sidewalk on Main Street, the eerie stillness of the morning washed over her. She could hear the waves breaking on the shore, a sound she could rarely hear this far from the beach. With no noise of traffic, no voices calling out, no doors opening and closing, the surreal feeling of the dream surrounded her. The sun had been up more than an hour, but the people of Marble Cove still slept. Most of them, anyway. Lights were on in the Cove, and she could see someone moving about at the back of the shop.

She hurried to the rear entrance of the Shearwater and unlocked the door. *"Calm down,"* Allan would say. *"Take your time."* But Margaret didn't want to put the brakes on. She wanted a brush in her hand, now.

In her backroom studio, she placed a new canvas on her easel and positioned it beside the window. She wasn't used to working in this light—not this early in the day—and she adjusted her artificial lighting until she was satisfied.

Color. She took out tubes of orange, red, black, and yellow. The colors of fire and shadow. But she needed water too, and she added three blues, two greens, and white. For a moment, she closed her eyes and tried to summon the images of the dream to her. The colors seemed right. At last she picked up her brush.

An hour later, she stood and stepped back a couple of yards.

Her creation was odd, not at all like her usual style, even since she'd been going a little more abstract. This painting was blurry and splotchy. The left side was dominated by a mishmash of orange and gold erupting out of black—the fire. Near the top was a thin suggestion of a cross, black sticks etched against the shadowed gold of flame. The foreground was dark, roiling blues and greens, and toward the background on the right was a shapeless dark hulk.

Margaret frowned at the canvas. Where was she in this picture? What had she forgotten from the dream? The only precise detail she remembered was the cross. Was she swimming? Yes, the water had threatened to overwhelm her. But the picture didn't feel like that. She hadn't captured the terror she'd felt at the moment of awakening, or her urgent need to move toward the glowing church. She couldn't even tell that it was a church—or any sort of building—except for the cross that seemed to float high above the building.

She sighed and began to clean her brushes. The painting wasn't right. It was an impressionistic tangle, a chaotic depiction she barely recognized.

What had she hoped for? A clear representation of a dream she barely recalled now?

Her dissatisfaction stayed with her as she walked home. People were moving about on Main Street now, and cars rolled past her and pulled in to parking spaces. The Mercantile's manager was unlocking the front door. Three men talking loudly headed for the Cove's entrance. She no longer heard the waves on the rocks. She turned onto Newport Avenue and passed the Wheelands' house. Detective Fred Little was coming out of his house.

"Morning, Margaret."

She returned Fred's wave and shuffled on to her own driveway. She went to the door that opened on the kitchen. Allan looked around brightly as she entered.

"Well, how did it go?"

Margaret shrugged. "I lost it. Maybe I shouldn't have gone to the gallery. Next time I'll just paint here. On the back deck, maybe." The natural light would be good there early in the morning.

"I'm sorry," Allan said.

She sighed and sat down at the table he had set for three. He brought two golden brown pancakes, balanced on his wide spatula, and slid them onto her plate.

"Syrup or strawberries?"

"Berries. Thanks."

Adelaide came into the kitchen yawning. "Hi, Mom."

"Good morning."

Adelaide would spend some time at the community center today, and she chattered on about a sewing project she was involved in there. The regulars were making a quilt together.

Margaret tried to listen, but in the back of her mind the water, the fire, and Buddy lingered, always ready to leap to the forefront. Somehow, all of this was connected to him, but she wasn't sure how.

CHAPTER NINE

Beverly pulled into the parking lot at the pet store on Tuesday afternoon. She almost never came here, as she and her father had no pets. She'd gone in once when she was shopping with Diane. Hanging inside the glass of the door was a computer-printed flyer with a photo of Lee Waters, smiling. *Waters for Mayor,* it read in large, purple letters. *Test the New Waters.* She grimaced and pushed open the door.

When she entered, the smells of wood shavings and pet food met her. Chirping birds kept up a continuous background serenade. A bank of aquarium tanks holding tropical fish drew her interest, and dead ahead was a raised enclosure that held three fat, wriggly puppies.

Lee turned from the display he was arranging—flea collars and worming medicine, by the look of it.

"Hello."

"Hi." She stepped forward.

Lee studied her for a moment. "We've met, haven't we?"

"Yes, I was in here once with Diane Spencer."

"Of course. Her neighbor."

"I'm Beverly Wheeland." She held out her hand.

Lee shook it, smiling. "How can I help you today, Beverly?"

"Oh, nothing for pets. I don't have one."

"Would you like one?"

They both laughed.

"Actually, Diane told me you were running for mayor, and I wanted to talk to you."

"Oh. Sure."

He straightened his shoulders, and Beverly could have sworn he was preening a bit. She'd better speak up before he launched his sign-my-petition speech.

"I was thinking of running too, and I didn't know anyone else had made that decision."

He blinked at her, obviously regrouping mentally. "Okay."

"I haven't taken out papers yet or anything. I thought I'd see you first and find out your thoughts."

"Well, I just finished getting signatures, and I took my papers in first thing this morning."

"I see. Do you have a lot of plans for the town? I mean, if you're eager to do this and have put a lot of thought into what you'll do, I—"

Lee shrugged. "I don't know. It's not like I spend every minute thinking about it. I mean, the economy's been bad, but there's not much we can do about that locally. Things seem pretty good here in Marble Cove. We've had a few new businesses open in the last couple of years, and the Cannery seems to be making a go of it."

"That's true," Beverly said. She, Margaret, and Shelley had all started new businesses and were showing a profit in each one.

"See, my mom's been the mayor for over twenty years, and before that, it was my grandfather. It just seemed like it might be good to step up and carry on with things, you know? But I'm surely not against someone else coming in, either. There's probably a lot of people out there with ideas of how to promote the town. Some of them would most likely do a better job than I would."

"You shouldn't say that," Beverly said with a smile. "Keep it positive when you campaign."

He chuckled. "Okay, I'll try. Thanks for the tip. So...are you going to run?"

"Still not sure. But I'm glad we talked."

"Me too. Thanks for letting me know, and...well, whatever you decide, stop in anytime."

Beverly left the store deep in thought. Lee seemed happy with the status quo in town, but she wasn't sure that was good enough for Marble Cove. She was mildly surprised he hadn't recognized her after the way she'd publicly taken on Dennis last month.

She believed in keeping on top of things and preempting events that could harm the town, whether they affected the economy, the environment, or the common heritage. Like Dennis Calder's plan to build a high-class vacation destination on the edge of town. That might have been good where money was concerned, but it would have been disastrous on several other fronts. How would Lee have stood on that issue? Hadn't he followed it closely? How much did he really care about the town?

She pointed her car homeward, but at the last minute turned toward the town office. It wouldn't hurt to get the necessary paperwork and take it home to study. Then if she decided to go ahead with it, she'd be prepared. She set out for the town office with her pulse aflutter. She wasn't sure why her nerves were kicking up. This wasn't a final commitment. Today she would only set things in motion. She could still change her mind.

As she drove into the parking lot at the municipal building, Evelyn Waters was coming out the door. Beverly sat in her car for a moment, giving Evelyn time to get to her vehicle and drive away. It was silly, she supposed, but the outgoing mayor—Lee's mother—was the last person she wanted to encounter this morning. For some reason, Beverly's professional coolness had fled. That didn't bode well for launching a campaign.

When Evelyn's car was out of sight down the street, she pulled in a deep breath and opened the door. She would take this step and continue to think about the rest of the journey.

★ ★ ★

Diane's doorbell rang, and Rocky let out a yip. Diane laid aside the book she was browsing and went to the door. She'd bought it online, rather than raise eyebrows at the library by asking for a book on lethal poisons.

Terri and Gallant stood on the front porch, and Gallant let out a little yelp when he saw her.

"Hi! Going for a walk?" Diane asked.

"Yes." Terri raised her eyebrows. "I wasn't sure I should bother you. If you're too busy to go, that's all right."

"I think Rocky and I could both use a break." At the sound of his name, Rocky pressed against Diane's leg and woofed happily. Gallant wriggled in reply, his ears flicking and his whole body shimmying with eagerness.

"Just let me grab the leash," Diane said. "Want to go to the beach, or should we take a different route?"

"I'd like to go by the old church," Terri said. "After you told me about your fund-raising efforts, I paid particular attention to the damage from the fire, but I didn't go up close. What a shame."

"Yes. It's a beautiful old building. I don't attend there, but I do know the minister, and my friend Beverly is a member. Their congregation is holding services over at my church until they can at least repair their roof."

"Well, that's kind of nice," Terri said.

"We can go browse around outside Old First if you like. It'll give the dogs something new to look at."

They headed up Newport Avenue for Main Street, and Diane steered Terri along the shortest route to Old First.

Terri covered a yawn. "Sorry. I overslept this morning. Somebody's book kept me up late last night."

Diane laughed. "Did you finish it yet?"

"I sure did, and you kept me guessing until the very end. I absolutely loved it."

"Thanks."

"And I did send a copy to Jack's e-reader. He said he'd look at it last night if he wasn't too tired out."

"That's nice," Diane said, "but I won't be insulted if Jack doesn't read it. Not everyone likes the same kind of books."

"Oh, he loves mysteries." Terri smiled but said no more on the topic. Diane hugged the bit of encouragement to herself.

"My son called me yesterday too," Terri said. "Guess what he's doing now?"

"I have no idea."

"He's putting solar panels in his house. *On* it, I guess I should say. He thinks it will save all kinds of money, but the cost of those things is so outrageous to begin with, I don't see how he'll ever make it back on his electric bill."

Diane laughed. "You may be right. But if he does the installation himself, it might work out well for him."

They were passing the Cove, and Terri paused on the sidewalk. "Didn't you tell me that Shelley bakes the pastries for that place?"

"That's right."

"Well, I'm telling you, those muffins she brought me were out of this world. In fact, they're *truly* out of this world now, because I've eaten them all."

Diane couldn't hold back a guffaw. "Shelley will take that as a great compliment."

"*Hmm*, well, I might just have to go into the Cove later and buy some more. Of course, I'll have to do a lot more walking to work off the calories."

"Let's get moving, then," Diane said. "We'll go have a look at Old First, and then we'll come back here for coffee and a scone, how about that?"

"Scones?" Terri's eyes twinkled. "She makes scones?"

"Delectable scones. And Danish and cookies and..."

★ ★ ★

Margaret awoke suddenly on Wednesday morning. She'd half expected to dream again, and she'd hoped she would get used to it, but the same nameless terror had overpowered her, making her throat tighten and her heart race.

She slipped out of bed and pulled on her robe. In ten minutes she had assembled the painting supplies she kept at home and set up her old easel on the back deck. The sun was just rising, and the indirect lighting increased as she made her preparations.

She began to paint, more realistically this time, as the birds began to twitter in the maple trees. After applying a wash of light blue, she began to form waves, shaded and highlighted until they seemed almost to be moving. She capped the nearest one with a suggestion of white spume. She was seeing the cove—she knew it was Marble Cove—from the level of the water's surface. The viewpoint was just high enough for the person observing to see shore in the distance. Two-thirds of the painting was foreground—all water. In the distance was a prominence of land with Orlean Point Light jutting up, almost black against the sky.

She kept on painting, prodding her memory for what she'd seen in this dream—and for ways it was different from the last one. After an hour, she heard Allan moving in the kitchen. She sat back and studied the canvas. It wasn't finished yet. She wasn't sure it ever would be. She hadn't gone back and added finishing touches to the other "dream paintings," as she had begun to think of them. They were nothing she would ever display or sell. So why did she do them?

She smiled to herself. Some people wrote down their dreams so they would remember them. Margaret Hoskins painted them.

The door leading into the dining room slid open, and Allan surveyed her. He arched his eyebrows. "Good morning."

Margaret smiled at him. "Hi."

"May I look?"

"Sure."

He stepped out onto the deck and stood beside her chair, silently regarding the canvas. After a moment, he asked, "Same as before?"

"No fire this time. Just water."

"Looks like the swimmer's a long way out."

"Yes," Margaret said. "I still have no idea what it means, or if it means anything at all."

"Well, I hope it stops interrupting your sleep soon. I've been praying about this."

"Really?" She looked up at him in surprise. "You know, I never thought to pray about the dreams. Buddy, yes—I've been praying for him this last week or two. But I hadn't considered this a matter for prayer."

Allan shrugged. "The way I see it, either God is sending these dreams for a reason, or else He's not. In the first case, it would be nice to know why. In the second case, if they're not doing anything constructive, then maybe if we ask Him, He'll take them away."

"That would be nice. Thank you."

He nodded. "I'm figuring on scrambled eggs this morning. That all right with you?"

"Sounds lovely. I'll clean up here."

Allan went inside, and she began to put away her paints and brushes. She liked his practical assessment. If God was using the dreams to tell her something, what was it? And why didn't He just tell her straight out? She'd love to get a clear message, instead of this frightening mishmash of images haunting her sleep.

Was she going to need rescuing again? Or was she being called to rescue someone else? Buddy, perhaps? He'd been on her mind a lot, and since Beth's call she felt guiltier over her neglect of Buddy. Or maybe this wasn't about her cousin at all. Maybe God was calling her to help rescue Old First. Or could it be something else, something totally unrelated? Another swimmer, maybe. That would fit with the dreams. Sort of.

She put away her easel and paint box. Leaving the canvas propped on her dresser to dry, she went to the kitchen.

"Hi, Mom." Adelaide was already at the table, wearing a bright pink-and-white top that she loved, with black jeans. Her shoulder-length hair was pulled back in a pink scrunchie.

"Hi, honey. You look nice. What will you be doing today at the center?"

"Working on our quilt, mostly. It's really pretty."

Margaret continued chatting with her and Allan as they ate breakfast. Afterward, she showered and dressed for her day at the gallery. When she was ready, she dropped Adelaide at the community center and went on alone. She had some time before she needed to unlock the front door. At first she tried to work on her consignment ledger, but after ten minutes, she gave up and picked up the phone. Calling Buddy was still a bit daunting. Maybe she should start with the AA sponsor. Odd that the thought of calling a stranger made her less uncomfortable than that of calling her cousin.

She had put the sponsor's phone number into her purse, and she rummaged for it and found the old envelope.

All right, Lord, here goes nothing. If this isn't what You want me to do, please let him not answer.

But after only two rings, a hearty voice said in her ear, "Hello, Greg Hathorn speaking."

"Oh. Hello." Margaret gulped and squared her shoulders. "My name is Margaret Hoskins, and we've never met, Mr. Hathorn, but I'm a cousin of Buddy Gordon. I've been concerned about Buddy, and our mutual cousin, Beth Dufour, suggested that I call you. She thought that perhaps together we could find a way to help Buddy."

"I'm glad you called," he said. "I was starting to think that I was the only one in the world who cared about Buddy, and he's not talking to me right now."

"I'm sorry to hear that."

Mr. Hathorn sighed. "I tried to call Buddy yesterday, but he didn't pick up. I've gone by his place twice in the last week, but either he wasn't home or he pretended he wasn't."

"Do you think he's all right?" Margaret asked. "I mean...what if he needed urgent help?"

"Well, the first time I went by, his pickup wasn't in the driveway, so I'm pretty sure he wasn't around. The second time—which was Saturday—the truck was there, but he didn't come to the door. I thought I saw movement at the window when I first drove in, and I tried the doorbell and knocking, but nobody answered the door. I think he just plain didn't want to see me."

"*Hmm.* You may be right, if he's embarrassed and depressed." Margaret ran her hand through her short hair. "I hate to pester anyone, but sometimes people need a shove to break off a bad habit."

"Ain't it the truth. Do you have any suggestions, Mrs. Hoskins?"

"Call me Margaret. If we both want to help Buddy, we'd better be friends."

"All right. I'm Greg. How far from Buddy do you live?"

"At least thirty miles. I've never been to where he lives now. Thomaston, isn't it?"

"Yes. He's got half a duplex. I take it you haven't called him recently?"

"Not yet. I thought I'd talk to you first. Beth didn't really give me much information, just that Buddy's drinking again. How long has this been going on?"

"He missed an AA meeting last month. I called him, and he made excuses. The next week, I went to pick him up and he wasn't home. It's been all downhill since then. I actually caught him home once, but he was pretty well stoned."

"I really don't know what I can do," Margaret said.

"Sometimes just knowing family does care makes an impression."

She sighed. "I'll try. But he may not want to talk to me either." She glanced at her watch. "It's time for me to open my business, but I will try to get hold of him later today." Just saying it made her accountable, and she needed that—it had been too easy to put off making the call.

"Let me know how it goes," Greg said. "And don't give up on him."

CHAPTER TEN

Shelley lifted the stroller onto the boardwalk and paused to dump sand out of her shoe.

"Come on, Aiden. Daddy will be home in half an hour, and I have a lot to do first."

Aiden scampered up from the beach with Prize at his heels and took hold of the handlebar. "Can I push?"

"Wait until we get up to the sidewalk, where it's smoother." The renter from next door was coming toward them, and Shelley didn't want any chance of Aiden slamming the stroller into her ankles. "Hello, Mrs. Glazier."

"Hi! It's Terri." She pulled up and held her leash with both hands, forcing her little brown-and-white dog to stay against her leg. "Can you get by? Because I can back up."

"Oh, there's plenty of room." Shelley glanced behind her. "Aiden, get Prize. Don't let her go back down to the beach." She'd forgotten the leash but had told herself they wouldn't need it. As usual, she regretted not taking time to do things right. She smiled sheepishly at Terri. "Sorry—I forgot the leash today. Are you enjoying the cooler weather?"

"I certainly am," Terri said. "Last week was almost as bad as August in California. But I was actually chilly last night."

"Do they have a way for you to heat the house?" Shelley hadn't thought about that when she and Diane had visited.

"The Simpsons said I can turn on the oil furnace if I need to, but they also left the wood box full, and I had a little blaze in the fireplace last night. It was cozy once I got the chill off the room."

"Nice," Shelley said. "We took the kids to a cottage that had a fireplace a few months ago. I was afraid it wouldn't be childproofed like ours is, but the owners had left a screen, and we didn't have any trouble with *that*."

Terri smiled. "Your tone says you had other problems to deal with."

Shelley laughed, remembering their weekend getaway. "The power was out almost the whole time we were there. It wouldn't have been too bad if it was just Dan and me, but with kids..."

"That must have been a real challenge."

Three teenagers came up from the beach and approached the lower end of the boardwalk.

"Guess we'd better get out of the way," Shelley said. "Nice to see you again."

"Thanks," Terri replied. "Same here. Drop over anytime for a glass of iced tea. The children are welcome."

That was nice of her, Shelley reflected as she pushed for home. Aiden bounced along beside her with Prize, and for once the dog waited for them when they reached the sidewalk, instead of bolting for home. Someday she'd dash into the street in front of a car, Shelley feared.

When they reached the safety of their own yard, she parked the stroller by the steps and crouched to face her son. "Aiden, you did a good job with Prize. I should have gone back for the leash, and I'm sorry that I didn't. It's not safe for Prize or for us to let her loose up here on the street."

Aiden put his grubby hand on her shoulder. "It's okay, Mama. You weren't bad."

She smiled. "Well, I did something that wasn't smart. So I hope you'll help me remember next time. If I start to go without Prize's leash, you can remind me how important it is, all right?"

He nodded solemnly. "But Prize was good today. We were all good."

"Yes, you were."

"Mama," Emma called.

Shelley rose and turned to unbuckle her. "Come on, kiddo. Let's get our stuff inside and change out of our swimsuits. I need to get supper ready." She was glad she had cooked potatoes and eggs for a potato salad that morning. It shouldn't take long to put that together.

When Dan walked through the door a short while later, she had bratwurst ready to throw on the grill and a big bowl of potato salad waiting in the refrigerator.

"Hi, honey." She met him near the door and kissed him. "How did things go today?"

"Good."

Aiden and Prize tore in from the living room. Dan ruffled Aiden's hair. "Hi, buddy." He looked around. His gaze lingered on the stroller, the heap of crumpled towels on the kitchen linoleum, and the plastic toys Emma and Aiden had scattered.

"Sorry it's a little cluttered," Shelley said. "We went to the beach this afternoon, and I haven't cleaned up everything."

He nodded. "I don't mind, but I hope you'll be able to get things organized by Friday."

Shelley stared at him. "Friday?"

"Dinner. You know. Wayne and his wife."

Shelley opened her mouth, but nothing came out.

"What's the matter?" Dan set his lunch box on the counter.

"Nothing. I—did you say Friday? As in day after tomorrow?"

"Yeah. What did you think I said?"

"Uh…"

"Shell, what's the matter?" Dan scowled at her.

"I thought it was next week."

His shoulders drooped. "Oh, come on. We talked about this—what—a week ago?"

"No. We talked about it last Friday. Today is Wednesday. And for some reason I thought I had another whole week."

He shrugged. "Well, you've got two whole days."

"Two days." Her voice rose in panic, and she gulped in a deep breath. "Dan, I don't even know what I'm serving yet. I'll have to shop and clean and bake." She clapped a hand to her forehead. "Allie said she'd babysit for me, but I told her the twenty-fourth."

"I'm sure Mom can do it if your friend can't."

"You're probably right." Shelley sighed. "Okay, can you grill the brats? I need to make my shopping list."

"I need to get washed up," Dan said.

"All right, I'll do it, but I need to go to the market after supper."

"Tonight? Can't you do that tomorrow?"

"No. Tomorrow I'll be cleaning and cooking all day."

"Aw, Shell! Did you really think it was next week?"

"Yes. You said 'next Friday,' and I thought you meant *next* Friday."

"Man! I was hoping we could all walk down to the beach tonight. I've been working all day."

"You can. The kids would probably love to go again. You'll have them all tired out. Prize too."

"No way. I can't handle both of them and the dog down on the beach. Take Emma with you."

Shelley grimaced. What did he think she did every day? She always had to handle both children and the dog alone. "You shouldn't have any trouble. I do it all the time."

"No, really."

She sighed. "What if we go to the beach for an hour after supper and then you put the kids to bed while I head for the store? You can study after they're in bed if you want."

Dan frowned, but he said, "Okay. Seems fair."

She gave him a little push. "Go get washed up. You've got ten minutes."

★ ★ ★

Beverly helped get supper to the table, and once again she was glad she hadn't needed to prepare it. Mrs. Peabody's homemade chicken stew and biscuits smelled delicious.

"Thank you so much," she told the older woman as they carried the hot dishes to the table. "Won't you stay and enjoy this with us?"

"No, thanks. My granddaughter's picking me up in a few minutes. We're going over to Willow's Corner this evening."

"Well, all right. I hope you won't skip supper, though."

Mrs. Peabody waved a hand. "We're eating out. Belinda insists on treating me now and then." She smiled as though anticipating a guilty pleasure. "I'll probably have a milkshake."

Father ambled into the dining room. "*Mmm*, smells good." He sat in his usual place at the head of the table. "Beverly, did you tell Mrs. Peabody you're going to run for mayor?"

Beverly glanced at the older woman. "Well, no. I haven't completely made up my mind yet, to be honest."

"We talked about that before." Mrs. Peabody raised her eyebrows. "Is it official now?"

"Not yet," Beverly said. "Lee Waters is running, and I'm still trying to decide."

"I believe I told you I think you'd do all right. You're awfully busy already, though, aren't you?"

Beverly shrugged. "I have plenty of work now, but I think I could spare a few hours a week for town business."

"I think you should do it." Her father reached for the water pitcher and filled his glass.

"Well, I don't know. Since I talked to Lee Waters..."
Beverly let it trail off. She still wasn't sure she wanted to
run against Lee. Would other people take it as criticism of
the Waters family?

"What did he say?" Mrs. Peabody asked.

"Not a whole lot. I just don't want to step on anyone's
toes."

"Who, Lee?" Mrs. Peabody scrunched up her face.
"I doubt he'd be offended just because someone else ran
against him. Might even welcome the competition. Now his
mother, that might be another story."

"You think Evelyn would be upset if Lee had an
opponent?"

"Well, I saw her yesterday at the Mercantile, and she was
in a bit of a tizzy because Dennis Calder had gone into the
town office and taken out papers."

Beverly stared at her. "Dennis is running?"

Mrs. Peabody shrugged. "All I know is what Evelyn
told me. She wasn't happy about it. I think she was hoping
Lee wouldn't have any competition. Someone as good-
looking as Dennis—well, maybe she doesn't think Lee will
have a chance now. Or maybe she doesn't think she'll like
how Dennis would run things if he won." She glanced at
the clock. "I'd best get across the street so I can freshen
up before Belinda comes. Beverly, the cranberry sauce and
pickles are all laid out in dishes in the fridge."

"I'll get them. You go on. And have a nice time." Beverly
watched her take off her apron and head for the door.

"So," her father said. "Dennis."

"Yes. That was a surprise." Beverly looked at him carefully. "Did you know?"

"Nope. No idea. But he's got a right, just as you do."

Beverly gave a little chuckle. "And here I was worried about hurting Lee's feelings if I ran."

"Sounds like Lee will have some stiff competition, either way. But do you want to run against Dennis?"

She frowned, thinking about that. "Forget about Lee—do you think *I* would stand a chance?"

"I do. Some people sided with Dennis on the development issue, but don't forget your side won."

"True. But he's lived here all his life. I'm a newcomer."

"Don't start doubting yourself now." Her father smiled gently. "You can be as charming as Dennis if you try. And you can bring a lot to town government, Beverly. Believe in yourself. The rest of us do."

"*Hmm*. I don't know." She brought the pickle dish and the cranberry sauce and sat down next to him.

"I'll tell you one thing," her father said. "If it was just Lee against Dennis, I think Dennis would win hands down. But you're the one person who could give Dennis a run for his money."

Throughout the meal, he kept up a stream of conversation about the neighbors, the town, and the seminar Beverly would be teaching that weekend, but her mind was only half on what he said. She kept mulling the question of running for mayor. If she did, she'd have to face off with Dennis. She wasn't sure she wanted to do that.

After supper, when she'd cleaned up the kitchen and started the dishwasher, she went up to her office and looked up Charlotte Vincent's phone number. She pulled in a deep breath and called the chamber chairperson.

"Hello, Mrs. Vincent?"

"Yes."

"This is Beverly Wheeland. Do you remember mentioning to me after the big meeting last month that I should consider running for mayor?"

"I sure do," Charlotte said, "and I still think it's a great idea. Are you game?"

"Seriously thinking about it."

"Fantastic. Oh, did you hear that Dennis Calder and Lee Waters have both taken out papers?"

"Yes," Beverly said. "Are there any others?"

"Not that I know of. Not yet, anyway. Beverly, I'd be happy to help you in any way I can."

"Thank you. I wondered if maybe we could get together for coffee, and you could give me an idea of some of the main issues the mayor will face this year."

"I'd be happy to talk about it. Are you busy tonight?"

"Well . . . not really."

"Great! I live not far from the Landmark. My husband and I are just finishing supper, but I could meet you there in an hour."

"Sure, I can do that. Thanks."

They signed off, and Beverly puttered about her desk for a few minutes, laying out the work she wanted to get done the next day. She opened a small notebook and jotted a few notes about things she hoped Charlotte could enlighten her on.

After a half hour, she put on a sweater, pocketed her cell phone, and picked up her purse. She went downstairs and found her father watching television in the living room.

"I'm going over to the Landmark to have coffee with Charlotte Vincent."

He craned his neck around and blinked at her. "Okay. What's up, if I may ask?" Beverly smiled. "We're going to discuss why I should or should not run for mayor." He settled back in his recliner with a smile. "Great. Talk to you later."

★ ★ ★

Margaret lifted the telephone receiver and stared at it for a moment, then put it down. Allan strolled into the kitchen and glanced at her.

"What's up?" He opened the refrigerator.

"I was working up my nerve to call Buddy."

He turned with a container of yogurt in his hand. "Any way I can help?"

"Don't think so." She grimaced. "I just need to do it."

"In that case, I'll leave you alone. But I'm proud of you."

"Don't be until I actually make the call."

He smiled and took a spoon from the cutlery drawer and then ambled back toward the living room.

Margaret lifted the phone again and carefully punched in the number. She hauled in a deep breath and listened to it ring. One ... two ... three ...

Four would be enough. She could hang up after that without feeling too guilty.

"Hello."

She plopped down onto a stool. "Buddy?"

"Yeah."

Margaret gritted her teeth. "Buddy, this is Margaret. I want to talk to you, but not when you've been drinking. Can you call me back when you're sober?"

"*Hmm*, doubt it."

She scowled. "Buddy, listen to me. Call me tomorrow, after you've slept it off. Do you hear me?"

A long pause followed, and she feared for a moment that he'd abandoned the call.

He breathed out heavily. "Who'd you say this is?"

She sighed. "Margaret Hoskins. Your cousin."

"Oh yeah, Margaret! Hi!" He sounded genuinely surprised and delighted.

Obviously her first approach hadn't worked. She said quietly, "Listen, Buddy. I want to talk to you. I know you've been drinking again."

"Who told you?" he asked distinctly, as though making great effort to pronounce each word.

"That doesn't matter. I just ... I want to help you."

"Thanks, Margaret. You can't help me. Nobody can help me."

"Don't say that. Why don't you just tell me what happened? What got you started again? You were doing really well."

"Yeah, I was. But then Pete died."

Margaret frowned as she tried to decipher his slurred words. "Pete? Who's Pete?"

"He's an old friend. Was. Dead now."

"I'm sorry to hear that."

"Yeah." Buddy sniffed. "He was a good friend."

"Well, I'm sorry that your friend passed away. I'd like to call you again tomorrow, Buddy. Maybe we can talk about Pete then. What do you say? If I give you a ring tomorrow— say around ten o'clock—will you be sober enough to talk to me?"

After a pause, Buddy sobbed. "Better make it later. I'm in awful lousy shape."

"I know, but you get some rest, and we'll talk, okay?"

He sniffed. "'Kay."

"Good. I'll talk to you tomorrow. About noon, all right? And don't you drink any more liquor until then. Not one drop."

He didn't answer, and a dial tone hummed in her ear. Margaret hung up the phone. A shadow fell on her, and she looked up. Allan stood in the doorway.

"Did you get hold of him?" Allan asked.

She winced and nodded. "He'd been drinking, but he understood who I was. After a while, that is."

"Was he coherent?"

"Oh, sort of. He said a friend of his had died. I'm not even sure if it's a person or a pet or what. Pete died, he said. That may be what made him stumble and take that first drink."

"Sounds like he's really depressed."

"I think so."

"Maybe Beth would know who Pete was."

"Yeah, she might." Margaret stood. "I feel wrung out, like a limp old dishrag."

"You'd better get to bed, sweetheart. Adelaide and I will finish up our movie, but then I think I'll hit the sack too. Things will look better tomorrow."

"I hope so. I told him I'd call him around noontime."

Chapter Eleven

At breakfast the next morning, Beverly's father's first words were, "Well, are you going to do it?"

She smiled as she removed the tea bag from her cup and squeezed it gently against a spoon. When she'd returned from her meeting with Charlotte last night, he'd already retired. "I think so, yes. At least I'll start filling out the papers."

"Do it today," he said. "And I'll be happy to be the first to sign. Mrs. P will probably put her name down too."

"I think she will too. She sort of surprised me with that. I never thought she was especially fond of me."

"She respects you, and I'm sure she'll back you. Just fill out the paperwork, and we'll see, shall we?"

Beverly finished breakfast and washed up their few dishes. She didn't like to leave a messy kitchen for Mrs. Peabody to face when she came to prepare their lunch. Up in her office, she put in two hours of work on a client's annual budget and was going over her notes for the seminar when she heard the elderly woman arrive.

When she came down the stairs, her father was asking about Mrs. Peabody's outing with Belinda the night before.

"Oh, we had a grand time," Mrs. Peabody said. "Belinda likes to have fun. We had supper, and then she took me to her sister's house. We played games and caught up on all the family news. And they gave me some new photos of my great-grandchildren."

"Sounds like a nice evening," Beverly said. "I'm going to go downtown to run some errands. Is there anything I can get for either of you?"

"Toothpaste," her father said. "You know the kind I like."

"I'm all set," Mrs. Peabody said. "You'll be home for lunch, right?"

"Wouldn't miss it."

★ ★ ★

Shelley was resigned to groveling if she had to, but she hoped she wouldn't need to tell Frances about her mistake in getting the date of her dinner party wrong.

"I'd be happy to babysit tomorrow evening," Frances said. "But isn't this a little short notice, dear? You must have been planning this dinner for weeks."

"Oh well, a week or so, but I thought my friend Allie was going to sit for me. But something came up, and so I thought I'd see if you were free. I'm very thankful that you are." She realized she was babbling and closed her mouth.

"It's not a problem. Now if you'd said *next* week..."

Shelley grimaced. "I guess it's a good thing it's not next week, then. Thank you so much."

"You're welcome. I must say, it was rather inconsiderate of your friend to cancel on you at the last minute."

"It wasn't like that...exactly." Shelley swallowed hard. She didn't want to give the wrong impression of Allie, but she didn't want to look stupid, either. Her pride, that was it. She hated to look bad, especially with Frances. *Lord, help me to be honest.* "Actually, it was my fault," she blurted.

"Oh?"

The silence chilled Shelley for a moment, and she steeled herself for criticism. "Yes. I had confused the date, and I told Allie the wrong day. She was perfectly willing, but as it worked out, tomorrow night was bad for her."

"I see. Well, those things happen to all of us."

Her affable tone surprised Shelley. "Thank you for understanding, Frances. I can have Dan bring the kids over—"

"Don't worry about that. I'll pick them up. Is five o'clock soon enough?"

"That's perfect." Shelley hung up humbled but extremely grateful. She'd dodged that bullet. Now, if she could just get the house thoroughly cleaned and the meal prepared. Last night's run to the market had helped, but she'd forgotten the rosemary she would need for the chicken dish.

"Mama! Emma's eating a leaf."

Shelley jerked her head toward Aiden's voice. What on earth? She'd removed her few houseplants to high places that toddlers couldn't reach. She ran to the living room doorway.

Emma sat on the rug near the sofa, chewing on something dark, with spittle running down her chin. Shelley ran over and snatched her up.

"Spit it out, Emma." She held her hand under the toddler's chin. "Icky. Spit it out."

A dark mass plopped into her hand and she grimaced.

"Good girl." She set Emma down and carried her prize to the window. It appeared to be a very mangled wrapper from a chewy candy. "Where on earth did that come from?"

Aiden came and peered at it. "Is it a leaf?"

"No, it's a candy wrapper."

"Bryce's mommy gave me one the other day."

"Oh, and you didn't get it into the trash?" Now Shelley vaguely remembered Allie asking if she could give Aiden a piece of chewy candy.

"I'm sorry, Mama."

Shelley sighed. "Okay. But you can see how important it is to put trash in the trash can. Emma could have choked on that."

Aiden nodded, tears in his eyes.

Shelley pulled him close for a hug. "Well, thank you for keeping a close eye on your sister. You're a big help to me in that way, Aiden. And you told me right away when you saw that she had something in her mouth that she shouldn't, so that was good."

"I thought it was a leaf." He blinked up at her.

"I know, honey." She kissed his forehead. "Come on. Let's take Emma into the kitchen. She can play under the table while you while I load the dishwasher."

★ ★ ★

Margaret called Buddy's number with shaking hands. She had dreamed again last night, and had risen early to paint before coming to the gallery. Now she had another unfinished canvas at home in her bedroom. This one was from the vantage point of a ship's deck at sunset, and the town was visible on shore, catching the late rays of sun— but the church was intact this time, with no fire marring the horizon. She'd known Buddy stood beside her on the ship, though she couldn't see his face. She wasn't sure how to put that in the painting, so she hadn't tried, but she still thought about it. It wasn't a rescue situation. This dream had felt more peaceful, and Buddy's presence did not alarm her.

Allan had come by to tend to customers during the noon hour so that she could have as long as she needed for the call. She'd gone into her office and shut the door, grateful for the promise of uninterrupted time.

As the connection processed, she sent up a quick prayer. *Lord, tell me what to say. Show me how I can help him!*

She found that she truly did want to help Buddy, and the annoyance and fear she'd felt earlier had vanished. She cared about her cousin, and anything she could do to steer him back to sobriety would be well worth her time.

"Hello?"

"Buddy? It's Margaret."

"Hi." Relief filled his voice, and to Margaret's joy, he sounded like himself—sober.

"Hey, how are you doing today?" she asked.

"Not too good. My head aches. I…I wasn't sure you'd call."

And I wasn't sure you'd remember, she thought, but out loud she said, "Well, I'm here. I want to talk to you."

"What about?"

"Well, can you tell me more about your friend, Pete? What happened to him?"

Buddy let out a shaky sigh. "It was real sudden. He just… One day I was talking to him about going fishing together, and the next day he was gone."

Margaret picked up enough clues to determine that Pete was a person, so she felt a little more confident about the conversation. "I'm so sorry, Buddy. Now, how did you and Pete know each other?"

"We were friends in high school. His family lived just down the road—a couple of miles, that is. They moved in when I was in tenth grade. We rode the bus together. Then, my senior year, when I got a car, I would pick him up every morning, and we'd ride together. We were cool then, I'll tell ya. Not too many of the kids had cars."

Margaret smiled. "That's a nice memory to hang on to. And you stayed friends with Pete all these years."

"Well…yeah, I guess. We had some times when we didn't see each other for a long period. Pete was in the army for a while, and I went to UMO. Then he lived in *Indianner* for about ten years."

Margaret laughed at his exaggerated accent on "Indiana." "Sorry—it's not funny, but I know you're being funny on purpose and—well, you are. You have a great sense of humor now."

"Not like the old days, huh? Margaret, I never meant to be mean to anyone."

"I know. I don't think you realized how much you hurt people back then. But let's forget about that, shall we? I want to know more about Pete."

"He was a great guy. Oh, sometimes he did things he shouldn't—but didn't we all? We got in trouble together a few times in high school. Nothing real serious. But when Pete came back from 'Nam he was different. I think that changed him. In fact, he sort of told me off one time, that I should grow up..."

Score one for Pete, Margaret thought. It was too bad Buddy hadn't listened to him back then, instead of annoying most of the people in his life for another forty years.

"Anyhow, since I'd been...you know, going to AA..."

"Yes," Margaret said, "I know."

"Well, we got close again. He lived in Waterville, and we only got together a couple of times a year, but we'd talk on the phone some, and when we did see each other... Those were some of the best times I've ever had. Just good, clean fun. In May I went up there and played baseball with Pete and his grandkids, and we went to see his grandson in a play. And last winter, we took a snowmobile trip together, clear up into Aroostook County."

Margaret shivered. Snowmobiling wasn't her idea of fun when she could curl up in front of a fireplace with a good book. "Sounds like Pete knew all your foibles and was still a good pal."

"Yeah. He was great in that way. And he…he brought out the best in me. When I heard he'd died, I just…I lost it, Margaret. I couldn't stand the idea that I'd never see him again. That I didn't have a true friend anymore. Somebody who'd seen me at my worst and stuck by me. But now—well, I look at Pete's life and all the things he did—the army, and his business, and he's got three kids that really love him. And then I look at myself, and all I see is a failure. I dropped out of college, and then I couldn't get a decent job. The jobs I had, I couldn't keep because of my drinking. And Sandra left me, and my own kids hate me, and…and my life is worth nothing. Absolutely nothing."

A lot of things swirled through Margaret's mind. Buddy's marriage had ended in divorce thirty years ago, and his ex-wife had fought hard for sole custody of the two children. Though she had purposely not learned the gritty details of the breakup, Margaret knew that Sandra had made the process difficult for Buddy. It sounded as though the children weren't on good terms with him either, but she wondered about his relationship with them.

"Why do you say Peggy and Joe hate you?" she ventured. "Do you hear from them?"

He barked a curt laugh. "Peggy hasn't spoken to me in years. She said I teased her too much when she was a kid, and her mother let her spread rumors about me. We never talk now."

Margaret winced. She could well imagine that Buddy had brought his daughter to tears many times over the years. It didn't seem profitable to dig into that.

"Joe's not quite so bad," Buddy went on. "We talk once in a while, and he sends me a Christmas card. He's living down in Virginia now, though. Haven't seen him for about three years."

"Does he know about…about this latest trouble you've been having?"

"What, that I'm drinking again? Might as well say it, Margaret. I'm still a drunk. I thought I could beat it, but I've proved I was kidding myself."

"Buddy, no. Don't say that. You stayed sober for—what? Six years?"

"Yeah, about that."

"That was wonderful. *That's* the person you are now, not the last few weeks. This is a setback, yes, but it doesn't mean it's all over."

"I dunno," he said. "I don't feel like I've got the strength to go through that again. It was great when I'd made it and things were going well, but I remember how hard it was when I quit."

"You can do it again," Margaret said. "I know you can. Buddy, you've got to go back to your AA meeting. Don't put it off."

He sighed. "I can't face people there. Not after this."

"Oh, and you think they haven't been through the same thing? Buddy, some of those people have fallen off the wagon dozens of times. But they pick themselves up again. You can help them and encourage them. Show them that even a mistake this big will not get you down. You're still the man I saw last fall, the one who was considerate and generous and helpful at the reunion. That's the Buddy all your friends want to see again."

"I'm not so sure about that."

"What? You think they're happy you started drinking again?"

"Maybe."

"You misjudge them. Nobody wants you to go back to your old ways. Not even to make themselves look good."

He let out a deep sigh. "It's too hard."

"Don't say that again. I want you to call Greg today. Right now, as soon as we hang up."

"You know Greg?" Buddy sounded startled, and Margaret wondered if she'd made a mistake in mentioning the sponsor's name.

"Well, yes, I do, slightly. In fact, I spoke to him on the phone a few days ago. He wants to see you succeed, Buddy. Greg cares about you. And so do I."

"Thanks. That's...well, it's hard to believe, but thanks for saying it."

Margaret was beginning to feel exasperated, as though nothing she said mattered. "Listen, there's another reason I called you. I've...I've dreamed about you lately. Several times. I'd wake up, and I'd be shaking from this dream."

"What kind of dream?"

"Usually I was in the water. I think I was remembering that day I nearly drowned. The day you saved me, Buddy. And when I have the dream, I get up and paint. I've done five or six paintings the last couple of weeks, trying to get my dreams on canvas. And I felt like I needed to call you. Even before I knew what was happening in your life, there was this strong urge to contact you and make sure you were okay. I'm sorry I didn't call you sooner."

"Wow."

They were both silent for several seconds.

"I mean it when I say I care about you," Margaret said gently. "I can't help wondering if God has been telling me to reach out to you, the way you did once to me."

"But...I didn't even know it was you." Buddy's voice choked.

"I know," she said. "But God knew. And He knew it was high time we connected again. So...will you call Greg?"

"I...I guess so."

"No, no guessing so. Promise me," she said firmly.

"Okay. I'll do it."

She smiled. "Good. I'd say thank you, but I don't really want you to feel you're doing this for me, Buddy. Do it for yourself. You need this. Now let's say good-bye, and you call him. Now."

"Will you call me again?"

"I will."

He exhaled. "Okay then. Bye."

"Talk to you soon. Bye." She clicked off and sat holding the phone for a moment. She hadn't noticed until that moment, but her eyes were filled with tears. She reached for a tissue and wiped them away. She took a sip from the cup of tea she'd carried into the office with her, but it was nearly cold now. How long had they talked? She set the mug aside, stood, and went to the door.

Allan was just ringing up a customer, and two more were browsing the gallery. He threw her a glance and arched his eyebrows in question.

Margaret smiled and gave him a small nod.

Allan grinned at the customer. "And here's your change. May I carry that out to your car for you?"

Only then did Margaret realize that he had a wrapped painting lying on the counter. She glanced around quickly to see which one had sold and relaxed when she saw the empty space on the wall in the neighboring section of the gallery. One of her friend Louellen Lumadue's framed "hidden angel" paintings. No sale could have made her happier today.

CHAPTER TWELVE

Margaret awoke from another dream on Friday morning, but this time she was not afraid. The dreams were taking on the nature of a series, she realized. With each episode, she learned a little more.

In this latest one, she stood on the deck of an old sailing ship on a stormy night. The wind blew with a ferocity that tumbled waves over the gunwales and across the deck. The ship tilted and lunged, and rain pelted her face. Margaret clung to the rail and stared toward shore. A light flared up—not a guiding beacon, but once more a blaze devouring a building. As the ship plunged up and then swooped low, she couldn't focus on the shore. Was the fire consuming the church again? Or was it a bonfire? Maybe it represented a warning to flee this coast. Or could it be an invitation to safe harbor? Or an ominous siren call?

The waves sloshing over her feet felt real, as did the relentless wind, and the pocks of rain on her upturned cheeks. She shivered and yet, even though she was far from shore, she fancied the heat of the fire singed her face.

She opened her eyes. It was daylight already. She grabbed a notepad from her bedside table and sketched the scene as she had viewed it. The ship from her vantage point on the deck, the waves, the distant shore—it was Marble Cove, she was certain this time—and the fire. The real fire at Old First must be triggering the dreams, or at least that part of them. Buddy wasn't in the dream this time. Was that because she had contacted him, so she'd let go of that worry? And the fire seemed closer, more immediate.

She wanted to remember the details, but she wouldn't paint yet, just get them into the sketch. She would wait until she got to her studio at the Shearwater to get out her paints. If customers were sparse, she would work on it today. If it was busy, she would have to wait, but she wanted to do this one right. She wanted the emotion and the sensations she had felt to spring at the viewer from the canvas. To make that happen, she would paint more slowly this time, choosing her colors and strokes with care.

★ ★ ★

Shelley woke in the gray light of dawn and peered at the alarm clock: 5:15. She closed her eyes for a moment, opened them again, and jumped out of bed. She scurried around in the dimness, looking for jeans and underwear and a suitable shirt, trying to be quiet, but Dan rolled over and squinted at her.

"Shell? Why are you getting up so early, babe?"

"Tonight's the dinner with Wayne and his wife. I've got a bajillion things to do."

Dan moaned and rolled over. Shelley patted the rug under the edge of the bed, looking for her sneakers. When she left the room, Dan was sitting up on his side of the bed, rubbing his eyes. She hoped he wouldn't be upset with her for waking him up a half hour early. Maybe he could still go back to sleep.

In the kitchen, she pulled butter from the refrigerator to soften and set a big bowl of dough out on the counter. She'd mixed yeast rolls the night before and let them rise once, then covered the bowl and put it in the fridge. After washing her hands, she began shaping the dough into balls and placing them in a baking pan.

Dan walked into the room yawning as she covered the pan with a clean dish towel.

"What are you doing?"

"Putting the rolls out to rise again." She opened the cupboard above the coffeemaker, wishing she'd started Dan's coffee first.

"Oh. What do you want me to do?"

She whirled and stared at him. "Really? Well, I have a list of stuff I need to do today. It's right here." Hesitantly, she held out her lengthy to-do list.

Dan took it and frowned. "What can be done now? I don't have a lot of time, but...hey, I can vacuum the rugs for you."

Shelley's heart leaped. She hated vacuuming. "That would be great, but it would probably wake up the kids."

"*Hmm*." Dan scowled down at the notepad. "Well, a lot of this stuff you have to do yourself."

"Yes, and some has to wait until afternoon." She scrunched up her face, thinking. "Maybe they'd sleep through the vacuum if you keep away from the hall. Just do the dining room and living room. It would help me a lot."

"Sure. I'll shut Emma's door first. You've got the monitor on, so you can hear her, right?" He actually looked relieved as he headed for the closet where they kept the vacuum.

"Teamwork," Shelley whispered. "Thank You, Lord."

To her relief, Aiden slept until almost eight o'clock, and Emma gave her another hour's respite beyond that. After Dan left for work, Shelley was able to square away the laundry and dusting.

When the kids were up, dressed, and fed, she took them into the backyard, with Prize tagging along. Her daylilies had bloomed a little late this year, but that was good. Probably transplanting them after the kitchen addition was built had set them back a little, and they would be perfect for tonight.

She was just returning inside to change Emma's sodden diaper when Maddie Bancroft called.

"Hey, I wondered if Aiden could do a playdate with my kids tomorrow."

"Thanks, Maddie. I'm sure he'd like that. Right now, I'm pretty frazzled, but tomorrow should be okay."

"What's going on now?" Maddie asked.

"Oh, Dan's boss and his wife are coming to dinner tonight. I've never met Mrs. Stover, and I thought the dinner was next week. To put it mildly, I'm a little stressed."

"Anything I can do?"

"I doubt it, but thanks," Shelley said. "You've got enough on your hands, I'm sure."

"Well, I'm just starting lunch, but I might be able to run over for a little while after I feed the kids."

"You don't have to."

"No problem. We'll see how it goes."

The prospect of Maddie "Mrs. Perfect" Bancroft popping in gave Shelley a new burst of energy. She liked Maddie now that she knew her better, but the woman's stamina and talents were still a bit intimidating. She led her church choir, homeschooled her children, and was considered by many to be the ideal hostess. Maybe she would be able to give some pointers, but Shelley felt she'd do just as well on her own. Maddie would only make her nervous.

★ ★ ★

As it turned out, a fair amount of traffic came through the gallery that morning. The sky was overcast, threatening rain and keeping folks away from the beach. Summer people meandered along Main Street, picking up odds and ends for their cottages and souvenirs to send home. Margaret sold one of her prints, a pottery vase, and some of Bernadette Lassiter's beach glass jewelry. One woman ordered an occasional table from Allan's line, but with custom inlay. She loved one of the models in the gallery, but wanted different woods. Margaret made copious notes and took the customer's phone number for Allan so that he could talk to her himself and make sure he had it right before he began. That could keep him busy for several weeks.

At last, about one o'clock, she had a lull and went to the back to eat a sandwich. She'd told Allan she wouldn't come home for lunch, since she wanted to work in her studio for a while. As she munched, she began setting out the supplies she would use. She'd just polished off the sandwich and was ready to sit down at the easel when her cell rang.

With a sigh, she pulled it out. "Hello?"

"Margaret?"

"Buddy?"

"Yeah."

She couldn't judge from his brief words what condition he was in.

"Buddy, how are you doing today?"

"Uh..."

She didn't like that response. "Buddy, did you call Greg? Talk to me."

He sobbed. "It's too hard, Margaret."

"Oh no. Come on, you know you don't want to be this way. Do you, now? I know better."

"I just...I just..."

"You just had a few drinks again, didn't you?"

"I was tryin' to get ready to call him, really."

She sighed. "How about if *I* call Greg? Is there a meeting tonight?"

"I can't remember."

"Well, try. Are you at home?"

"Yeah."

"Okay, listen, I'm going to hang up now and call Greg. If he can, he'll probably come over and talk to you. Or at least call you. Don't go anywhere, and whatever you do, stop drinking that stuff. Do you hear me?"

She heard a tiny sob or a hiccup, and then, "Sure, Margaret. I'll be here. But don't call Greg."

"And why not?"

"I let him down. I can't see him now."

"Of course you—"

"No, Margaret. I let you down. I let everybody down."

"Stop that. I'm calling him now, Buddy, and you do whatever Greg tells you."

"'kay."

She closed her phone and let her shoulders slump. Babysitting her cousin was not the way she'd envisioned this day. She had lost her patience, and she regretted that. Still, with Buddy's brain in a fog, the kind, soothing approach would probably not have been effective.

She decided to call Greg from the landline to ensure a good connection, but just as she reached for the phone, the bell on the front door jingled.

★ ★ ★

Shelley managed to straighten up all the rooms, even Aiden's, in case the Stovers wanted a tour of the house. She hated that, but Dan would probably think it was a great idea. At last she sat the kids down for lunch. Emma was still in her booster seat when Maddie drove in. She let her three older children get out of the car and join Aiden in the backyard. She carried the youngest, who was Emma's age, inside.

"Hi," Shelley said. "I'm just cleaning up from lunch." She wiped Emma's face and set her down beside little Jenny. "Wow, she's getting big!"

"Isn't she?" Maddie grinned. "She's taller than her cousin, who's six months older than she is."

"Amazing."

"So," Maddie looked around, "what can I do?"

"I'm not sure. I think I actually have things under control. I'm going to arrange my flowers with some driftwood we picked up on the beach, and I still have the salad and chicken to fix."

Maddie nodded and walked to the living room doorway. "You've done your floors."

"Yeah, Dan did the vacuuming before he left for work. I just need to do a last-minute wipe-up in the bathroom now and put out fresh towels. And I fixed a fancy dessert that I need to decorate," Shelley said. "It's individual tortes. They look fabulous, and they're not that hard to make."

"It sounds scrumptious."

"Of course, I still have to get *me* ready." Shelley blew a strand of blonde hair up off her forehead and looked down disparagingly at her jeans and stained Patriots shirt.

Maggie pulled a long face and shook her head. "Shelley, I don't think I can help you."

Shelley stared at her. Was it that bad? She'd felt pretty good about the menu, and the house was clean now, or nearly. Of course, keeping it clean until this evening with Aiden and Emma in residence would be a challenge. Sure, the decorations would be a little sparse, but was she really hopeless? She gazed bleakly at Maddie. "Oh."

★ ★ ★

Diane and Rocky walked toward the Cannery after lunch. She'd hoped to connect with Terri, but as she left her house she noticed that her friend's SUV wasn't in her driveway. Diane missed Terri, and Gallant too. Their company had made her walks with Rocky more interesting. With him on the leash, she strolled along through residential neighborhoods feeling a little down. The sky was clouding up to match her mood.

Her phone rang as they were passing the elementary school, so Diane guided Rocky into the parking lot and answered it.

"Hi, Diane. Frieda here. How's the weather in Maine?"

"It's cool and cloudy this afternoon. I've got Rocky out for a walk before the rain comes. How's New York?"

Frieda laughed. "It's okay. I wish I could get outside. Listen, I've got some exciting news. There's a company interested in optioning your book for film rights."

Diane froze. She gulped and asked, "What did you say?"

"WMN—the Women's Movie Network—is talking about optioning the film rights for your book."

"Wow. I don't know what to say. This is … unexpected."

"Yes, well, don't get stars in your eyes quite yet. It's only an option, and ninety-five percent of those options never get used. But if they do take this step, it will mean a small bit of income for you, and if it does go forward … well, you just never know, do you?"

"Yes—I mean, no. Oh boy. Tell me more."

Frieda chuckled. "Somehow one of their film producers got hold of your book, and he thinks it's good for a TV movie."

"I think so too," Diane said. "But I never really thought it would happen."

"It still may not. In fact, it probably won't. I want to be sure you understand that. This is just a first, formal step of securing the possibility of doing it."

"Okay. So now what?"

"They're supposed to send me an agreement. I'll look it over, and if it seems all right, I'll send it on to you to sign. You send it back, and then forget it."

"Forget it?"

"Yes. Because if you put too much stock in it, you'll probably be disappointed. Like I said, ninety-five percent of those who take this step never go any further."

"I'll keep it in mind."

"Good. I don't have the details yet, but I'll let you know when I do."

"Great," Diane said. "Thank you so much. This is … it's a real encouragement."

"It should be. I'm proud of you and your book, Diane. I'll talk to you again soon."

Diane exhaled deeply and put her phone away. Rocky was sitting patiently on the pavement, looking up at her with his big brown eyes. Diane laughed out loud and crouched beside him.

"Did you hear that, boy? Some TV company may option my book."

He woofed, and Diane ruffled his fur. She laughed again and hugged him. "Hooray! I don't care what Frieda says, I'm going to be happy about it. Come on!"

They took off in a victory jog around the empty playground.

★ ★ ★

Hurrying out into the gallery, Margaret spotted a woman who had been a frequent browser this summer, and it appeared she had brought a friend along. Margaret put on her best smile.

"Good afternoon, ladies."

"Hello," said the repeat customer. "I brought my friend in. We were getting out of the rain, but I knew we'd enjoy spending a few minutes in here."

"That's fine." Margaret glanced toward the window. A light rain was falling, and pedestrians were dashing for cover. She'd better make that call to Greg and just give him a quick update, or she might find herself tied up without an opportunity all afternoon. "Help yourselves to coffee, ladies. I have a brief call I must make, but I'll be right with you."

She used the phone behind the counter, and in the three minutes it took for her to get hold of Greg and tell him Buddy was in immediate need, two more customers came in, laughing and folding their umbrellas.

"As it happens, I can go over there now," Greg said. "I'll do my best to persuade him to go to a meeting with me tonight."

"Thank you so much." Margaret hung up and approached the new customers. "Welcome. We keep this antique umbrella stand here by the door just for days like this one. Feel free to use it." She'd found that this approach kept most customers from dripping all over the gallery on wet days. Many were intrigued by the hundred-year-old ceramic jar in the shape of an elephant. Several people had tried to buy it, but Margaret had decided to keep it, at least until she found a replacement she liked as well.

The perennial browser's friend came around one of the dividers and hovered, obviously waiting for her attention.

"Excuse me," Margaret told the newcomers. "Help yourselves to coffee if you'd like, and I won't be far away if you have questions." She turned to the waiting woman. Too bad she had no helpers today. "May I help you?"

"Yes," the woman said. "I was wondering about that sailboat painting. Is that a local scene?"

"It was done by an artist who lives in Lincolnville." Margaret walked back toward the painting as she spoke and told the shopper a little about the artist. The woman seemed very interested, but did not say the magic words—"I'll take it." After a few minutes, Margaret left her to help a couple who requested a box for a pottery bowl they were buying.

An hour later, she decided she must have some assistance. More and more shoppers had entered, and they all seemed reluctant to leave because of the rain. They struck up conversations in corners and went through three pots of coffee and all her cookies. It was worth it—she'd handed out lots of brochures and business cards.

The woman who liked the sailboat painting approached the counter.

"I do believe I want that picture."

"Wonderful," Margaret said, and went to remove the sailboat watercolor from the wall. She was especially pleased about this transaction, as it was the first piece she'd sold for that particular artist. She wrapped it carefully and saw the buyer and her friend to the door—and then stood aside for three more people to enter.

After ringing up another purchase of a ceramic plaque, she grabbed a moment to call home and beg for aid.

Chapter Thirteen

Maddie stood in the doorway between the dining room and the living room and gazed slowly around each room.

"Wh-what do you mean, you can't help me?" Shelley asked. "Am I that hopeless?"

Maddie swung around, her eyes widening. "Hopeless? Of course not! Sweetie, everything looks perfect. I can't think of one thing I'd have done differently!"

Shelley puffed out a breath and collapsed her rigid stance. "Thanks."

"You don't need me. But I'll tell you what: would it help you out if I take the kids away for a couple of hours?"

"Really?"

"Yup. We're headed to the new playground in Willow's Corner. Have you been there?"

Shelley shook her head.

"Aiden will love it. And there's a special fenced play area for toddlers, so if we can fit Emma's car seat in my van, she can go too."

"You . . . you'd take six kids to a playground by yourself?"

"Sure. Roger's old enough to help me keep track of the little guys. It would give you time to do those nitpicky things like the centerpiece and the tortes without interruption. What do you say? Last call."

"Well—yes. And thank you."

Maddie grinned. "I'll wear them out so that they're ready for a good nap when they get home too." She turned to the door and yelled outside, "Roger! Katelyn! Time to go. Aiden and Emma are going with us."

Aiden came puffing in, red-faced. "Mama, am I really going with them?"

"It seems you are. Just for a little while, but I think you'll have fun. Help me get your booster and Emma's car seat into Benjamin's mom's van."

Shelley squeezed every minute out of the next two hours. Refusing to worry about the kids or Maddie, she put them out of her mind and went down her remaining to-do list at a brisk clip. By the time Maddie's minivan returned, she had completed all but her personal grooming and the cooking that had to be done at the last minute. She dashed out to the driveway, exhausted but triumphant, to help Maddie get her children and their car seats out of the vehicle.

"Hey," Maddie said with a grin. "We had a great time."

"Thank you so much," Shelley said.

"No problem. Oh, that's grape juice on Emma's top. Sorry about that."

Shelley shook her head as she viewed the small stain. "Don't worry about it. And thanks for giving them a drink."

"Do you have a good stain remover?"

"Uh, yeah."

Maddie nodded. "Hey, I'm still open to a playdate tomorrow. I was serious about that."

Shelley stared at her. "That would be too much for you."

"No, just drop Aiden off around two if it works for you."

"Okay. I'll call you if he's not coming."

Maddie gave her a thumbs-up. "You can be proud of yourself, Shelley. You've done a terrific job. I hope all goes well tonight."

As the Bancrofts' van drove out, Emma began to fuss, and Shelley held her close.

"You're tired, aren't you, honey? Well, I know just the remedy for that."

She grinned to herself as she took the children inside. She was holding her own with Maddie Bancroft, the best hostess in Marble Cove.

★ ★ ★

Surveying the crowded gallery, Margaret held her breath while the home phone rang. To her relief, Allan picked it up on the third ring.

"Thank goodness you're there. Can you possibly come give me a hand? I'm swamped!"

"Be right there," he assured her.

The look on Allan's face when he arrived ten minutes later told Margaret he'd thought she might be exaggerating. She waved, and he hurried to the counter.

"Wow. What do you want me to do? Man the register?"

"That couple over there was asking about your tables. Why don't you tend to them first?"

Margaret breathed easily for the first time in an hour. She turned to smile at a young woman approaching the checkout with a small print in her hands.

Allan was a great help in taking inquiries about the wooden items, and then he managed a dash next door to the Cove for more pastries. After that, he got behind the counter while Margaret replenished the refreshment table. By the time he left at four to pick up Adelaide from the community center, the rain had slacked and the crowd began to thin. Margaret was exhausted. She felt almost as drained as she did on days when they had special showings. Her sales for the day were healthy—no need to worry about next month's rent and electricity—but she had never gotten back to her easel. Now she was too tired.

"Well, Lord," she said out loud as she cleaned up the used coffee cups and napkins in the refreshment area, "if You want me to do that painting right, I guess You'll have to find me some extra time for it. And thank You for all the people You sent in today."

All in all, it had been a good day, but not at all the one she'd anticipated when she awoke that morning. Turning the deadbolt on the front door, she wondered whether Buddy would go to the AA meeting. She decided to leave that question to Greg Hathorn and God.

★ ★ ★

Beverly drove to Portland on Friday afternoon and checked into the hotel where the seminar would be held. Her nerves fluttered a little, but not too badly. She settled into her comfortable room and made sure she could access the Internet easily. At six, she freshened her makeup and went down to the hotel's restaurant. She'd agreed to meet the event's organizer, Rachel Conley, for dinner. When she entered the dining room, Rachel was waiting for her at a corner table.

"We have more than sixty women registered," Rachel said eagerly as they scanned their menus. "I'm so excited! I know the skills you're going to teach them will help them in their new ventures."

"I hope so," Beverly said. "I spoke to someone at the Small Business Administration Tuesday, to make sure I'm up-to-date on regulations. You said several of the attendees are hoping to start catering businesses, so I zeroed in on that for a few of my visuals."

"Terrific. Yes, we've got at least five women who listed that as their target business. And four want to either open a gift shop or start an online gift business."

"*Hmm*, there's a big difference. I'll be talking about overhead and how to succeed with and without a physical retail location."

"Good. I know some of the women think they'll have easy sailing if they don't have to rent a physical space."

"Well, I have a friend who's running a custom bakery out of her home," Beverly said, "but she still had to put in a commercial kitchen and jump through some official hoops."

"I guess it depends on what sort of business you have," Rachel said.

"Yes. I have to admit that with a home office instead of a downtown location, I find my own overhead is minimal. But for some businesses a commercial space is a necessity."

They continued to talk shop while they ate. After the meal, Beverly excused herself and returned to her room. She opened her briefcase but didn't take her notes out. She knew the material cold. A sheaf of loose papers caught her eye, and she pulled out the information she'd picked up at the town office. Did she really want to commit to a stint as mayor—assuming she could win the election, of course? Rachel Conley had mentioned several corporations she would recommend Beverly to if tomorrow's seminar went well, including a prosperous company that manufactured and exported computer chips. Beverly might soon have all the financial consulting that she could handle.

She wondered where Jeff was tonight. He'd said he would call her, but she hadn't heard from him yet. She took out her phone and put in his number. It rang, but then went to voice mail.

"Hi," Beverly said, feeling a bit embarrassed. Should she have waited for him to call? "I...uh...I got to Portland okay, and I just wanted to let you know. The hotel is nice. The classes will start at eight in the morning. Everything looks good. I hope you've had fun in the Allagash. Talk to you later. Bye!"

She wished she'd had a chance to talk to him in detail about the election. She picked up the papers from the town office and fluffed up the pillows on the bed. If she read through everything again, maybe she'd have a better idea of what she wanted to do about that.

★ ★ ★

"Shell? Where are you?" Dan called.

Shelley poked her head out of the bedroom. "In here. I hope you took your boots off on the porch."

"Oops."

She grimaced and turned back to take the clean underwear she would put on from her dresser. Emma cooed at her from the bed. A moment later, Dan appeared in the doorway.

"It's awfully quiet here. Did you manage to do everything you wanted?"

She smiled at him. "Sure did. Can you just watch the kids until your mom picks them up? She should be here any minute, and I have a bag all packed for them. Aiden is in his room."

"Okay," Dan said, looking a bit puzzled. "What are you going to do?"

"I'm getting into a bubble bath, thank you."

"Well, I brought you something." He brought his hands from behind his back, and Shelley gasped.

"Oh, Dan! Flowers? They're beautiful!" She hurried over and took the paper cone of blossoms from his hand. A florist's name was stamped in script on the holder—so they didn't come from the grocery store. No way would she ask how much they cost. "Roses! Wow, I didn't expect this. Thank you!" She stood on tiptoe to kiss him.

Dan smiled sheepishly. "I thought it was a great idea, but I see you've got flowers already."

"Oh, those are just lilies the kids and I picked. They're nothing special. I'll put these in that pretty vase your aunt gave us for our wedding present and set them in the living room. They should impress Mrs. Stover."

Dan laughed. "You don't need to impress her. She's just a regular, down-to-earth person."

"Glad to hear it. Would you mind just sticking these in some water while I have my bath? You can use that plastic pitcher I use for lemonade. I'll get the vase out when I'm done."

"Sure. I'll put this on the counter, okay?" He held up a bright red foil sack.

"What's that?"

"Fresh-roasted coffee. From the Cove." He shrugged. "I just thought it might be good with dessert or something."

She grinned at him. "It's perfect. I made those fancy-schmancy little tortes, and they came out wicked nice." She thought she heard tires on gravel and raised her chin, listening. "I think your mother's here. Help her get the kids buckled, okay? And then do the flowers."

"Got it." He scooped Emma off the bed and headed into the hallway, calling, "Aiden! Meemaw's here. Come give me a hug before you go."

Shelley spent twenty heavenly minutes in the bathtub, thinking about what a terrific husband she had and going down her list of last-minute tasks in her mind. She vacated the bathroom reluctantly so that Dan could shower and get ready. Over her dress, she donned a big wraparound apron and put the vegetables on simmer.

A few minutes later she carried the elegant vase of roses into the living room and set it on the end table. She looked around her clean, pretty home again and smiled. "Thank You, Lord!"

Just as the Stovers arrived, Dan came from the bedroom with shiny, blow-dried hair. He wore clean, pressed tan pants and a short-sleeved cotton shirt. Not dressed up, but certainly a couple of cuts above what he wore to work.

They went to the door together. Wayne and his wife were waiting on the porch.

"Hey, come on in," Dan said. "Mrs. Stover, this is Shelley."

Wayne's wife smiled at her. "Hello, Shelley. Please call me Eileen. Oh, and this is for you."

Speechless for a moment, Shelley gazed down at the small box of swanky chocolates. "Wow! Thanks so much."

"Those do wonders on a stressful day." Eileen winked at her.

Next to Wayne's big, burly form, Eileen seemed petite, but she was as tall as Shelley. She looked about fifty but "well preserved," as Dan's dad would say. She wore her blonde hair cropped short, and judging by her tan, Shelley would have guessed she lived in Florida, not Maine. Wayne looked different than he usually did when Shelley saw him—for one thing, he wasn't wearing his blue work clothes. He had on a navy polo shirt and khaki pants, and he looked nearly as squeaky-clean as Dan did.

They spent a pleasant evening together, and both the guests exclaimed over the meal. Eileen asked for Shelley's chicken recipe. At the sight of the chocolate tortes with raspberry glaze, she let out a low moan.

"My dear, I don't know how I can possibly do it, but I can't say no."

Shelley smiled at Dan and poured out the extraspecial coffee. To her relief, the conversation wasn't all wiring and sports. Wayne wanted Eileen to see the commercial kitchen Dan and his father had helped install. Later they settled in the living room and discussed topics ranging from the Stovers' grandchildren to the upcoming Lobster Festival.

"I'm having a cookie booth at that festival," Shelley said. "Dan's going to help me."

"That sounds like fun," Wayne said.

"It sounds like a lot of work, though," Eileen added.

"It will be, but it's only one day." Shelley smiled. "It's a big event in town, and I want the Lighthouse Sweet Shoppe to be visible."

"I'm sure everyone will be glad you're offering your cookies." Eileen smiled. "You're a fabulous cook, Shelley. I hope it ends up bringing you a lot of new business."

"Thank you," Shelley said.

"She's freezing cookies ahead," Dan said. "How many have you made so far, Shelley?"

She smiled. "I've got thirty dozen earmarked for the festival so far, but I want to start out with about three times that many."

"Wow," Eileen said. "Just thinking about baking that many cookies makes my head swim. You must really love to bake."

"I do," Shelley said. "Ever since I was a little girl, it's been one of my favorite things."

"Now, will you be showing your woodworking at the festival?" Wayne asked Dan.

"Sort of. My friend Allan Hoskins is the one I work with on that—and he'll be there." Dan looked at Shelley. "Are Allan and Margaret setting up a booth?"

"I don't think so." Shelley looked at the Stovers. "Allan's wife owns the Shearwater Gallery on Main Street, and they both sell their work there. I think they plan to keep the gallery open extra hours and maybe just have a display over at the festival, instead of trying to sell things in two places."

"The Shearwater," Eileen said. "I went in there once. I loved it!"

"Margaret's a wonderful painter," Shelley said. "She opened the gallery last year. But she and Allan live right across the street from us. They're good friends, and Dan helps out with Allan's furniture when he's busy." She glanced at Dan, wondering if he'd rather she would be quiet and let him tell Wayne about his off-the-clock pursuits.

Dan shrugged. "I used to work for Allan more, before you hired me on. I still go over there some on weekends and help with the finish work."

"Your skill shows in that new kitchen," Wayne said. "The detail work on the cabinets is terrific."

"Thanks," Dan said.

"Well, I'm glad you mentioned the gallery," Eileen told Shelley. "I need a special gift next month. I think I'll go back there and see if I find something. I remember they had prints of your lighthouse . . ."

Shelley sat back in the curve of Dan's arm, feeling content. Her lighthouse. Her friends, her town. And her home had passed muster. Next time Wayne and Eileen came to visit, she might get brave and keep the children around.

With Dan's help, she could probably do that without having a disaster. It felt good to know that she could organize a complicated event of her own, and that she could count on Dan to work with her. They made a great team.

When the Stovers left about nine thirty, Dan called his mother.

"Hey! Our company's gone. I'll be over soon to get the kids." He frowned and listened for a minute, then turned to Shelley. "Mom says they fell asleep and she'd be happy to let them stay till morning. What do you think?"

Shelley hesitated. Dan listened to some further information from Frances, and said, "Shell, she says Emma's sleeping on a quilt on the family room floor, but she can move her into her and Dad's room. And Aiden's sacked out on the couch. It'd be okay."

Shelley tried to think of a reason to say no, but both kids had an "emergency" change of clothes in their bag, and if they woke them up now, they might come home cranky. "Well . . . I guess. It's getting late."

Dan took that as consent and said into the phone. "Okay, Mom. And thanks."

Shelley gulped. Shouldn't she have put up more resistance? She'd hardly done anything with the kids today.

Dan hung up and turned to her, smiling. "How did this happen?"

"What?"

He walked slowly toward her. "Think about it, Shelley. We're alone."

Chapter Fourteen

Beverly awoke with a fluttering of nerves. Today was the seminar. She knew from experience that once she stood up in front of the group, she would be fine. She loved presenting, and she'd become quite good at it over her years with the state. But beforehand, there was always that "what if they don't like me" moment.

She got up much earlier than she needed to and sat down at her computer for a few minutes. After checking her e-mail, she decided to shower and go down to breakfast early. She'd have some extra time to set up and chat with any attendees who came in early.

She was about to turn on the shower when she heard her cell phone and dashed back into the bedroom, where she'd left it on the nightstand.

Jeff.

A warm feeling started somewhere near her heart and diffused throughout her. When she raised the phone to her ear, she felt a little breathless.

"Jeff! Thanks for calling."

"Hi," he said. "Am I too early?"

"No, I'm up and puttering around. This is a good time, actually."

"Great. I got your message last night, but I figured it was too late to call. Are you ready for the seminar?"

"Yes, so far everything's going smoothly. And the organizer has some great corporate contacts. If this goes well, I may be able to meet some potential clients through her."

"Sounds like some good networking. Are you nervous?"

"Maybe a little, but I think that keeps me on my toes."

He chuckled. "You'll do great."

"Thanks." Beverly sat down on the edge of the bed. It was nice to have someone who was there for her and who truly believed in her.

"I miss you," Jeff said quietly.

She smiled. "I miss you too. I was thinking about you."

"Good thoughts, I hope."

"Yes. Even better now. How was your trip?"

"It was great. Lots of fun, and I got some really good wildlife pictures."

"Yeah?" She smiled at the eagerness in his voice.

"Oh, Beverly. We were like three yards from a moose in that canoe!"

"*Hmm.* Not sure I'd want to be that close. But I can't wait to see the photos."

"I'll come see you soon. We just got in last night, and most of the time we were so far out in the boonies that we didn't have phone service. The story of my life."

"No problem." She could tell Jeff loved that life. While it would be nice to be able to check in with him more often, she wouldn't change any of it. How could she even think of it, when he so obviously loved his work?

"Well, you've probably got things to do," he said, "but I'll be thinking of you all day and praying that it goes well."

"Thanks, Jeff. I hope you have a great day too."

"Thanks. See you soon."

★ ★ ★

Margaret greeted Shelley at the door of her home on Sunday afternoon.

"Come on in, Shelley! I can't wait to hear how your dinner went Friday night."

"Very well, thanks. I kind of like the boss's wife." Shelley stepped inside and held out a plastic box. "I had a few imperfect muffins this morning."

"Great—they'll go with our coffee. Thanks." Margaret glanced toward the sidewalk. "Oh, here comes Beverly. Just set that on the kitchen table, would you, Shelley?"

Soon Beverly and Diane had joined them. They fixed mugs of tea or coffee to suit them in the kitchen and moved into the comfortable living room to talk. Margaret took Allan's recliner and set the throw pillows on the floor before she sat down.

"Tell us all about your seminar, Beverly," Diane said. "That must have been quite a day for you yesterday."

"You could say that. Several people came in to register at the last minute, and we ended up with seventy-five attendees. The organizer had to go and copy extra handouts for me." Beverly glanced at the cat that had resettled beside her.

"I'm guessing that was a good thing," Diane said.

"I think so. Of course, most of those people are just starting out—or just *thinking* about starting a new business. But I met some very interesting entrepreneurs, and the variety of businesses was astounding. One woman makes collages—what they call 'found art.' And another one designs lace patterns. She wants to sell them online and possibly compile a pattern book. On the opposite end of the spectrum were two ladies who want to open an upscale restaurant in Portland's Old Port."

"That's ambitious," Margaret said.

"Yes, it is, but both of them have restaurant experience, and one has a business degree. I was surprised they came to my seminar, but they both said afterward that they'd learned a lot. And everyone seemed to appreciate the resources I'd listed in the handout."

"Hey, that's great," Shelley said.

"And...there is one other thing," Beverly said hesitantly.

Diane's mouth opened, and she clapped her hands together. "You're going to do it!"

"Do what?" Shelley asked, looking from Beverly to Diane and back. "Tell us."

"Well, it's not set in stone yet, but I went to the town office this week and took out papers for the mayor's race."

"Well!" Margaret rose and went over to the couch, her hand extended. "Congratulations, girl. That's fantastic."

"Thanks," Beverly said, her face flushing. Margaret took her seat once more.

"I think it's wonderful," Diane said, "but I made the mistake of signing for Lee Waters before I knew she was doing it. If you two haven't signed a candidate petition yet, make sure you sign Beverly's."

"Think of it," Shelley said. "Mayor Wheeland!"

"Well, as I said, I got the papers, but I haven't turned them in yet."

"But you seem pretty sure that you will," Diane said.

Beverly shrugged. "I guess I am. It's just the finality of it. Once I start telling people and asking for support, I can't back out."

Shelley laughed. "Why would you want to? I think it's great."

"Thanks. How about your dinner for the boss's wife?" Beverly asked her. "Did that go all right?"

"Yes, I was just telling Margaret. Very nice."

Margaret smiled at them. "You young ladies have had some exciting stuff going on."

"I don't know if I qualify in that age bracket," Diane said, "but I have a bit of news myself. Everybody was so busy this weekend, I didn't get to tell anyone."

They all watched her expectantly.

"Spill it," Margaret said.

Diane laughed. "All right. Now, this sounds a little more glamorous than it really is, but—"

"Come on," Shelley said. "Just spit it out."

"Okay, a production company may option the film rights for my book."

"Wow!" Shelley's shout was so loud that the cat jerked her head up, then rose and jumped off the couch.

"Diane, that's really something," Margaret said.

Beverly nodded. "Excellent."

Diane held out both hands in protest. "See, I told you, it's not really all that fantastic—though it is good—but it's not a done deal yet, even for the option. And my agent says that ninety-five percent of these things never go anywhere. It's only an initial step in case, down the road, they want to do something with it."

"Well, it's still something," Margaret said. "I've never known anyone who had their book optioned before."

"Yeah," Shelley said. "This is wonderful, Diane, even if they don't ever make the movie. Let yourself celebrate."

"I think that's good advice," Margaret said.

Diane shrugged. "Okay, you talked me into it. Any excuse for a celebration, right?"

"Well, yeah," Shelley said.

Beverly smiled. "I think it's fabulous. And now I'm wondering what Margaret has going on."

"What do you mean?" Margaret gazed at her, baffled.

"I know you're busy at the gallery. Is anything else happening?"

Margaret frowned. "Well, yes, now that you mention it. I hate to put a damper on the mood, but I'm afraid my news isn't as cheerful and exciting as all of yours."

"Can you tell us about it?" Diane asked, setting down her tea mug.

"It's my cousin, Buddy Gordon. I told you all about him last fall, when I went to the family reunion."

"Yes," Beverly said. "That's when you learned he was the one who rescued you from drowning."

"You told me a couple of weeks ago that you'd dreamed about him," Diane said slowly.

Margaret nodded. "I've had several more dreams and thought maybe I should contact him. And then our mutual cousin, Beth Dufour, called me with some disturbing news." The three friends sat in silence, their expressions sympathetic. Margaret pulled in a deep breath. "Buddy started drinking again. After several years of sobriety, he fell back into it."

"Oh, how sad," Diane said.

"I'm sorry to hear that," Beverly added.

"So was I. Beth gave me the phone number for Buddy's AA sponsor, and I talked with him a few days ago. He said he'd tried to help Buddy and get him to a meeting, but Buddy wouldn't go. The dreams kept bothering me—waking me up and nagging at me. So I finally called him."

"What did he say?" Shelley asked.

"It was hard talking to him. I hope I helped a little. And he told me he would call Greg, but he didn't. I talked to Buddy again the next day, and I told him I was calling Greg. That's his sponsor's name. Greg said he would go right over, and I haven't heard anything since. But I haven't dreamed again, either, for the last few days. At least, not that I've remembered."

Diane sat forward and said earnestly, "You mentioned to me you tried to paint your dream. How did that work?"

Margaret shrugged. "The first two were pretty awful. But this last one has more substance. I think it may turn out to be interesting."

"Interesting?" Shelley cried. "I think it's fascinating. Do you have it here?"

"As a matter of fact, I do. I started it in my studio, but I brought it home this weekend. Would you like to see it?"

They all seemed eager to view the painting, so Margaret rose. "I'll bring it out." She'd neglected the housekeeping somewhat during the busy season at the gallery, and she had no desire for her friends to see the cluttered room where she kept her painting supplies at home.

She carried the latest canvas out and propped it up on top of the entertainment center. Her friends stood and gathered around, gazing at the painting.

"Wow, that's dramatic," Diane said.

Margaret chuckled. "It's all right if you don't like it. I wanted to get the feel of the dream down, not so much to make a pretty painting."

"I sort of like it." Beverly pointed to the blaze in the background. "Is that a church burning?"

"Yes. It's happened in several of my dreams lately. Not always. I don't think it's the one that burned in 1789, though.

Well, I suppose it could be. But in every painting the church looks different."

"Maybe that's because we don't really know what it looked like," Shelley said. "The colonial church, I mean."

"You may be right," Margaret said thoughtfully. "But I think maybe this is the modern church. I've thought so much about the fire they had in June that I think it's found its way into my dreams. And each dream is different in other ways."

"What do you mean?" Diane asked.

"Sometimes I'm in the water, either swimming or fighting the waves. Buddy has been there a couple of times, and once I'm pretty sure Allan was on the ship with me. Twice I've had the distinct impression that I was standing on the ship's deck, looking toward shore. And that's what I see—a fire. It's usually stormy, though not always, and—well, I wake up shaking, like I got drenched with icy water."

"Ouch. I'm so sorry." Diane slid an arm around Margaret's shoulders.

"That must be pretty harrowing," Beverly said.

"Sometimes it is. And you know what's really funny?" She looked around at them, and they all shook their heads. "When I wake up, I feel this urgent need to paint it. It's not just a whim. It's like I *have* to."

Diane frowned. "Maybe subconsciously, you feel that if you don't, you'll lose part of the memory."

"That could be."

"Yeah," Shelley said. "Sometimes when I wake up, my dreams seem real, but a couple of hours later, I can barely remember them."

"I put a notepad beside my bed," Margaret told them. "That way, I can sketch it as soon as I wake up. But I think it's more than that. And even though Buddy's not in every dream, I sort of feel like he's connected to them."

"They say the things we're dwelling on in our conscious hours show up in our dreams," Diane said.

"Are you going to see him again?" Beverly asked.

"I don't know. I was thinking about inviting him here for the Lobster Festival. I need to talk to Allan about it, though. If he thinks it's a terrible idea, I won't do it. And even if I do, Buddy might not come." Margaret grimaced. "I certainly don't want him to come if he's not sober."

"Maybe you could invite him and his sponsor," Diane said. "If they came together, you'd know he would be on his best behavior—and he'd have a safe driver."

"That's a thought."

"Well, I hope he beats this thing." Diane gave her a squeeze. "I'll be praying for him, Margaret, and for you."

"Me too," Shelley said, and Beverly nodded.

Margaret smiled. "Well, let's not be so glum. I think this is the best of the paintings inspired by my dreams, and it's not very good. So I'm just going to put it away and then we'll top off our drinks, shall we?"

"I think that painting's not finished," Diane said.

"Do you?" Margaret eyed it critically. "Probably not. But will I finish it or not? That's the question. If I have the dream again, I'll probably start a new one." She lifted down the canvas. "You all head out to the kitchen if you want more tea or coffee. And I'm sure there are more muffins out there." She paused in the doorway. "Did I tell you all that Allan is entering the cooking contest at the festival?"

"No, you didn't," Beverly said.

"That settles it. I *have* to go to that festival." Diane grabbed her cup. "Who else wants more tea?"

CHAPTER FIFTEEN

Diane, are you sitting down?"

Diane caught her breath at Frieda's words. "Should I be?"

"I think so, yes."

In light of the erratic reports her agent had given her lately, Diane pulled out a kitchen chair and sat down.

"Is this about the movie option? Because I can't imagine what else it would be. I've been on pins and needles since you called me on Friday."

"Yes, it is. I have the contract in hand, and I wanted to talk to you about it."

Diane blew out a deep breath. She was never sure with Frieda whether she was bearing good news or bad. Last week it was the film option, but a couple of weeks before that, it was the possibility that her third book might not be published. "Thanks so much for not having bad news."

Frieda laughed. "No, this is another dose of good news, so I hope you can just forget about that earlier report."

"You mean the one where they're not going to publish book three?"

"That's the one. Because I spoke with your publisher this morning. Not your editor, your publisher."

"Oh, wow. That's significant, isn't it?"

"It surely is. Diane, we've received this film option offer from the Women's Movie Network. That carries a lot of weight with a publisher."

"So they'll give me a chance with all three books?"

"Yes. They don't want to lose you now."

"Thank you so much!" Diane sent up a quick prayer of thanks too.

"I have the contract here, and I've read through it. It's not fabulous, but you are a new writer. I think it's fair. Let me just run down the details with you."

Diane listened as Frieda talked through the major points of the contract. After a couple of minutes, she had the presence of mind to grab a piece of scrap paper and pen and jot a few notes.

"Sound good?" Frieda asked.

"Yes. I'll trust your judgment on this."

"Okay. I'm going to e-mail the file to you. Print out three copies, sign and date each one, and mail them to me, all right?"

"Got it," Diane said. "Thanks again." When at last they signed off, she sat still for a moment, staring down at her scrawls.

"Heavenly Father, I don't know what to say," she murmured.

Rocky woofed, and she glanced down at him. He'd come over to stand beside her chair, eyeing her anxiously. Diane patted his smooth head.

"I wish you could understand this, Rocky. It's...unbelievable." She checked the e-mail and waited while the file came in. When she'd opened it, she clicked the buttons instructing the printer to give her three copies. She laid the pages on the desk and signed them carefully. It was only an option, not a promise of a film, but it brought so many possibilities with it that Diane felt a little light-headed. The small payment the film company was giving her to cement the deal would come in handy too.

Preparing the envelope took a few more minutes, but at last she was done. She jumped up with it in her hand. "Come on, Rocky! Let's get your leash and walk to the post office. I want to get this in the mail today!"

She decided she needed to talk to someone human about the new development too. She looked across the street. Shelley's car was missing from the Bauers' driveway, but one house up, Terri's SUV was parked in its usual place. She decided to stop in at her friend's house on the way home. Nothing would distract her from mailing the contracts first.

By the time they reached the post office, she was nearly ready to burst. She hoped the postal clerk would say something that would give her an excuse to share her good news, but the woman was very businesslike.

Margaret would understand. But a glance inside the gallery told her that Margaret was very busy with several customers in the store. She was bending over the counter writing something, and didn't even look up when Diane stuck her head in and the bell on the door rang. If Diane hadn't had Rocky in tow, she might have offered to stop and help her friend. This was clearly not the time to bounce in with happy tidings.

Back on Newport Avenue, she noted that Beverly's car was not in its usual spot. "That's right," Diane said to Rocky. "She told me she was meeting with a client on Tuesday, and that's today."

Terri's rental was still in the same spot. Diane checked for traffic and hustled Rocky across. She rang the doorbell and bounced on her toes while she waited. It was after nine o'clock. Terri must be up—after all, she had a dog.

As if echoing her thoughts, Gallant's high-pitched bark sounded inside. A moment later, Terri opened the door.

"Good morning, Diane! Come on in. Hello, Rocky. You can come in too." Terri threw the door wide, smiling.

To Diane's relief, her friend was fully dressed in gray Bermuda shorts and a white top with turquoise embroidery.

"Hi! I'm sorry to come so early. I ought to have called you."

"No, this is fine. Come on into the kitchen. I was just finishing my coffee, and then I thought I'd take Gallant down to the beach. Maybe we can go together, if you're not busy this morning."

"Well, I have some news, and I was just bursting to share it." Diane followed her into the kitchen with its speckled green linoleum and butcher block laminate counters. She released Rocky from his leash.

Terri kicked a plastic ball with a jingle bell inside toward Gallant. "Here, play ball with Rocky." Gallant yipped and chased the ball into a corner. "Coffee? There's plenty."

"Sure," Diane said.

Terri brought her a mugful and topped off her own cooling coffee. "Cream or sugar?"

"No, thanks."

"Well, what is this exciting news?" Terri settled in her chair before an empty cereal bowl.

"You'll never guess."

Terri's eyes sparkled. "Must be something good."

"Oh, it's super." Diane shook her head. "I can't believe how blue I was after my agent told me the publisher might not print my third book. I've been moping around for a week and a half. And all the time, God had a huge blessing in the works."

"So tell me!"

"Well, Friday my agent calls me again and tells me that someone might want to option the film rights for my book. I was flabbergasted. I probably should have told you, but I wanted to be sure it was real."

"Is it?"

"Yes! Frieda called me again this morning. This film outfit—Women's Movie Network—is buying the option. They're talking about making a TV movie out of my first book. Is that unreal or what? I mean—oh, I just can't believe it!"

Terri's smile deepened. "Oh, I can believe it."

"Thank you, flatterer."

"The truth is…" Terri's expression sobered. "Diane, I hope you'll forgive me, friend, but I've been holding out on you."

"What do you mean?"

"Did your agent give you the name of the producer who wants to make your movie?"

"She did, and I wrote it down. John something."

Terri laughed. "Does John Bowman ring a bell?"

"That's it! How did you know?"

"Uh...I'm married to him."

Diane set her mug down with a thud. "What?"

"He's my husband. Please don't be upset with me. I didn't want to get your hopes up, so I didn't tell you, but when I sent your book to Jack, I told him I thought he should look at it seriously as a potential basis for a film."

Diane sat in silence for several seconds, taking in what Terri had said.

"Are you upset?" Terri asked.

"No, I...I think God had a hand in this."

"Really?"

Diane smiled. "I surely do. I've been agonizing over the situation with my publisher. I told you about it, how they might not print my third book."

Terri nodded. "I think they're nuts, because you're a fine writer. That lighthouse mystery was so deliciously creepy!"

"Well, thanks. This is a real blessing for me. I'm *very* thankful that God brought you here, and that He used you in my life."

Terri smiled then. "I wouldn't have thought of it that way. I was just glad Jack loved the book as much as I did. He told me he read it all the way through the night he got it. And I'm glad I got to know you."

"So am I." Diane reached for her coffee and stopped. "Wait a minute, *Bowman*? Did you keep your maiden name?"

"That's right," Terri said. "I did some acting before we were married, and Glazier was my professional name, so I kept it."

"What were you in?"

"Nothing you've ever heard of, so far as movies go. In fact, most of my income came from commercials. I did a six-month stint on a daytime drama too."

"Wow. If this gets out, people will be beating on your door for autographs."

Terri laughed. "Then let's make sure it doesn't get out."

"Well, I have to say, your Jack is a man of many surprises." Diane took a sip of her coffee.

"I didn't tell you the best part," Terri said.

"Oh? What's that?"

"He's going to try to come to Marble Cove for a few days, and he hopes to meet you."

Diane gulped. "Wow. Did I already say that?" Things were moving so fast, she felt like she was on the Tilt-a-Whirl at the state fair. "That'd be great. Maybe you two can have dinner at my place one night."

"Sounds good."

"Wait until I tell Frieda!"

"That's your agent?" Terri asked.

"Yes. She's very calm, but this has got to get her excited." Not to mention what her friends in Marble Cove would say when they heard the news. Diane could imagine Shelley hopping up and down, and Beverly and Margaret planning a party.

"I just hope he follows through," Terri said with a frown.

"On the movie?" Diane's hopes plummeted.

"No, on the trip. I'm pretty sure he's serious about doing the film, but I was a little bit surprised that he would actually take a week off to come here when he's so busy. I guess you're a big attraction for him. He always likes to meet the authors and discuss their stories with them."

Diane let out a slow breath. That put a lot of responsibility on her, it seemed.

"I pushed him a little last night, telling him to book his flight right away," Terri said. "I sure hope he did. I told him to come to Portland, and I'd go pick him up so he wouldn't have to rent another car."

"Keep me posted," Diane said. "And I won't tell Shelley that Jack is coming until you're sure. She'd get really excited if she knew she'd have a movie producer in the house next door."

Terri laughed. "I like Shelley. She's so genuine."

The two dogs had come into the kitchen, and Rocky stood by Diane's chair, looking up at her adoringly.

"I suppose I'd better go do some work, in case they decide to publish my third book after all."

"Is there any doubt now?" Terri asked, rising.

"Frieda thinks it's in the bag. We'll see."

"I sure hope they will. They won't be sorry." Terri reached out and hugged Diane. "You deserve lots of good things."

"Thanks." Diane wanted to protest that she deserved nothing, but this wasn't the right time for that discussion. Her friend had done her a great kindness, and she didn't want to lessen Terri's satisfaction over it. "Rocky and I just had a walk to the post office, but maybe we can meet later today for that walk on the beach?"

"Sure. I'll take Gallant a different way this morning. When's good for you?"

They set a time in the afternoon, and Diane headed for home with Rocky, determined to put in some solid work before then.

★ ★ ★

Several days had passed since Margaret had succeeded in reaching Buddy by phone, and she decided to call him again on Wednesday. She'd had no word from him since she'd told him she would talk to his sponsor, but Greg had called her briefly on Monday to let her know he had finally gotten Buddy to an AA meeting. By now they should have attended a second one—Greg had said the more the better for a few weeks, until Buddy had at least a little self-control back.

She decided to call him about halfway through the morning, reasoning that if he hadn't completely stopped drinking, she wanted to catch him fairly early in the day. After seeing a customer out the door, she looked around the gallery and confirmed that she was momentarily alone. She picked up the phone.

When Buddy answered, she smiled. She could tell by his voice that he was sober, though he sounded a little wary.

"Hi! It's Margaret."

"Oh, hi. I was afraid you were Greg, wanting me to go to another meeting tonight. I told him two in one week was good enough."

"Well...is it enough? Or don't you really know yet?"

Buddy sighed. "I haven't had a drink since Saturday, if that's what you mean. Four days."

"That's good, Buddy. I'm so glad."

"I was a real idiot, wasn't I?"

"I wouldn't say that."

"Beth did."

Margaret grimaced. "Did she?"

"Uh-huh. I guess I was pretty rude to her when she visited me. I don't remember."

"I see. Well, listen, I was wondering if you'd like to come down to Marble Cove for a visit. We're having the Lobster Festival on Saturday."

"Lobster Festival?"

"Yes. The food will be fabulous, and there's a parade. They have lots of contests and things. Allan is entering the cooking competition."

"Is that right?"

"Yes. We've had seafood dishes every night this week because he was trying to decide what recipe to use. I never thought I'd say this, but I'm getting tired of shrimp and clams. But he's having fun. And Adelaide has volunteered to help with the children's activities that day."

"What are *you* going to do?"

"I'm going to keep my gallery open all day, but I have friends who will give me a break, so I could take some time off to go and eat with you and Allan and Adelaide. Oh, and Greg—I was thinking maybe he would come with you."

"Greg?"

"Well, he might be busy."

"Actually, he asked me if I wanted to hang out this weekend. I think he's hoping to keep me busy so I won't want a beer."

"Hey, whatever works," Margaret said. "Do you want to suggest it to him? It could be a fun day."

"I don't know, Margaret."

"Come on. They'll have a bonfire on the beach and steam the lobsters down there."

"I'll think about it."

"Okay, you do that. And let me know, won't you?"

"Sure."

The bell on the door jingled. "Hey, I've got a customer, so I have to go now, but call me soon."

"Yeah, yeah." Buddy sounded grumpy but a little amused. Margaret hoped he was getting his sense of humor back—though not too much. She didn't mind if he never resumed his teasing habits.

The next time she had a break in traffic, she went to her studio and gazed at the last "dream" painting. The dream hadn't returned since she'd talked to Buddy, but after Diane's suggestion that the painting wasn't done, she had done more work on the canvas. She'd thought this morning that it was finished, but now she wasn't so sure. She studied the shoreline from the vantage point of the ship's passenger.

She could see buildings in the town, surrounding the flaming church. Off to the right was a high bluff or cliff. She wasn't certain which it was in her dream, but she'd painted it in dark browns and rust, with ochre highlights. It looked like the cliff north of the Marble Cove beach. But something was missing. She'd thought the church was the focal point of the scene, but that dark bulk on the right begged for...what? Tilting her head to one side, she puzzled over it for a moment, but the ringing bell summoned her back to the showroom.

Nearly two hours later, she locked the front door and turned the "closed" sign outward. Her customers had come in bursts today, but overall she'd had a satisfying number of sales. Even better, she thought she knew what her painting needed.

She hurried to the back room and pulled on a smock, then got out her brushes and her pad of thick palette paper. She squeezed blobs of paint from several tubes and mixed a couple of hues together. Slowly, precisely, she stroked in a small figure on the cliff.

None of the "dream paintings" had contained people. Still, she felt this was right. In her last dream, she must have seen a man on the cliff. But wouldn't she have noticed something so different and recalled it when she awoke? No matter—she saw it now, in her mind's eye. Was it Buddy? She stepped back and eyed the figure critically. Most decidedly not Buddy. Not Allan either, or anyone else she could recognize. And it still wasn't quite right. She lifted her brush and added a few more strokes to the figure on top of the cliff.

Chapter Sixteen

On Friday afternoon, Diane was right in the middle of a scene where her heroine confronted a ne'er-do-well when her phone rang. For a second, she considered ignoring it—her concentration was all too easily broken, and she had the tone just right for a suspenseful encounter. But she couldn't stand the thought that it might be Frieda or one of her children calling, and she couldn't let it ring.

"Hello?"

"Diane, it's Terri. Jack is coming in to Portland tonight! I'm about to leave to pick him up."

"That's wonderful," Diane said. "Drive carefully."

"I will. His plane lands about seven. I thought we'd have dinner in the city. We'll be late getting home, so I wanted to let you know now."

"Will I see the two of you tomorrow at the Lobster Festival?"

"We'll be there. If you don't run into us, give me a call. See you!"

Diane hung up with a prayer of thanks on her lips. She was eager to meet Jack, but most of her pleasure was for Terri. She hoped all went well for the couple. She would like to think that Jack had left his work behind in California, but the fact that he wanted to meet her and discuss the movie option put that thought to rest. She would just have to make sure he wasn't too fixated on that. She'd suggested to Terri that morning that the two of them should do some exploring along the coast. She hoped they'd relax and enjoy this time together.

Determined to finish her scene, Diane turned back to her keyboard. She had to stay in the suspenseful mode for this one, and she found it difficult after the brief phone call. Outside, a perfect afternoon was going to waste. Every fiber of her body wanted to get up and walk downtown with Rocky. Maybe stop in at the gallery, or browse at the bookstore. Get a frozen yogurt cone.

"Stop that," she told herself sternly.

Rocky looked up at her and whined.

"Oh no, don't you start. I refuse to leave this house until this scene is done. I need at least another two pages, and I'm going to tear into it now, so quit making eyes at me!"

Rocky sank down onto the rug and laid his chin mournfully on his paws.

Half an hour later, Diane shoved back her wheeled chair.

"Okay, boy! It may not be great literature, but the scene is at least roughed out. And my reward is to get out with you and get some air and talk to some real, breathing people!"

As they walked toward the beach path a few minutes later, she couldn't help thinking once more how great it would be if her book was made into a film. And what if they used

Orlean Point Light as a location? She supposed that was far-fetched. She wished Terri was on hand to walk with her and share her excitement. But that was silly—Terri had gone to Portland to retrieve the cause of Diane's euphoria, so she shouldn't wish her here.

Her cell phone rang, and she pulled it out of her jeans pocket. Jessica. Diane's spirits rose. Her daughter was just the one to chat with. Diane had told her about the film option, but now she had another snippet of news to share.

"Hey, Mom. Just checking in. Are you down off cloud nine yet?"

"Not really," Diane said. "And, honey, guess what!"

"You're so full of surprises lately, I'm sure I couldn't imagine what you're up to now."

"The producer is coming here."

"Oh, wow. He's your new friend's husband, right?"

"Yes." Diane laughed. "Terri's thrilled because he's coming to vacation with her after all, and he wants to meet me. Of course, I won't see much of him, but I am looking forward to meeting him. I'll at least have one dinner with him and Terri."

"Hey, that is terrific, Mom. Wouldn't it be wild if your whole series got made into movies?"

Diane looked ahead as Rocky bounded down the beach toward the lighthouse. "Now you're dreaming."

"Why not?" Jessica asked. "If you're going to dream at all, might as well dream big."

★ ★ ★

"Wow," Dan said, surveying the kitchen. "Looks like a hurricane hit."

Shelley grimaced. "Yeah, I know. Sorry. I figure we need at least a hundred dozen cookies for tomorrow. I'm nearly there." She glanced around at the cooling trays of ginger gems and macadamia–white chocolate chews. Stacked on the counters were boxes of chocolate chip, date-filled, and oatmeal-raisin cookies, and more varieties filled her freezers.

"Where are the kids?"

"Adelaide's got them in Aiden's room, building a rocket factory."

Dan's eyebrows shot up. "A rocket factory?"

"Aiden's idea. You should go see it. And I suppose we need to send Adelaide home. She's been here all afternoon."

"Are you going to keep working?"

Shelley gritted her teeth. "Well, yeah. I need to do pastries too. For us and for the Cove. They want extra for tomorrow."

Dan set his lunchbox down in the corner. "Let me guess. The best way I can help is to keep the kids out of your hair tonight."

"Is that awful?"

"No. This is a once-in-a-while thing. After I get them to bed, should I go over to the field and set up your stand?"

"We can do that tonight or in the morning. The festival officially opens at nine, but I don't think many people will buy cookies until after the parade."

"Let's set up in the morning. Dad can probably help me then. You fixed it with Mom, right?"

Shelley nodded and reached for a can of shortening. "Yeah, she'll keep them all day. They'll walk around the festival grounds after the parade and ride the merry-go-round. And after lunch, she and Ralph will bring them home for their naps."

Dan leaned against the door jamb. "Do you think it's better if I keep them and you have Frances help you in the booth? She said she could do either."

Shelley looked up. He was contemplating her with a serious expression. "I think it would be less stressful for me to have you helping me. They'll be fine with your folks. Unless you truly would rather—"

"No, that's okay. I guess I was wondering if you really thought I could keep up. Mom is so efficient..."

Shelley walked over to him. "Dan, we make a great team. Remember the dinner?"

"Yeah."

"We work well together. And I love having a chance to do that."

He gave her a crooked smile. "I think it will be fun too. A hundred dozen cookies!"

"Well, I could be wrong and wind up with ninety dozen in the freezer afterward, but I don't think so. A cookie is an inexpensive impulse purchase. This town always gets a lot of tourists for the Lobster Festival. And our booth will be right next to the lemonade and iced tea stand. Is that God's work or what?"

He laughed. "Okay, I'm going to go see the kids and tell Adelaide she can go. What's for supper?"

"Hot dogs on the grill?" Shelley asked with a hopeful smile.

"I can do that." He bent to kiss her. "Maybe I'll take the kids over to Allan's after we eat."

"Oh, you'd better not do that. Adelaide told me he's as harried as I am, getting ready for the cook-off. They've eaten seafood every night this week."

"Really? And that's bad?"

"Yes, and since he's settled on the recipe he's going to use, they've had it three times. She says that she and Margaret are sick of it, but they don't have the heart to tell him. Don't you tell him, either. Just leave the poor man alone in his creative madness. This will all be over tomorrow."

"Okay," Dan said. "The beach it is."

★ ★ ★

On Saturday morning, Margaret woke at dawn. Allan was up and pulling on his clothes in the dim light.

"What are you doing?" she mumbled.

"I can't sleep anymore. A little nervous, I guess. I'm going to go pack up my things for the contest."

"Want me to help?"

"No, go back to sleep."

It was the answer she'd wanted, and she rolled over and snuggled into the pillow.

She dozed off again, and some time later awoke to find Adelaide and Lizzie, one of the cats, on the bed with her.

"Hey. What's up?"

"You have to get up, Mom. We're going soon."

"Oh. Really?" Margaret squinted at the clock. It was nearly eight. "Goodness! I've overslept!" When was the last time she'd done that?

"Dad is taking me with him. He says you can wait for Buddy."

"Okay. I'd better get dressed. I don't really expect him for another hour or so, but I'd better get ready just in case he comes early."

"Dad made French toast."

"Oh, is it good?"

Adelaide grinned at her and scooped up Lizzie. "Yummy." She headed for the door.

Margaret peeled back the covers. Might as well face the day. Ten minutes later, she padded out to the kitchen wearing navy pants, a long blue-and-white print blouse, and her slippers. Allan had packed his spices, his cooking pot, and his utensils in a box, and his already baked pie sat on the table in the plastic carrier. Adelaide had on the striped capris and oversize T-shirt she had picked out for her day as a children's activities helper, and she had a tote bag in her hand. Allan was just closing the dishwasher.

"Looks like you two are ready to shove off," Margaret said.

"Oh, there you are. Yes, we're all set. Now, I've loaded all the dishes except yours, and the soap is in. Just put your breakfast things in when you're done and start it, will you?"

"Sure." Margaret walked over to kiss him good-bye. "What time does the judging start?"

"Not until ten thirty for the pies, or after the parade disbands—whichever comes first—and the seafood contest starts at one. But we want to get Adelaide there in plenty of time. I'll drop off my pie and hang out with whoever's around this morning."

"Great. I'm opening the gallery at ten. I hope Buddy gets here well before that."

"If he's not here when it's time, call him and tell him to go straight over there."

"Good idea."

Margaret stood on the porch and waved, then went back to the kitchen to enjoy a solitary breakfast—solitary except for the cats watching her. She lingered over her coffee, then topped it off with hot brew, tucked her plate and silverware into the dishwasher, and carried her mug to the bedroom to make the bed and get her shoes. She'd just put them on when she heard a car drive in.

Hurrying out to the porch, she watched Buddy unfold his tall frame from the passenger seat of a black pickup truck. He looked lean and tired, but he was smiling. Another, younger man with fading blond hair and sharp blue eyes got out of the driver's seat.

"I'm so glad you made it." Margaret scurried down the steps and into Buddy's embrace. She was happy to realize that she meant every word.

"Thanks for making me come," Buddy said, folding her close for a moment.

"Making you?" She stepped back and playfully slugged his shoulder. "As if I could ever make you do anything." She turned to his driver. "You must be Greg."

He stepped to her and shook her hand. "Great to meet you, Margaret. What's the plan?"

"We have about a half hour before I need to go over to my gallery. I thought maybe you and Buddy would like to see it. I have some chairs there that we can take out onto the sidewalk for the parade. That begins at ten, and the route goes right past the front door, so I thought we'd watch it there, and then I'll open up for business."

"Sounds like fun," Greg said.

"Yeah." Buddy grinned. "I haven't sat still to watch a parade in ages."

"Well, the locals take it seriously, and they make floats. The theme this year is 'Over the Bounding Waves,' so there will probably be a lot of nautical entries. When it's over, I'll point you in the direction of the festival events. Allan is entered in the cooking competition this afternoon, and he's in the pie contest being judged this morning too."

"I had no idea Allan was such a good cook," Buddy said.

"Well, I'm lousy at it, so it works well for us," Margaret said with a chuckle. "They make the seafood dishes on the spot, with the judges watching. I think Allan's feeling a bit of pressure this morning, but he'll love every minute of it."

While they talked, she walked them into the living room, and they all sat down.

"Where's Adelaide?" Buddy asked.

"She's helping the woman who's organizing games for the children." Margaret turned to Greg. "Adelaide is my daughter. I'll have to stay at the gallery for a while, but some of my friends are going to come in and tend the store for me around one, so if you fellas want to get by on snacks until then, I can eat a late lunch with you on the beach."

"Lobster?" Buddy asked.

"Yes, or hot dogs for those philistines who don't like seafood, and corn on the cob, bean hole beans, and desserts coming out your ears."

"Yum, sounds like a real diet-buster," Greg said.

"Yes, the butter that goes with the lobster and corn does me in every time," Margaret said with a laugh. "But it's once a year, right?"

For the next twenty minutes, they caught up on family news, and Margaret asked Greg a few questions. She learned that he taught high school math. A recovered alcoholic himself, he sponsored Buddy and one other AA member. He blamed the dissolution of his marriage on his alcoholism.

"By the time I'd gotten hold of myself, Melissa had moved on," he said with a tinge of regret. "But I'm truly glad she's happy. We didn't have any children, and she has a nice family now."

"Aren't you dating someone?" Buddy asked. Margaret thought him a bit rude to ask such a personal question, but it seemed they were on "friend" terms.

"Well, you know I've been seeing Karen for a few months. We're taking it slow, but I like her a lot." Greg shrugged.

"I hope it works out for you," Margaret said. "You must be heading back to school soon."

"Yes, as a matter of fact, I have two teacher in-service days next week. Fortunately, math at the high school level doesn't take a whole lot of preparation once you've taught it for several years."

"I used to be an accountant," Margaret said. "I think I was in the minority, being a girl who liked math."

"It sure wasn't my best subject," Buddy said with a grimace.

Greg laughed. "A lot of people say that. It doesn't have to be your best. I just try to make sure my students leave my classroom understanding it. Liking is not a requirement."

"Where were you when I was a sophomore?" Buddy asked.

Margaret chuckled. "Well, I suppose we'd better get over to the Shearwater. Buddy, would you mind carrying this box of cookies for me?"

"Cookies?"

"I serve them with coffee, to my customers. You two can enjoy them when we get there. It's not far, and I thought we'd walk. We can't park on the street because of the parade, and I figured it would be simpler to just leave the vehicles here."

Her tote bag was loaded with a new can of coffee, the consignment ledger she'd brought home the night before, and her wallet. She picked it up and led the men out, locking the door behind them. They walked up to Main Street, where people were already gathering and staking out their spots for watching the parade.

★ ★ ★

Beverly opened the front door to Jeff, and she couldn't hold back a smile. He looked great in his Dockers and casual olive drab shirt with rolled sleeves—like a man who had just come in from an outdoor assignment in a remote place and loved every minute of it. His eyes lit when she smiled at him.

"Hi." He bent and kissed her cheek. "You look terrific."

"Thanks. It's great to see you again." She was glad he approved of her appearance. She'd decided not to go completely casual, since she'd be presenting herself as a mayoral candidate today. She'd chosen tailored capris, a new linen blouse, and leather sandals she knew were comfortable enough to stand in most of the day. "Come on in. I think Father's almost ready."

They went into the kitchen, where she offered Jeff coffee.

"No, thanks. I thought we could get something there."

"Great. Shelley's having a cookie booth, and she's right next to a coffee, iced tea, and lemonade stand run by the middle school students."

"Perfect," Jeff said. "So tell me more about the seminar and whatever you've been doing this week."

"Well, I took on my first corporate client."

He arched his eyebrows. "Really? That's fantastic."

"Yeah. Computer chips. I'm going to Portland next week to meet with the partners and discuss their budgetary needs."

Jeff grinned. "I'm proud of you. Not just that you landed the client. I'm really impressed you understand all that stuff."

She laughed. The marvel to her was that he wasn't intimidated by it. A lot of men would feel nervous around a business-savvy woman, but not Jeff. He was comfortable in his artistic niche.

"Do you remember when I e-mailed you about the mayor's race?" she asked. "You know—the election?"

Jeff eyed her keenly. "I sure do. Are you going ahead with it?"

"I think I am."

"Great! After that development controversy you had last month, you're a natural for this. I meant what I said then—I think you'd be very good at it."

"Well, I've been thinking about it ever since. I'd like to get involved in some meaningful work that will contribute to Marble Cove's prosperity. Outside my business, I mean."

Jeff nodded. "You understand finances and government and . . . yeah, I think it's a terrific idea."

Beverly smiled back. She'd known she was capable of doing the job. What was holding her back? Was it the time involved, or was it the perception of the people she loved? So far, their verdict was unanimous—she should pursue it.

"I got the paperwork from the town office. I . . . I seriously think I'll do it."

"Wonderful!" Jeff gave her a quick hug. "Let me know if there's any way I can help. Head shots for press releases? Posters?"

She chuckled and gave him a little squeeze before stepping back. "Thanks. It's only a small campaign. I wouldn't want to overwhelm the locals. On the other hand, Dennis is running against me—"

"Dennis Calder?" Jeff's reaction seemed a bit strong, and she faltered.

"Well, yes. He and Lee Waters, the current mayor's son, are both running. I admit I see Dennis as the real competitor though."

"You've got to win this, Beverly."

She laughed. "Okay. I'll give it my best shot. And I'll definitely let you know if I need anything by way of photos. I thought maybe the festival would be a good place to start collecting signatures."

"For what?"

"That's part of the election process. I need to get the signatures of fifty registered voters to have my name put on the ballot."

"Well, sure. Bring the papers along, and I'll help you. I'll bet we can get most of those today."

Her father came to the doorway. "Hello, Jeff. How are you doing?"

"Just great. How are you, sir?"

"Fair to middling, as my father used to say." He had a pair of sunglasses tucked into his shirt pocket, and his favorite straw hat was in his hand.

"Beverly just told me she's venturing into politics," Jeff said.

"Yes, isn't it grand? I'd be related to the mayor. I could park anywhere I wanted at next year's festival."

Beverly laughed and waved a hand through the air. "Oh, stop it. If you're ready, we should get going. It really might be hard to find parking near the lobster feed."

"Don't forget the paperwork," Jeff said.

"Right." She turned to her father. "I'm going to take the petition for the election. Jeff says he'll help me collect signatures today."

"Aren't you going to be at Margaret's gallery this afternoon?"

"Yes, for two hours."

"That's okay," Jeff said. "I'll keep stumping for you."

"You'd do that?" Beverly asked.

"Of course."

"And I'll hit the senior-citizen crowd," her father said. "Do you have more than one copy?"

"I'll make extras." Beverly dashed up the stairs to her office. She had two men in her life who were absolute princes. She found the paper she needed and stuck it in the printer to make copies. As she waited for them, she smiled to herself. *What does that make me? I think princess is a notch higher than mayor.*

CHAPTER SEVENTEEN

Margaret unlocked the door of the gallery and started the coffee, then gave Greg and Buddy a short tour of her office and studio, as well as the exhibit areas.

"Wow, Margaret, this is a classy place," Buddy said, looking over the merchandise with his hands shoved into his pockets. She wondered if he did it to make sure he didn't touch or break anything.

"Thanks, Buddy."

"It sure is," Greg said. "When did you say you opened up?"

"Last year, in May."

"I knew her before she was famous," Buddy said with a boyish grin.

Margaret chuckled. The rich smell of coffee wafted through the rooms, and she looked over to see if the pot was full. "I think the coffee's ready now. Help yourself to that and the cookies." She had ordered several dozen from Shelley for today, expecting a bumper crop of browsers during the festival.

"And you said your husband makes all these stands and tables?" Greg asked.

"Yes, and most of the shelves and displays too." She sensed more than a casual interest. "You'll get to meet Allan soon. Do you do woodworking?"

"I putter at it, but nothing as beautiful as this." He leaned down to closely examine the inlay on one of Allan's end tables.

Buddy came over with a cup of coffee in one hand and a macadamia nut cookie in the other. "I always liked Allan. Say, Margaret, did you make these? They're terrific."

"No, I told you, I'm not much of a cook. A friend of mine did. She has an online bakery, and you can order them from her." Margaret stepped to the counter and picked up one of Shelley's brochures. "Here you go. She'll ship them right to your doorstep. She has a booth today at the festival. Lighthouse Sweet Shoppe."

"*Mmm*. I'll look for it when we're over there."

The activity outside seemed to be increasing. "We'd better grab our chairs and get out there," Margaret said. They were just in time to find a strip of sidewalk wide enough for all three folding chairs.

A brass band began to play down the street, and Margaret leaned forward to watch for the marchers. The scouts, 4-H, veterans, and other community groups had marching units. Several horses strutted along in colorful parade gear, with their riders waving to the crowd. A troupe of clowns came tumbling down the street. At last the floats arrived. Several of the creators had used trailered boats as the bases. The people riding in them ranged from some young "merpeople" to crusty fishermen in their yellow slickers. One float featured a stack of lobster traps with a big stuffed lobster on top. It reminded Margaret of the Lobster Trap Christmas Tree the town built each December.

Buddy pointed to the fishermen on a passing float. "It's a little warm for that getup, don't you think?"

"Yes, I do." Margaret was glad for the sunshine, though. A couple of years back, the festival was pretty much rained out, and the local businesses had suffered.

A farm family had contributed a float that had two little boys in ragged jeans and straw hats, fishing off the side of their raft—which looked suspiciously like a hay wagon with its stake sides removed.

"There's Tom Sawyer and Huck Finn," Greg said with a laugh.

"Looks like they're catching plenty of fish," Margaret said. "That must be Becky Thatcher with them." A girl dressed in a long frilly dress and starched white pinafore threw handfuls of penny candy at the spectators.

"Hey, fireballs!" Buddy scrambled after them and bumped heads with a child. "Oops, sorry, fella. Here, you can have mine." He looked anxiously for the boy's parents, but the tyke scurried off to keep pace with the raft float.

The next entry was decked out as an old sailing ship, with a square-rigged sail made from sheets and a little crow's nest at the top of the mast. A boy of about eight sat in the crow's nest, peering about with a brass telescope.

"Wow, he's pretty high up," Buddy said. "Do you think he's safe up there?"

"Well, that's his father right below him," Margaret said. "I expect he built that mast himself and made sure it was sturdy."

After the twelve floats came a section of new boats on display by area marinas. The lineup included two lobster boats, a couple of cabin cruisers, and four gleaming sailboats. Last of all came the fire trucks. Several towns had sent an engine, and when the drivers turned on their sirens, Margaret clapped her hands over her ears.

"Time to go inside," she yelled to Greg and Buddy.

They nodded and gathered up the chairs. Margaret opened the door, and they all slipped in. Allan came in behind them.

"Well, hi," Margaret said. "Where did you come from?"

"Thought I'd come see if Buddy and his friend want to go up to the field with me and watch the pie judging." The area where the tents, booths, and rides for the festival were set up lay in a stretch of open farmland, and the residents referred to it as simply "the field."

"Sounds great," Buddy said. He introduced Greg to Allan.

The door opened and several people came in, one of them Penny Tyler from the community center.

"You're open, right?" she asked, looking expectantly toward Margaret.

"Yes, come right in."

"We'll get out of here," Allan said. "Call my cell when you're ready for lunch."

"I'll do that," Margaret told him.

"Thanks for the coffee," Greg said with a smile.

Buddy grinned at her and handed her his empty cup. "We'll see you later."

"You sure will. Have fun, boys!" Margaret turned to greet the shoppers.

★ ★ ★

The pie judges took their time. They examined each of the fourteen entries. Appearance seemed to count for a lot, and one of the judges even bent down to sniff each pie, which made Beverly shudder. Then each one received a tiny piece of the first pie on a small paper plate. They ate it pensively and then scribbled notes on their clipboards.

"This could take a while," she whispered to Jeff.

"I'll bet by number ten or twelve they won't be as thorough." He looked around. "Maybe I can work the fringe of the crowd and get a few signatures."

"Is that good etiquette?" Beverly asked. She would hate to offend anyone.

"I think it's the kind of thing people expect at an event like this."

She glanced about and nodded. "Okay, there's quite a crowd near Shelley's booth. Maybe I'll mosey over there and see if I can get a few."

"Back here in ten minutes?"

She nodded and strode quickly over to where Shelley and Dan were dispensing cookies and Danish and directing customers who wanted a drink to the lemonade stand next door.

Beverly decided to speak to people leaving with their treats. She wouldn't want to keep them talking when their turns came and interrupt Shelley's business.

"Excuse me," she said to a couple who turned away from the counter with chocolate chip cookies in hand. "Are you registered voters in Marble Cove?"

"No, we're from Ellsworth," the woman said. "Just came down for the day."

"Oh, sorry." Beverly eyed the next few customers anxiously. This could be trickier than she'd thought. A lot of out-of-towners, and even out-of-state visitors, came to town for the Lobster Festival. She picked out a gray-haired man she recognized and targeted him next.

"Hi, I'm Beverly Wheeland."

"Oh, sure. Harold Wheeland's daughter, right?"

"Yes," she said with gratitude in her heart. "I wondered if—well, you're a registered voter here in town, aren't you?"

"I sure am."

"I've decided to run for mayor, and I wondered—"

"Really! Now, that's interesting."

"Is it? I mean, thank you." She gulped. "I'm collecting signatures in order to get my name on the ballot."

He laughed. "You caught me just right, young lady. My wife told me she signed one of those things for Dennis Calder, and that I should sign his sheet if I saw him. But I haven't seen him yet, and I think I'll put my John Hancock on yours instead. How about that? A split vote from the Sewalls. That will make for some debate at the dinner table tonight." He signed his name with a flourish.

"Thank you so much!" Beverly told him, encouraged. When she spied Maddie Bancroft's husband walking along with a child holding each of his hands, she stopped him. "Excuse me, Mr. Bancroft. I'm Beverly Wheeland, and I'm running for mayor."

"Hi, Ms. Wheeland." He glanced at her clipboard. "Congratulations, but I'm afraid I can't help you. I signed for Lee Waters last week."

"Oh. That's all right. Thanks, and have fun!" She smiled at the children and turned back to the pie judging.

On the way, she saw Reverend Locke and his sister approaching. Beverly put on her best smile.

"Good morning, Reverend. Priscilla, good to see you again."

"Hello, Beverly," the minister said.

"Isn't it a beautiful day?" Priscilla noticed her clipboard. "Are you working today?"

"I'm trying to collect a few signatures. I'm running for mayor of Marble Cove."

"Bravo," Priscilla said.

Reverend Locke's eyebrows rose. "Indeed? I wish you the best."

"Would you care to sign my petition?" Beverly asked.

"I would, but I'm afraid Mr. Calder found me first. So sorry."

"It's all right," Beverly said. Dennis and Lee couldn't have gotten to everyone in town. She'd just have to work harder and maybe go door-to-door next week.

"I can't, of course, since I'm not a resident," Priscilla said, "but I'd be happy to otherwise."

"Thank you. I'm sure I'll get enough names. My father and Jeff Mackenzie are helping me, so if you see one of them coming at you with a clipboard, watch out!"

Priscilla laughed. "I'll keep it in mind."

Beverly headed back to the pie contest. Jeff found her on the edge of the throng a few minutes later where she was watching the judges.

"How'd you do?" he asked.

"Only one," Beverly said glumly.

"I got three. Don't be discouraged. You're in this for the long haul."

She smiled. "Thanks. I'm guessing eighty percent of the people here aren't residents, and half the ones who are have already signed a petition for Dennis or Lee."

"We'll root out the ones who haven't," Jeff said.

"Well, just so you know, if you see Reverend Locke, he signed for Dennis."

"Check. Oh, look. Something's going on with the pies."

The head judge turned on a portable microphone. "Ladies and gentlemen, we have concluded the first round of judging, and we have selected the best three pies. We'll do a final tasting and consult before placing them in order. We hope the bakers are present. For your information, the three top-rated pies from the first round, in no particular order, are numbers three, five, and twelve."

"Which one is Allan's?" Jeff asked.

"I have no idea." Beverly frowned as she watched the judges accept more little plates of pie. "They're not going to want any lunch, are they?"

Jeff laughed. "Say, there's Allan over there. Shall we ask him which one is his pie?"

"Sure."

They sidled around the spectators until they were close to Allan.

He smiled when he saw them. "Well, hi, Jeff. Beverly. I'd like you to meet Margaret's cousin, Buddy Gordon, and his friend, Greg Hathorn."

Beverly and Jeff greeted the two men, and Jeff said, "We wondered if your pie is one of the finalists, Allan."

He smiled and said in a low voice, "Number three."

Beverly smiled and nodded. "Good luck."

"I'm sure these are discriminating judges," Allan said.

Beverly recognized Rusty Garrison from the Cove, but the other two judges didn't look familiar.

Jeff looked over at Buddy and Greg. "I don't suppose either of you gentlemen is a registered voter in Marble Cove?"

"No," Greg said. "We're just here for the day."

Jeff nodded. "Well, Allan, have you signed a mayoral candidate's petition? Because Beverly has decided to run." He held up his clipboard.

Allan broke into a grin. "You don't say! No, as a matter of fact, I haven't, but I'd be happy to sign for you, Beverly."

"Thank you, Allan." She watched in satisfaction as he signed Jeff's sheet. "Only forty-five to go."

"We'll get them," Jeff said.

"Ladies and gentlemen, we have made our decision."

Everyone stopped talking and looked toward the judges under the awning.

The head judge said, "Third place, number twelve."

One of the other judges placed the white ribbon beside what was left of the pie. Beverly held her breath, hoping Allan would win. She could feel his tension, even though he was so easygoing that she knew he would laugh it off if he didn't get the blue ribbon.

"Second place, number three."

She and Jeff, along with Allan and his companions, let out deep sighs.

"And the winner is, pie number five."

"I think that's Mrs. Peabody's." Allan smiled. "Well, she's not entering the seafood cook-off this afternoon. Maybe that's my event."

The judge read off the names of those who placed in the contest and offered congratulations.

"Better luck next time," Greg said.

"What now?" Buddy asked Allan.

"Shall we go over and see how Adelaide is doing? She may be getting tired, and I want to make sure she's wearing her sun hat."

"Sure, let's go," Buddy said.

"Jeff, Beverly, we'll see you later," Allan said. "Are either of you entering the lobster crate run?"

"Not me," Jeff said. "I think I'm too heavy."

"What's that?" Greg asked.

"They have fifty lobster traps tied together in a line in the water so that they're partially submerged," Jeff said. "You have to run along on top of them. The one to get the farthest without falling in the drink wins."

Greg laughed.

"Not my sport," Buddy said.

"Mine either." Jeff shook his head. "I think it will be a lightweight who wins it. Beverly could do it."

"Yes, you run a lot, don't you Beverly?" Allan asked.

"And she's a lot lighter than I am," Jeff added.

She felt the blood rushing to her cheeks. "Stop it, you guys. There is no way you'll get me to do that in front of hundreds of people. I prefer to run in solitude. And without the probability of getting a ducking."

"All right, we'll let you off the hook this time," Allan said. "But when you're mayor..." He attempted an evil grin.

Beverly barked a laugh. "I'm pretty sure that's not one of the mayor's duties. See you later!"

★ ★ ★

When Diane entered the gallery at quarter to one, she was surprised to see Terri Glazier standing at the counter with a lithe man whose iron-gray hair and aquiline nose gave him a distinguished look. His dark Jamaica-length shorts and striped shirt had a designer stamp to them, and she knew before Terri turned toward her that this was Jack.

"Diane!" Terri ran to her and grasped her hand. "You've got to meet my husband."

He turned toward her and smiled easily, but his eyes gave her a quick, shrewd appraisal. "So this is our author?"

"She sure is," Terri said. "Jack Bowman, Diane Spencer. It gives me great pleasure to introduce you two!"

"I'm very pleased to meet you, Mr. Bowman." Diane stepped forward and offered her hand.

He laughed as he grasped it. "Please—Jack. And I can't tell you how glad I am that Terri talked me into reading your book. It's just what we need for a mystery for our spring lineup. Fast-moving, a little romance, and the killer's not obvious."

"Spring? Do you mean next spring? Would it happen that fast?" Diane asked.

"I hope so, but probably another year would be more realistic. Of course, I'll have to convince about fifty other people first, and that takes time."

Terri asked, "Can you have dinner with us tomorrow night, Diane? You and Jack could talk about it then. You could just walk across the street and join us."

"I'd love to. And I see you've both met one of my dearest friends, Margaret Hoskins." Diane smiled at Margaret, who was waiting patiently to give Jack or Terri a sales slip. The wrapped item on the counter boded well for Margaret's sales of the day—Diane was sure from its size that it was a painting.

"Yes," Margaret said. "I was delighted to meet Terri. It's been rather a fluke that we hadn't collided on the sidewalk before this."

Terri chuckled. "I absolutely love this gallery." She glanced at Diane. "Jack does too. He's bought one of Margaret's paintings for his office, and I'm going to have her ship that table right over there"—she pointed to one behind Diane—"to our home in California. I have the perfect spot for it, and I want that exact arrangement, the table, the vase, and even the doily. It will be stunning in my entry."

"Better than that old hat rack that's there now," Jack said.

"Yes, I think that was a mistake." Terri shrugged. "Anyway, we should get on over to the beach, I'm told, before all the lobster is gone."

"I just came from there." Diane put a hand to her stomach. "Talk about good food!"

Jack and Terri left, but several other people were browsing in the gallery.

"Do you think I ought to go?" Margaret whispered. "It's been busy all day."

"Yes, you should," Diane told her. "Beverly will be here any minute. We'll be fine. Go and enjoy the day. And by the way, I met Cousin Buddy."

"You did?"

Diane nodded and smiled. "He's larger than life, isn't he?"

"You might say that. I do hope he stays sober."

"I can't guarantee the future, but he and his friend and Allan were drinking root beer when I saw them."

Beverly came through the door with Jeff, in the wake of a few more shoppers.

"Hi, Margaret." Beverly took a quick look around. "You'd better get out of here quick, or you'll never leave."

"I can stay and help if you want me to," Jeff said.

"That's great," Diane said, nodding at Jeff. "I was just telling Margaret to skedaddle myself, and an extra helper would be nice."

The next two hours were hectic. Diane and Beverly took turns manning the checkout and mingling with the customers. Jeff extolled the virtues of the artwork to the shoppers and carried out a bulky parcel for a woman who bought one of Margaret's lighthouse paintings. Diane was overjoyed when she also sold one of the prints, and a woman and her daughter purchased four pieces of jewelry. Meanwhile, Jeff managed somehow to collect half a dozen signatures for Beverly's petition.

Allan arrived at three o'clock in high spirits.

"Hey, how did it go?" Diane asked as he came in and shut the door.

"Great. You're looking at the new seafood cook-off champion!"

"That's wonderful!" Diane gave him a quick hug. "Say, there's a couple over in the other part of the gallery that's very interested in one of your shelf units. I told them you'd be right in, and they said they'd wait a few minutes."

"Thanks, Diane."

"Oh, and before you go talk to them, Jeff's out back looking for a framed print to hang in place of the one we sold. Do you know right offhand where they are?"

"Check the storage area next to the restroom. There are a couple of big cartons with framed ones in them."

"Right. We'll find them."

"It's pretty busy," Allan observed. "I hate to ask, but could one of you stay?"

"No problem."

Beverly was behind the counter, and Diane waved to her as she headed toward the storage room. She met Jeff as she rounded the corner.

"I think I found them," Jeff said. "I don't want to put out the wrong thing, though."

"Allan's here. As soon as he's done talking to a customer, we can have him check it."

When Allan had a free moment, she asked if he had connected with Margaret for lunch.

"I sure did, and she got to watch the cook-off. She's with Buddy and Greg now, and they were going to see if Adelaide is finished with her job and ready to take in some of the rides."

More people came in the door, making over a dozen browsers in the gallery.

"Has it been like this all day?" Allan asked.

"Yes, and I expect that after the crate race and the other events wind down, even more folks might stop by before heading home."

"Well, I appreciate you all staying."

Jeff was hanging the replacement print, but a consignment artist's painting was now lying on the counter, and he had another blank spot on the wall to fill. Allan hurried to get another framed piece from the storage room. Diane went from customer to customer answering their questions as best she could. Nothing could have pleased her more than to see the gallery so busy.

"Should we send Jeff to Shelley's booth and see if she has any more cookies?" Beverly asked in her ear. "We're nearly out."

Diane turned to survey the refreshment area. "Oh, looks like I need to make more coffee too." She glanced at her watch. "It's almost four thirty. We can try, I guess, but she may be sold out."

Beverly frowned. "Are we closing at five?"

"Six, I think. Margaret wants to take full advantage of the tourist mob today."

Beverly nodded. "Oops, there's someone at the counter again. Can you ask Jeff to check on my father when he makes the cookie run?"

"I can take the register if you want. See what Allan thinks about refreshments." Diane hurried over to the checkout.

A silver-haired woman held up a beautiful blown glass vase. "Do you have another one just like this? I want two."

"*Hmm*, I don't know," Diane admitted. "I think each one is unique, since they're handmade. But we may have something very similar by the same artist. Let me check with Mr. Hoskins." She took the vase and glanced about for Allan.

"I'll have to look," he said in reply to her query. He took the vase and headed out back.

Beverly met her back at the counter. "Jeff's going to Shelley's booth to try to get more cookies. I told him if she's out of cookies, get anything she has left."

"What about your dad?"

"If he wants to go home now, Jeff will take him." Beverly smiled and looked around at the still-packed rooms. "I don't think this place has ever been so mobbed, even when Margaret had Ms. Lumadue in to speak."

"I think you're right," Diane said. "I love it, and the fact that we'll have a good report for Margaret. But I'll be glad to go back into my quiet little cave tonight."

CHAPTER EIGHTEEN

Margaret and Adelaide yelled themselves hoarse at the lobster crate race. After several young men and two girls tried to run the unstable course and wound up in the water of the cove, a middle school boy succeeded in skimming over all fifty crates and claimed the trophy.

"That was fun," Adelaide said. "He went really fast."

"Yes, he did. Would you like to get something to eat now?"

"I'm still full." Adelaide rubbed her belly.

"Yeah, that late lunch filled me up too," Buddy said. "Not to mention the ice cream we got afterward."

"Do you want to go over to the gallery with me?" Margaret asked. "It's nearly closing time."

"We should feed the cats," Adelaide said.

"*Hmm.*" Margaret knew the cats could wait a while longer, but she suspected Adelaide was ready to escape the crowds. "You worked hard today. Are you tired?"

"Kind of."

Greg looked at his watch. "I hate to say it, but we should probably hit the road soon."

"I'd like to talk to Margaret a little more," Buddy said, eyeing her a bit anxiously.

"Do you two want to walk Adelaide home, and I'll stop in at the gallery?" Greg asked. "I'd like to see Allan again about his woodworking."

"I could bring your truck over there," Buddy suggested.

Greg smiled and fished the keys out of his pocket. "I'm happy to say I can trust you to do that today. I'm proud of you, Buddy."

"Thanks." He nodded gravely. "Come on, ladies. Lead the way."

Adelaide's steps were dragging by the time they reached the house on Newport Avenue.

"I think I'll go right to bed," she said.

"Your favorite program comes on soon," Margaret opened the door, and Oreo greeted them with a plaintive meow.

Adelaide scooped up the cat and buried her face in his fluffy neck. "Maybe I'll curl up on the couch with this ball of fur."

"All right. I'll ride over to the gallery with Cousin Buddy, if you think you'll be okay. I'm sure Dad and I won't be long."

"I'm okay," Adelaide said.

"Well, Adelaide, it was a pleasure to see you again." Buddy held out his hand.

She shifted Oreo in her arms and took his hand for a moment. "See you."

Buddy grinned. "Yeah. See you."

He and Margaret went out to the truck, and he opened the passenger door for her. Margaret climbed in and buckled her seat belt while he walked around to the other side. She yawned. Adelaide probably had the right idea—early to bed tonight.

He started the engine and backed out of the driveway. As they headed up the street, he said, "Today was really good, Margaret. Thanks for inviting me."

"I enjoyed it too," she said. "Greg seems like a great guy, and a good man to have on your team."

"He's been terrific as a sponsor. I felt so bad when I let him down."

"Well, that is over now." She turned on the seat and watched him.

He nodded and cleared his throat. "I was thinking... Well, I wondered if you and Allan might come over to Thomaston sometime and visit with me. Maybe in October. We get real pretty leaves where I live. Well, most years."

"I think that would be very nice," Margaret said. "We could take a foliage ride together. I'm not nearly so busy once the summer people leave."

He smiled. "Great. Let's plan on it."

"I'm going to call you next week and see how you're getting along."

"I won't be drinking. I promise you that."

"Good. But I want to stay in touch more than we have. Okay?"

"Yeah. I'll answer when you call. And we can e-mail too."

She nodded. Accountability. Maybe that would help Buddy, and it was something she could give him without a total disruption of her life.

They reached the gallery, and she could see that several people still moved about inside. Diane was just turning the Open sign to Closed. Cars lined the street outside.

"Drive around to the back," Margaret said. "There's a small parking area there."

"I wanted to tell you something else," Buddy said as he put the gearshift in park. "I talked to Joe the other night."

"Your son Joe?"

"Yeah. I had got to thinking about what you had said to me on the phone, and...well, I thought I'd give it a try, and he actually talked to me for about ten minutes."

Margaret smiled. "I'm glad."

Buddy nodded, his lips pressed in a flat line. "Me too. Haven't dared to try Peggy yet. I think I'll wait a while on her. Maybe practice on Joe again first."

Margaret touched his sleeve. "Don't give up on the kids, Buddy. Take it slow, like you said, but do try to rebuild those relationships. You'll be glad you did."

"Thanks. It's something to work on."

The first thing she noticed when she and Buddy went in through the back door and entered the main showroom was that one of her prints hung in a choice display spot.

"Hi, Margaret," Jeff said cheerily.

She grabbed his wrist. "Did you sell Dorothy's painting? The one that hung over there?" She nodded toward the wall in question.

He grinned at her. "That and two or three more."

"Goodness." She pressed a hand to her chest. "Have you and Beverly been here all afternoon?" Beverly was still behind the counter, and Diane and Allan were circulating among the customers.

"Yes, but don't worry about it. We had fun, and really, the time just flew."

"What about Mr. Wheeland?"

"Mrs. Peabody's granddaughter drove both him and Augie Jackson to their homes when she took Mrs. P," Jeff said. "I saw them all before they left, and they seemed to have had a good time today."

"Okay. That's good." Margaret looked around slowly and noticed several other changes in the displayed items. "The ruby vase—oh, and Allan's walnut occasional table!"

Jeff grinned at Buddy. "Hold her down so she doesn't get too excited. This was a banner day at the Shearwater."

★ ★ ★

Diane dressed with care and put on a favorite pair of earrings that Jessica had given her. Even though Jack had dressed beach casual yesterday for the festival, it was classy casual, and she felt that tonight would be a bit more formal. She'd decided to wear a sleeveless pink print dress and white sandals and hoped she'd chosen right.

Terri had set dinner time for seven, and Diane had snacked earlier so she wouldn't starve. She'd followed her neighbors' rural ways and taken to eating around five most nights, with a small snack in the evening. Jack and Terri probably ate late and stayed out until all hours in California—although after her many conversations with Terri, she didn't think the couple went out as often as she imagined most "film people" did.

At precisely seven, she shut Rocky in and walked across the street. Jack and Gallant met her at the door of the rental house.

"Hello, Diane. You look lovely tonight—nice and cool."

"Thank you. How was your day?"

"Oh, terrific. We drove up the coast and puttered around antique shops, mostly. Come on through to the kitchen. Terri's out there."

"Hi," Terri called as they entered. "I'm just about set with this chicken, but I think it needs five more minutes."

"Can I do anything to help?" Diane asked.

"Well, I thought we'd eat on the deck, it's so nice out. Why don't you choose what you want to drink, and we'll head on out there for a few minutes?"

Terri seemed to have all the dishes laid on the table, and she'd anchored the napkins so the ocean breeze wouldn't send them flying. Diane and her hosts settled in deck chairs near the small table.

"Can't believe you got such gorgeous weather all week," Jack said. "The last time I was in New England in summer, it rained the whole time, and I thought I'd freeze."

"It's been beautiful this month, if a little on the hot side," Diane said. "But we need it so we'll have something pleasant to look back on when winter hits."

"I don't think I'd want to stay here all winter, but this has been lovely." Terri sipped her iced tea.

"Now, Diane," Jack said, "I'd like to hear how you were inspired to write your mystery."

"Mysteries, plural," Terri put in.

"Is it a series?" Jack arched his silvery eyebrows at Diane.

"Well, yes. I'm writing my third now. The second book is in production." It felt so good to say that. Diane savored the feeling of contentment. Only a few days ago, she'd dragged around, quite certain the third book would be canceled, and wondering if the second one would really see print. Now she could speak confidently and sound very professional about it.

"That's great." Jack settled back in his chair. "You know what I liked most about the one I read?"

Diane shook her head and waited eagerly for his response.

"The ending. It just *made sense*. Even though you kept me guessing all the way through, and I had no idea who the culprit was, it made so much sense when I found out. Everything sort of fell into place in that last chapter. Good job!"

"Thank you," Diane murmured, feeling her cheeks flush.

"I thought that too," Terri said, "but I think what I liked best about it was that it really felt like Maine. And now that I've been here a couple of weeks, I'd say it really feels like Marble Cove, even though you didn't call your town that."

Diane smiled. "Thanks so much. It's still hard for me to sit and take praise, but I admit I love hearing that people enjoyed my story. I can't describe how that makes me feel, but it's good, and I'm thankful that I've been able to have this experience."

"Well, don't stop because you're so satisfied," Jack said.

Terri's eyes widened. "No, we want more books."

Diane couldn't help laughing. "With all this encouragement, I don't think I'll quit anytime soon."

For a while, as they ate dinner, they talked about their adult children and the scenic places they'd visited along the coast. The couple had plans to visit the Penobscot Marine Museum in Searsport the next day. After they'd discussed it, Jack swung the conversation around to Diane's book again.

"You know, Terri was right about the setting of your book. You have a gift for portraying the feel of a place, Diane. And when I got here—" He chuckled. "Well, not immediately, because it was dark, but the next morning, when Terri took me down to the beach, and I saw the lighthouse in the distance, I thought, 'This is it. This is where the story happened.'"

"He said that," Terri confirmed.

Jack nodded. "Yesterday things got a little crazy, with the festival and everything, but today we went down there again. Took the dog and had a nice, quiet stroll, all the way to the lighthouse and back. It's perfect."

"I like it myself," Diane murmured.

"Well, I took quite a few pictures," Jack said. "When it comes time to persuade my company's production committee that this story is for us, I plan to show them some photos of Marble Cove and that lighthouse. It's an ideal location."

"You don't mean you'd film it here, do you?" Diane's pulse raced. That would be wonderful—wouldn't it? Or would it disrupt the quiet little town and make it into something unrecognizable?

Jack shrugged. "If we did make the film, I think it would be super if we could shoot some of the exterior scenes here. But that's all in the dreaming stage."

"Oh, I know," Diane said. "But when you talk about it, I start to think it could really happen."

"It could." He nodded slowly, his eyes focusing on something far away. "I might just have a word with your town officials before I leave, to see how they feel about it. It might make a difference if I could tell the committee the town is open to allowing a film crew on the beach, and maybe even in town. That makes filming so much easier. And you have such a quaint little town."

"He means that in a good way," Terri said hastily.

"Wow." Diane shook her head, still not able to comprehend it.

Terri stood and reached for Diane's empty plate. "Jack makes it sound so simple, but there are about a million steps to go through before it becomes a reality."

"That's true," he said apologetically, handing her his plate. "It all comes down to the budget, and whether or not the committee likes the story. But I'll be pulling for you."

"Wouldn't it be wild if you *did* make the picture, and you came back here to film it?" Terri asked. "Diane and I could sit in our beach chairs and watch while you worked all day. Your friends would love that, Diane!"

"They sure would. We've all been working hard to help preserve the lighthouse, and having it in a movie would pretty much guarantee that the town would earmark some maintenance money. We've talked about ways to draw in more tourists, and it seems to me that would help a lot."

"You'd have so much fun," Terri said wistfully. "I hope it goes forward." She carried the plates inside and left the door open.

"Can I help with anything?" Diane called.

"Yeah, maybe. Do you like Black Forest cake?"

"*Ooh.*" Diane stood. "Can I bring you anything, Jack?"

"I'll take some coffee. Thanks."

Diane went inside. "Where did you get Black Forest cake?"

Terri laughed. "Where else? As soon as I knew Jack was coming, I hotfooted it over to the Lighthouse Sweet Shoppe, aka the Bauer house, and asked Shelley if she could make me one. It's his favorite."

"Should have known," Diane sighed. "I've really got to stop eating like this. You know, living across the street from a bakery is hazardous."

"Tell me about it! I've had her scones and Danish almost every day since I've been here. I'll bet I've gained five pounds."

"Don't say that. Or say you'll walk the dogs with me again after supper to work off some calories."

"Done." Terri grinned. "But I don't think going back to California will cure the problem. I've already ordered six dozen cookies for Shelley to ship out there for my next turn to host a charity committee meeting."

Diane poured the coffee while Terri fixed the cake plates and they went outside.

"Thanks," Jack said. "Diane, I hope we haven't pumped up your expectations to an unrealistic level."

She settled in her chair and smiled. "I don't think so. Yes, I'm excited about the possibilities, but you know what? This film option deal isn't the best one I've had this summer."

"Oh? Sold a new series?" Jack's eyebrows quirked.

"No, not that. I was talking about the new friend I found this summer—your wife."

Terri beamed. "I feel that way too. Diane's been a wonderful friend to me. She's a very good listener, and she's imparted some bits of wisdom that I think will stick with me. I'm very glad you got to meet her."

Jack reached for Terri's hand. "I am too, sweetheart. This trip has been good for me in a lot of ways. Thanks for keeping after me until I got on the plane."

Terri smiled at him and then winked at Diane. "I made him turn off his cell phone all day. You wouldn't believe what a difference that makes."

"That's right," Jack said. "I didn't realize how dependent I was on it. I had all my calls forwarded to my assistant.

When I called at five for an update, there was exactly one thing I needed to handle. He had dealt just fine with the other thirty-seven calls."

Diane laughed. "Isn't that the way? I know I let things like that distract me too. E-mail, phone calls—but in my case it's usually an excuse not to write."

She watched Jack and Terri as their conversation continued. The two seemed at ease with each other, and happy to be together. In fact, they seemed quite affectionate. That was an answer to her prayers for Terri.

Thank You, Lord, for letting me see that firsthand.

CHAPTER NINETEEN

On Thursday afternoon, Beverly walked toward the Shearwater with Diane and Shelley. Margaret had called the meeting, and all were eager to see the progress she had made on her dream painting.

"I was sorry to see Terri and her husband pull out this morning," Shelley said as they reached Main Street. "It was kind of nice having neighbors over there."

"I'll miss Terri too," Diane said.

"Not Jack?" Shelley asked with a laugh.

"Oh, sure, but I didn't get to know him well. But Terri's a real friend now. We'll keep in touch by e-mail. She told me she hopes to come back next summer."

"I hope she gets the Simpson house. She brought her dog over yesterday, and she let him play with Aiden and Prize in the backyard. They had so much fun!"

"I'll bet they did," Diane said. "What's up with you this week, Beverly?"

"I've been quite busy with some projections for my first corporate client. And tomorrow's the last day of the month. That's the deadline for turning in my election papers."

"Did you get all the signatures you need?" Shelley asked.

"Not quite. We got almost enough during the Lobster Festival, but then we ended up spending the afternoon at the gallery. I need seven more."

"Maybe we can help you after our meeting," Diane said.

Shelley frowned. "As usual, I'll have to go right home. My friend Allie is there with the kids, and we're taking them all—mine, and her son—to the beach afterward. But you two could probably scare up seven names in a short time."

"I think we could," Diane said. "Would you like me to help you, Beverly?"

"Sure." Beverly had put off going door-to-door alone, though that seemed like the most promising way to get the few names she still needed. With personable Diane at her side, it would probably be painless, and she wouldn't feel so much like she was marketing herself. She had unlimited confidence when it came to her business, but this seemed different somehow.

"Maybe we can go around to some of the people in your church first," Diane suggested, "and folks who voted your way on the development issue."

Margaret had customers when they arrived. While they waited, Shelley made a fresh pot of coffee, and Beverly and Diane circled the gallery, pointing out to each other new paintings and pottery pieces Margaret had on display.

"How do you suppose she got so many new pieces so quickly?" Beverly asked. "The festival was less than a week ago, and I think she's replaced everything we sold and then some."

"She's very good friends with most of the artists she represents," Diane said. "I expect she called them and begged for more."

Beverly laughed. "I'll have to remember that tactic."

"Well, the promise of a healthy check from the artwork she sold last weekend is probably a great motivator for her consignees."

They stopped before an abstract with the colors of seawater shimmering through it and lines suggesting an anchor off to one side.

"That's interesting," Diane said. "Is it Margaret's?"

Beverly's gaze went straight to the signature. "It is. She's getting more comfortable with this new style."

"I like it," Diane said.

"I do too. The colors are amazing."

★ ★ ★

A few minutes later, Margaret saw her customers out the door with the small framed print they had purchased and joined her friends out back in her office.

"Whew, it feels good to sit down for a minute." She plopped into her desk chair.

"Can I get you some coffee?" Beverly asked.

"Yes, please, and I'd love one of those molasses cookies out there. I've made myself stay away from them all day, telling myself I could indulge in one when you all got here."

As they all selected their refreshments, the door opened, ringing the bell. Beverly saw Margaret's frown before she quickly replaced it with a cheerful expression and went to greet the newcomer.

"Let's just take everything in back and have it ready," Shelley suggested, picking up the coffee cup Margaret had abandoned and an extra cookie for her.

The customer stayed a few minutes, and when he left Margaret bustled to the back room again.

"Quick! Give me that coffee before someone else comes in." She accepted her mug from Diane and took a sip. "*Ah.* Thank you. It's not usually too busy this time of day. I get a three o'clock lull."

"The season's winding down," Shelley said. "The Cove has ordered fewer pastries since the festival. It's a relief, in a way, not to be so busy."

"Yes, a lot of the summer folk have gone," Diane said. "The beach was quite sparse this morning."

"We saw the new painting out there," Beverly said. "The anchor abstract. It's nice."

Margaret smiled. "Thank you. Maybe the anchor is too obvious, though, if you noticed it right away."

"It made me feel...settled," Beverly said. "I like your lighthouses, but I'm really enjoying your new style."

They munched on Shelley's cookies and chatted for another minute and then Margaret rose.

"I'd better show you that dream painting while we have a chance. It's in my studio."

They moved into the area Margaret sometimes used for painting. She had the canvas propped on her easel, and she flipped on the track lighting overhead.

"Oh, now that's different," Diane said. The dark, brooding waters of the sea still filled the foreground, and the town on shore remained as she had seen it before, but on the right side of the painting, on a craggy headland, stood the figure of a man. He was as large as the church in the town below, and Diane wasn't sure if that meant the cliff was closer than the town, jutting out toward the viewer, or if Margaret had simply painted the man that way to emphasize his importance.

"Who's the guy?" Shelley asked, squinting at the figure on the cliff.

"You tell me," Margaret said, a bemused smile playing on her lips.

"Well, he's not a natty dresser," Shelley said. "He looks old-fashioned."

Margaret eyed him critically. "I've painted him four times. Each time I was sure I hadn't got it right. But this feels right. So who is he? He's not Buddy."

Beverly squinted a little. "It sort of reminds me of the statue in Rio of Christ the Redeemer. But instead of holding both arms out, it looks like he's pointing."

"Yeah," Shelley said. "Toward the sea."

"Or toward us," Beverly said quietly. Everyone looked at her.

Margaret ran a hand through her hair. "Now, that's a new thought that never would have occurred to me."

"I wonder," Diane said slowly. "Is it possible that he's Jeremiah Thorpe?"

No one said anything for several seconds. They all stared at the painting.

At last Beverly looked over at Margaret. "Was this man in your dreams?"

"I don't think so. They were all different. I know Buddy was there a couple of times. The last dream I remembered had me on the deck of a ship, looking toward shore. It was our Marble Cove shore, with the village and the cliff."

"No lighthouse," Diane said.

"No, which is kind of weird."

Margaret shrugged. "I don't know where he came from. It was just that while I was painting the scene, I felt as though it didn't have a focal point."

"Not the church?" Beverly asked.

Margaret shook her head, frowning at her own work. "I don't think so. It was definitely the focus of the one before this. And in that one, I made the town closer, and the fire bigger and more colorful. With this one, it's almost like it's just part of life on shore. He's what's important." She pointed back at the soberly garbed man on the cliff.

Diane made a face. "I wanted to say he doesn't look like Jesus, but do we know what Jesus looked like?"

"Not really," Margaret said. "But this guy's wearing pants. Breeches, maybe. And tall boots."

"He does look sort of colonial," Beverly said.

Margaret sighed. "It's probably just that everything's so muddled up in my mind lately, with Buddy and the festival and being so busy here this month."

"What if it's more than that?" Shelley asked.

Diane eyed her keenly. "What do you mean?"

"Well, Margaret's been having these intense dreams, and she said that when she woke up, she felt like she *had* to paint them."

"That's right," Margaret said. "It's been odd, but I did feel a compulsion, even though I had so many other things to do. And then this figure...I didn't know at first what he was supposed to be like at all. My first attempt to paint him in was just a blob with eyes. But now...now he looks more like a—a—"

"A wild, two-hundred-fifty-year-old preacher," Shelley said.

Diane laughed. "I don't know how wild. Wild-*eyed*, maybe. But he does seem to be wearing clothing from that era. And I almost think his white hair could be one of those powdered wigs."

"Heavens," Margaret said. "Did ministers wear those? I thought it was only the rich people and lawyers."

"To be honest, I don't know. But I have an idea."

"What?" Shelley asked.

Diane tilted her head to one side. "We could go up to the cliff and stand on the spot where this figure is standing, and see what we see."

"*Hmm*." Margaret stared thoughtfully at the canvas.

"I suppose we could," Beverly said. "We wouldn't want to get too close to the edge. It might be dangerous."

"Can you drive up there?" Shelley asked.

"Partway, I think." The bells above the door jingled, and Margaret turned her head toward the showroom. "I think that's a good idea. Excuse me." She hurried out into the main room.

"I think you can drive close to it," Beverly said. "And it shouldn't be too much of a hike the rest of the way. I'm not sure we could find the exact spot, though."

"I agree," Diane said. "The proportions seem off. If you took a ruler and measured that man's figure, he's probably about two inches tall. He's bigger than some of the houses in the town. I was wondering whether that meant he was closer—or more important."

"Good question," Beverly said.

Diane shrugged. "Either way, it makes it difficult to judge exactly where he's standing. But I do think we should go up there and just see what's there, if anything, and what the view toward the ocean looks like."

"I'm game," Shelley said. "But not today."

"Tomorrow?" Beverly asked.

"I can." Diane looked out toward the gallery. She could hear Margaret's voice. "We'll have to see if the artist can join us."

When Margaret returned, they told her what they'd discussed.

"I'll see if Allan will stand in for me here to give me an hour or so," she said.

They set a time, and Beverly said hesitantly, "Do you think we should tell Reverend Locke?"

The four looked at each other.

"You know," Diane said, "we probably should. That might be a way to reassure him we have good intentions."

"Yes," Margaret said. "We wouldn't want him to find out afterward and feel excluded. And even though the connection to Jeremiah Thorpe seems questionable"—she glanced at the painting—"I'd just feel better if we told him."

"Let's do it, then," Shelley said. "Now I need to go home. Who's going to make the call?"

"I will," Beverly said.

Diane appreciated her offer. "All right, we'll see you here at ten tomorrow morning." She took the empty Styrofoam cups and tossed them in the trash.

"What should we bring?" Margaret asked.

"Digging tools and metal detectors?" Beverly arched her eyebrows at Diane.

"Yes. And I'll bring along my binoculars."

"How about a camera?" Shelley asked.

"Good idea. I'll bring some plastic bags to put any interesting finds in." Diane smiled at them. "Beverly, shall we go stump for you and get those signatures now?"

"I'm ready if you are."

They walked outside, and Beverly said, "I'll have to go home and get the clipboards. Shall I bring the church directory for Old First?"

"Good idea."

"Oh, and I should call Reverend Locke as soon as possible."

"Tell you what," Diane said. "I'll go take Rocky out for a few minutes, and you give me a buzz when you're ready."

"All right. I've hit everyone on our street already, so maybe I should pick you up in my car."

"If you want."

They walked down Newport Avenue and separated at Beverly's house. When she went inside, her father was in his library, pulling out books from one of the shelves, looking at the covers, and shoving them back in.

"Hi," she said. "What's up?"

"Just looking for Bradford's *Of Plymouth Plantation*. I know it's here somewhere."

Beverly smiled. "Well, if it's okay with you, Diane and I are going to try to get the last few signatures I need."

"Fine, fine." He sounded distracted, and she knew he wouldn't stop searching until he found his book.

"If you need me, call my cell." Beverly hurried upstairs to get the necessary paperwork and made sure pens were attached to both clipboards. She sat down at her desk and picked up the phone. Silas Locke answered on the third ring.

"Hello," she said, striving for a cheerful and confident tone. "This is Beverly Wheeland."

"Oh, hello. How may I help you, Beverly?"

"There's been a development in the Jeremiah Thorpe matter."

"Oh? Did you find some more documents?" He sounded much more animated than he had when he first spoke.

Beverly felt suddenly a bit wary. Would he think they were flaky for mounting another search based on a painting inspired by a dream?

"No, not exactly. It's just that we plan to do some more hunting tomorrow, and we thought you should be included. That is, we wanted you to know, and if you want to come along, you're welcome."

"Where are you going?"

"Up on the cliff," Beverly said.

After a moment's silence, he asked, "What takes you there? Is there new evidence...?"

"Not hard evidence. It's more of a hunch that we don't want to discount. You certainly don't have to go if you don't want to. You see, Margaret Hoskins has been troubled recently by a series of dreams, and she began to paint them."

"Paint her dreams?"

"Yes." It did sound a little odd, and Beverly quickly went on. "She's had some difficulties in her family—with her cousin, but that's another matter. In these dreams, she saw herself in the water or on the deck of an old ship, and her view of the town included a burning church."

"Old First?"

"We believe so. And in the last one...well, Margaret said she's not sure it was actually in the dream, but she felt something was missing from the painting. After several days of dabbling with it, she showed us the result. And there's a figure on the cliff. We think it may represent Jeremiah Thorpe."

"Oh." He didn't say anything for several seconds, and Beverly wondered if he thought she was completely off her rocker. "I'm not sure I see the connection..."

"We're not sure we do, either," Beverly confessed. "But we do know that God works in mysterious ways. On the chance that this image means something, we want to go to the spot on the cliff where the figure in the painting is standing and see if we find anything there. If you don't want to go, it's all right—"

"I think I do. If you ladies are sure you don't mind, that is. I'd like to see you in action, so to speak. And I'll try to keep an open mind."

"Very good. Meet us at ten o'clock at Margaret's gallery. Her husband is going to mind the store for her while we're gone. Oh, and if your sister wants to go—"

"Thank you, but Priscilla has gone home. I don't think she could come back so soon, but I'll tell her."

"All right. She's invited, if it works out. We're taking a few tools and a metal detector. We'll see you at ten."

She hung up and inhaled deeply. That was almost as hard as cleaning out her father's attic had been. She glanced at her watch and jumped up. Diane must be waiting.

★ ★ ★

Two hours later, Diane and Beverly walked to the car in front of the Cannery, an old factory that now housed several craft and antique shops.

"That was a stroke of genius, coming here," Beverly said.

Diane smiled. "Well, it made sense. When we went door-to-door we either got people who had already signed or had some reason not to."

"That's out of the ones that were home." Beverly grimaced.

"Right. I guess a bright, sunny Thursday afternoon in August isn't the best time to find people at home." Diane climbed into the car and fastened her seat belt. "I think most of the ones we got here came from shopkeepers, not customers."

"Yes, a lot of the shoppers were from out of town. But it all worked out well." Beverly stowed the clipboards on the backseat and started the car.

"Want to get some ice cream?" Diane asked.

"Well...it sounds lovely, but I should probably get home. Mrs. Peabody doesn't usually get supper for us—just lunch, unless I ask her special. So it's up to me to see that Father gets a good meal."

"Okay. I shouldn't indulge, anyway." Diane smiled ruefully. "Not after eating some of Shelley's cookies earlier."

"Yeah, we need to find a way to get together without piling on the calories."

"I suppose we could meet at some place a mile or two out of town and insist that everyone walk to the rendezvous."

Beverly laughed. "I'm sure that would go over well."

As she drove onto Newport Avenue, Diane said, "You don't have to take me down to my house. I'll walk the rest of the way. That will burn ten calories or so."

"All right." Beverly drove into her father's driveway. "Thanks a lot for going with me. I'm not sure I'd have pushed myself to do it today if you hadn't encouraged me."

"Well, now you have no excuse not to get those to the town office tomorrow."

"Nothing like a last-minute candidate."

Diane glanced at her watch. "Well, I'm afraid we were a few minutes too late to get them in today. The office closed ten minutes ago."

Beverly reached back for the clipboards. "I know Lee filed his papers, and I assume Dennis did. I wonder if there are any other candidates."

"Ask when you take them in," Diane said.

"Right. I'll do it before we go over to the gallery."

"Why don't we take my car?" Diane suggested. "We can put the tools and things in the back."

"Sounds good."

"And I'll swing by the town office before we go to Margaret's to make sure you do your duty."

Beverly laughed at her stern tone. "All right, but we'd better allow an extra ten minutes for that."

"Will do. I'll pick you up at twenty minutes to ten."

Chapter Twenty

To Margaret's surprise, she received a call from Priscilla Abbott before she'd even left home Friday morning. She was moving the breakfast dishes from the table to the counter, where Allan was loading the dishwasher.

"I'm sorry to bother you," Priscilla said. "I'm at my brother's house, and I wanted to be sure you ladies didn't mind if I tagged along today."

"We'd love to have you," Margaret said.

"Oh, thank you! Silas assured me that Beverly mentioned me particularly when she'd called, but he assumed I wouldn't want to drive back over here so soon."

Margaret smiled. "I take it you disabused him of that notion."

"Yes," Priscilla said with a chuckle. "I find it very exciting. My genealogy research usually takes place in musty places like the state archives. The thought of hunting for treasure on a windswept cliff overlooking the ocean gives me goose bumps."

"I hope our outing lives up to your anticipation," Margaret said. "We're meeting at the Shearwater at ten, but you and Silas are welcome to come a few minutes early for coffee if you like."

"I'll accept for both of us. I'd very much like to see the gallery."

Margaret was glad Priscilla would join them. She liked Silas's sister, and Priscilla seemed to add a tempering influence to her brother's moods. Where Silas saw interference and sinister motives, Priscilla saw concern and a desire to help—which was what the women of Newport Avenue intended.

Allan raised his eyebrows as she hung up the receiver. "Is your scouting party getting larger?"

She laughed. "Not really. We invited Silas Locke and his sister, but he thought Priscilla wouldn't come. That was her, saying she'd be delighted. She sounds quite excited about it."

"Good. I'll be over at the gallery by ten—unless you want me there earlier. I have some work to do in the shop on that special-order table."

"That's fine," Margaret said. "I'll see you at ten."

The big question now was, should she show Priscilla and Silas the painting? The thought made her stomach tighten, but since it was the impetus for their hunt this morning, she probably should. They might see something in it the others had missed. Margaret sent up a quick prayer. *Lord, this whole thing seems a little wacky to me, but if You can use my painting to help us save Old First, I'm all for it. And if this is just our imagination, well . . . we'd still like to find a way to repair the church, if You want that.*

She still felt unsettled about the whole thing, but she couldn't think of one good reason why the Lord wouldn't want the church restored. And until she knew otherwise, she would keep on looking for a way to do that.

★ ★ ★

Diane pulled into the Wheelands' driveway right on time. Beverly gathered up her things.

"Bye, Father. I'll see you later." She hurried out to Diane's SUV, juggling her purse, a trowel, work gloves, and a camera. In addition, she carried a manila folder.

"Hi," Diane said when she opened the door. "Hop in."

Beverly stowed her things on the floor, except for the folder, which she kept on her lap.

"I hope I'm not late."

"You're not," Beverly said.

"Good. I took Rocky out early for a good, long romp on the beach this morning. I wanted to be sure we had time to get to the town office and still be on time at the gallery. Of course, Rocky wanted to chase gulls and sniff every clump of seaweed on the sand."

Beverly laughed. "Sounds like a typical, healthy dog."

Diane looked over her shoulder and backed out of the driveway. Beverly glanced back there and saw a spade lying on the backseat, along with a trash bag and a couple of leather cases.

"I brought my video camera," Diane said. "Not sure if we'll use it, but hey, I figured it would be fun to be able to look back at this and laugh, if nothing else."

"Oh boy. I see you brought a spade too."

"Yes, and a compass. I don't really know why I threw that in, but it seemed like the sort of thing to take on a treasure hunt."

"This is shaping up to be a real adventure," Beverly said.

"I hope so." Diane headed for the town office. "All set to officially become a candidate?"

"As ready as I'll ever be."

When they arrived, Beverly's stomach fluttered. They got out of the vehicle and went up the walkway to the municipal building's annex together. She was glad Diane was there. For one thing, she couldn't chicken out now. For another, Diane was the staunchest friend she could imagine, and if there were any glitches, she would jump in and smooth things out.

The building was an old Victorian house, and next to it sat the newer part of the municipal building, a modern brick facility that housed the police department.

"Your new office will be in this part," Diane said. "Aren't you glad?"

Beverly smiled. "You're making a huge assumption, as usual. But I admit, I like this better than the modern part."

The blue-gray building had several varieties of shingles in its siding, and a turret jutted up from the second floor. The trim was painted deep blue and vanilla, and Beverly wondered how the colors would look on her father's house—not that he would ever want to change it. Diane held the door open for her, and they entered the foyer, where a discreet sign said "Mayor's Office" and had an arrow pointing toward the stairway. She wondered if it was in the tower room. Wouldn't it be a kick to have her office up there?

Beverly stepped forward and opened the door to the reception room. No sense daydreaming about it. She had a lot of work to do before election day.

The clerk behind the counter looked up and smiled.

"Hi, Mrs. Spencer!"

"Hello, Angela," Diane said. "You've got a new haircut."

"Yeah." She smiled and ran a hand through her messy cropped cut. "Do you like it?"

"It's cute on you. Do you know Beverly Wheeland?"

"We met when she came in for nomination papers a couple of weeks ago. Does this mean we have another mayoral candidate?"

Beverly stepped forward and laid her folder on the counter. "It does."

"Great! The more the merrier, that's what I say." Angela opened the folder and gave each sheet inside a quick perusal. "These look okay at first glance. I'll go over them carefully and give you a call."

"Thank you," Beverly said. "My cell number is on the application. Oh, and . . . " She hesitated, but her curiosity got the better of her. "Can you tell me how many candidates there are?"

Angela grinned. "Two. You and Lee Waters."

Beverly stared at her.

"What about Dennis Calder?" Diane asked.

Angela shrugged and looked up at the clock. "He took out papers, but he hasn't brought them in yet. He's still got seven hours, though."

"Do you think he will?" Diane asked.

"To be honest, yes, I do. But we'll see." Angela smiled at Beverly. "Whether he does or not, you'll stand out, if for no other reason than that you're the only woman."

"She'll stand out anyway," Diane said. "Beverly has skills that would be very beneficial to the town."

"I'm sure she has." Angela glanced toward the door behind them. "Say, it looks as though you timed it right if you want to make an announcement in tomorrow's *Courier*."

Beverly turned toward the door as Gerald Kimball, the newspaper's reporter, entered.

"Hey, Gerald!" Angela called. "I've got a front-page story for you."

"Really?" Gerald smiled and glanced curiously at Beverly and Diane, as though he wondered if they were responsible for this newsworthy event.

"Yup, we now have two candidates for mayor, and the latest entry is standing right next to you."

Beverly opened her mouth to protest, but closed it. If she really wanted the position, she'd better not be shy about saying so.

"Hey, that's great." Gerald opened a small notebook. "Some days I get lucky. I just came from the police station, and they haven't had anything new on the cop log for three days."

"I believe it," Angela said.

"So you're running for mayor?" Gerald's blue eyes focused on Beverly.

"Yes, I am." Beverly mustered her most professional tone.

Gerald nodded and made a note. "It's not such a big step from opposing the Calder development to running for mayor. Would you like to make a formal announcement in the *Courier*? We'd love to run it in tomorrow's edition."

"Well, I..." Beverly glanced at Diane. They must be nearly late for their appointment at Margaret's already.

"I could sit down with you for a few minutes right now and do an interview," Gerald said. "I've already interviewed Lee Waters, and, of course, we want to treat all candidates equally."

"Actually, I have a ten o'clock appointment," Beverly told him. "Maybe later."

"How about one o'clock?" he persisted. "I could still make my deadline, and I'd bring my camera for a headshot. What do you say?"

"Well..." Beverly almost looked to Diane again, but made herself stop. She needed to do this on her own. "Sure. Would you like me to come to the newspaper office?"

"How about I come to your house? That way, I can take some pictures in your own environment."

"I guess that would be all right."

"Great." Gerald tucked his notebook away in his jacket pocket. "I'll see you at one."

Diane walked out through the entry with Beverly, and as she reached for the door handle, she said, "I'm so proud of you. That was great! What a fortuitous meeting!"

Beverly blew out a deep breath. "Wow. Gerald can sort of steamroll you."

"But it's good," Diane insisted. "You've got a few hours to think of what you want to say."

"Yeah, while I'm hunting for treasure." Beverly stepped outside and stopped in her tracks. Coming up the walkway was Dennis Calder.

He stopped two steps below her. Beverly heard Diane's sharp intake of breath behind her.

"Well, good morning, Beverly," Dennis said. "Diane."

"Hello," Diane replied.

"Are you here to turn in your nomination papers?" Beverly asked.

"That's right." Dennis returned her gaze with a challenge in his vivid blue eyes. He looked great, wearing a short-sleeved cotton shirt and Dockers. "How about you? I heard you were collecting signatures on Saturday."

"Yes. I just left them with Angela."

Dennis nodded slowly. "So we face off again. May the best man win."

"Or woman." Beverly didn't let her gaze waver, but she couldn't help thinking of their past friendly encounters and the times they'd laughed together over coffee at the Cove.

Dennis's mouth slowly morphed from its stern line into a smile. "This should be fun, Beverly. I think I'm going to enjoy it. I hope you do too."

"Knowing you're in the race will prod me to stay on top of the issues," she said.

"Same here. I don't think this will be a runaway for anyone. Well, ladies, I'll let you be on your way." He stepped aside so they could pass him.

"Good-bye." Beverly hurried down the steps and didn't look back. Diane caught up with her at the end of the walkway.

"Wow, talk about timing," Diane said.

Beverly glanced over her shoulder then. Dennis had disappeared inside. "Yeah. Just think, if I hadn't stopped to chat with Gerald Kimball, we'd have been out of here before he arrived." She looked at her watch. "Come on! We're late."

They both hopped into the SUV. On the short drive to the gallery, she said, "I'd better call the house and see if Mrs. Peabody can do a little spiffing up before the interview."

"Your house is always clean."

"Well, I don't know how much time I'll have to clean up, and I seem to recall leaving a few things in the living room. And I haven't dusted since—" She shook her head. "I'll just call Mrs. Peabody. I'll feel easier if I know somebody's on it. You go ahead in."

Diane found a parking spot in front of the Cove, just a few yards from Margaret's business.

"I'll tell them you're here but you had to make a call."

"Thanks," Beverly said.

Diane laid her hand on Beverly's wrist. "Don't let Dennis upset you."

"I won't. I thought he was in it to begin with, anyway. I hadn't had time to let it sink in that he hadn't filed his paperwork yet, and bang! There he was. Nothing's changed, really."

"Okay." Diane got out and leaned down to speak through the open doorway. "The interview is going to be terrific, Beverly."

"Thanks. I wish I had a shot of your confidence."

CHAPTER TWENTY-ONE

Margaret heard the bells above the door jangle and looked out into the gallery. Diane was just entering, and she stopped to greet Allan, who stood near the counter.

"There's Diane," Margaret said to the others in her office. "Excuse me." She hurried out front and smiled at her friend. "Glad you're here! Have you talked to Beverly?"

"Yes, she's outside," Diane said. "She had to make a phone call. Gerald Kimball waylaid us at the municipal building."

"Oh?" Margaret smiled. "I'll bet he wants to interview Beverly. That must mean she got the papers in on time."

"You're right on both counts."

The doorbell rang again, but instead of Beverly, two women entered.

"I'll handle this," Allan said softly. "You ladies get out of here."

Margaret drew Diane toward the back room. "Reverend Locke and his sister are here," she whispered. "Shelley too. We've had coffee."

Diane's eyebrows arched as if she was thankful for the tip-off. "Did you show them the painting?"

"No. I thought about it, but..."

Diane nodded in understanding and squeezed her arm. "That's fine." She entered the office smiling. "Priscilla! So good to see you again."

"Thank you." Priscilla shook Diane's hand. "I was delighted when Silas called and told me I was invited. This sounds like a real adventure."

"We hope it is one," Shelley said. "Hi, Diane."

"Hi." Diane chuckled. "I'm not sure if it's a 'real' adventure or just a cockamamy scheme for us to get together and have fun, but we've got a perfect day for it."

"Yes," the reverend said, with a nod of greeting. "Lovely weather we've had—all week, in fact."

The back door opened and Beverly came in, a little breathless.

"Hello, everyone. Sorry I'm late."

"You're fine," Margaret said. "I understand it was official business that kept you."

Beverly's cheeks went a becoming pink. "Well, yes. I had to stop at the town office."

Diane laid a hand on her shoulder and looked around at the others. "Since it's going to be in the *Courier* tomorrow, I think it's all right to make a little announcement right here, don't you think?"

"Uh—well, I suppose so," Beverly said.

Diane smiled broadly. "It gives me great pleasure to present to you the newest candidate for mayor of Marble Cove, Beverly Wheeland."

"Yay!" Shelley clapped and bounced up and down. Margaret and the Lockes joined her applause.

"This is excellent news," Silas said. "Does this make two on the ballot now, or three?"

"Three," Beverly said. "There's Lee, of course, and Dennis was heading into the office with his papers when we came out. I wasn't sure if I should do this, but—"

"Now, my dear girl, don't go second-guessing yourself," Margaret said. "You're in it, and I'm glad. I think you will do a fabulous job if elected. Now—shall we head out to the cliff?"

"Yes, let's, before it gets any later," Beverly said.

Margaret picked up a tote bag and a metal detector.

"Oh, let me carry that for you," Silas said, and took the metal detector from her.

"Thank you. Diane, I hope you brought a spade."

"I did."

"And I've got Dan's metal detector, so we can have two working at once," Shelley said.

"Then off we go." Margaret smiled as she led them out the back door. Like Diane, she had no idea what they would find. Maybe nothing at all. But the flutter of anticipation was worth it, no matter how the expedition turned out.

★ ★ ★

Shelley rode in Diane's SUV with Diane and Beverly, while Margaret climbed into Reverend Locke's car with him and his sister. The reverend led the way, as he thought he knew a place to park on the road that skirted the headland.

"I wouldn't have any idea how to get up there," Diane said as she drove along behind him.

"Me either," Beverly said, "but I think he and Margaret will be good guides. They've both lived here a long time, and I know Margaret rambles around to find good painting spots."

In only a few minutes, they reached the place Reverend Locke had mentioned and pulled off onto a flat, grassy strip beside the road. Just beyond, a neglected path meandered uphill. The ocean wasn't visible from that point, as the rise of the ground hid it, but Shelley could hear the waves breaking on the rocky shore.

"Doesn't look like many people go up here," she observed. They all got out, and Diane opened the back of the vehicle so they could get out their equipment.

They carried the tools over to where Margaret was taking Allan's metal detector from the trunk of the reverend's car.

"I've been up there before, but it's been a long time," Silas said, gazing up the hill.

"Same here," Margaret said. "We took Adelaide up there once, but the railing was in bad repair, and it seemed like a dangerous place to be."

"If it's not fixed, maybe we should tell the town council," Diane said.

Shelley grinned at Beverly. "Or our next mayor."

Beverly smiled. "I'll make a note. If I'm elected, I'll certainly bring it up. And if I'm not, I'll make sure His Honor is aware of the problem."

The others laughed. They walked up the path chatting and enjoying the cool breeze off the ocean.

"I think the hot, muggy weather is done for the season," Margaret observed.

As they reached the top of the hill, the splendor of the sea burst before them. The headland protruded on the northern end of Marble Cove, and the face dropped in a nearly sheer cliff to the rocks below, but the top was covered in grass, weeds, and low bushes. Near the edge was a railing about two feet high made of peeled logs. It leaned outward, and in one section the rail had come loose on one end and hung down, leaving a gap near the brink of the cliff.

"I didn't think it was right on the very edge like that," Margaret said, frowning.

Reverend Locke stepped closer. "Looks like there's been some erosion. We'll need to be careful and not go too close to the railing."

"You're right," Diane said. "It looks like more of a warning than a solid barrier."

Shelley looked out over the rail. The tide was high, and the surf pounded the rocks below. She backed away from the edge and turned on her metal detector. "Margaret, do you want to take that side, and I'll take this one?" She waved to indicate the areas she meant.

"Sure." Margaret hefted her detector and looked around at the nearly flat, grassy hilltop. "It could be anywhere, I guess."

"*Hmm*," said Priscilla. "If I were going to bury a treasure, where would I do it?"

"Nearer the edge than not?" Beverly suggested.

"I don't know about that." Silas shoved his hands into his pockets and gazed about. "I'd think it's pretty rocky under this soil. I'm not sure it's the ideal place to bury anything."

"What *would* be the ideal place?" Diane asked. She turned on the small video camera she'd hung about her neck on a strap.

He smiled. "I guess if we knew that, we'd be digging already."

"Think like a pirate," Shelley said.

As on their outing at the cemetery, Diane walked along with Shelley, and Beverly went with Margaret. Silas and his sister followed slowly along with Margaret and Beverly.

Diane carried her spade and stuck the handle of a trowel in one back pocket and an empty plastic grocery bag in the other. Shelley reflected that this bright, sunny day was far different from their nighttime venture into the cemetery a few months before.

The detector beeped, and she stopped, sweeping it over the ground. "There's something here," she said.

Diane was filming, she realized.

"Just a sec. I wanted to film a little bit of the setting and you working that thing. Do it again."

Obligingly, Shelley moved the head of the metal detector back and forth, and the beeps were clearly audible.

"Great." Diane crouched and pushed the grass aside. "Can't see anything. Let me dig."

She took her spade and stepped on the top edge of the blade, shoving it through the tightly woven grass roots and into the ground. She turned over two scoops of earth, and Shelley ran the metal detector over them and the hole.

"I think you got it," Shelley said.

Diane pulled out her trowel and chopped away at the clods she had turned over.

Shelley caught the glint of metal. "There we go."

Wearing her work gloves, Diane picked out a quarter and rubbed the dirt off. "*Hmm*. 1980. A not-so-old treasure."

Shelley laughed and went over the spot a couple more times. "I'm afraid that's it for that hole."

"Go on," Diane said. "I'll fill it in."

They continued slowly searching the ground. Diane picked up a few pieces of trash and put them in the plastic sack. Fifteen minutes later, they heard some chatter over Margaret's way.

"Find anything?" Diane called.

"Maybe," Margaret said.

Diane stuck her spade in the ground to mark the spot where they'd left off, and she and Shelley hurried over to the others.

"There's something down here," Beverly said. She and Silas were kneeling and poking in the dirt, while Margaret and Priscilla watched. Diane turned on her camera and focused on Beverly and Silas.

"I hope it's not just another can," Margaret said. "We've got three already."

"We found one," Shelley said.

"Wait, I've got something." Reverend Locke sounded downright excited. Beverly leaned in and scooped away loose earth with her trowel, and a moment later he held up his prize—the rusted chassis of a toy truck. "Well, that's seen better days."

"Guess we're about even," Diane said. She and Shelley went back to their area.

As they worked their way closer toward the railing, Shelley encountered more signals. Their trove grew to include several more cans, two pennies, a large bent nail, and a washer about an inch in diameter.

A strong beeping again sent Diane to her knees. She separated the grass and let out a yelp.

CHAPTER TWENTY-TWO

W hat is it?" Shelley crouched beside her.

"Maybe something good." Diane held up a ring with a stone that gleamed in the sunlight.

"Wow." Shelley peered at it. "Looks like gold. What kind of stone is that?"

"It might be a birthstone." Diane examined the purple gem mounted on the gold setting. "Could be an amethyst." She turned the band about and squinted at it. "Look right there, Shelley. Does that say 18k?"

Shelley took it and stared at the inside of the band near the setting for the stone. "I think you're right. This could be worth something."

"Yeah, but it wasn't even down in the dirt," Diane said. "Just lying in the grass."

"Maybe some girl got mad at her boyfriend and threw the ring at him," Shelley said.

"*Hmm.* That might make more sense if it was a diamond. Well, let's go show the others." Diane rose, and Shelley walked with her to where their companions worked.

"We found something," Shelley told them.

"It's not ancient treasure, but it may be worth a few dollars." Diane held out the ring.

"Wow. I'll bet someone misses that." Beverly took it and held it close to examine it better.

"Do you think it's an amethyst?" Diane asked.

"Maybe. Or a tourmaline."

"What's that?"

"It's a stone that grows in Maine," Reverend Locke said with a faint smile.

Shelley laughed. "Good one, Reverend. I've heard of it, but I thought they were green."

"Some are," Beverly said, "but they can be purple too. There's a display at the state museum. Seems like I read tourmaline is found in a few other places too—like Brazil, maybe."

"Is it valuable?" Shelley asked.

"Not as valuable as the precious stones, but well-made tourmaline jewelry can be pricey." Beverly handed it to her.

"Maybe we should advertise and try to find the owner," Diane said.

Margaret nodded. "I think that's a good idea. It may have sentimental value, even if it's not worth a lot in dollars."

Priscilla held out her hand to Shelley. "May I see it?"

"Sure." Shelley handed it over, and Priscilla studied the ring.

"It's lovely. May I make a suggestion?"

"Of course," Diane said.

"If you took it to a jeweler, he could tell you what type of stone it is and the approximate value. But it looks like a nice piece to me."

"Let's put an ad in the *Courier,*" Shelley said. "Don't they have a lost and found column?"

"Yes," Margaret said, "but we'd need to word it carefully. We'd want the person to describe it in detail before we'd hand it over, I should think."

Priscilla passed the ring back to Shelley. "Yes, and you might ask them where they thought it was lost, though they might not have an inkling."

"I think Diane or Beverly should write the ad," Shelley said. "Diane's a whiz with words, and Beverly has written tons of business ads."

The two women looked at each other.

"We could work on it together," Diane said.

"I'm willing." The wind ruffled Beverly's hair, and she pushed back a strand. "But we ought to agree right now—if no one claims the ring and it's valuable, we should sell it and put the money toward the repairs at Old First."

"Of course," Margaret said.

Diane nodded. "I agree. That's our purpose in coming here—to find something that will help fix up the church."

"Count me in," Shelley said.

Reverend Locke smiled. "I think that's a wise and compassionate decision. Thank you, ladies."

Beverly looked at Diane. "Why don't you hang on to it, and we'll take it to a jeweler when we both have time."

"Sounds good to me." Diane pocketed the ring.

"Well," Margaret said, "that's something. Shall we proceed? I have a good feeling about this day."

★ ★ ★

Margaret swept the metal detector's head over the grass, listening for another series of beeps. Were they all crazy to be out here looking for treasure? She remembered Reverend Locke's reaction when he'd found them searching the graveyard. But he'd changed his attitude now. He and Priscilla seemed nearly as enthusiastic about the hunt as she and her friends were. Maybe the hints they'd found in old documents supporting the rumors of treasure had swayed him—and, of course, finding the ring hadn't hurt. Everyone was upbeat now, almost expecting more.

She was nearly to the edge of the precipice and the sagging railing now. A couple of feet from it, she stopped and extended the metal detector's handle forward. The instrument gave a high-pitched stream of beeps, and she jumped. Moving it slowly back and forth in front of her, she stood stock still.

"Sounds like something's there," Beverly said.

"Yes, but we're close to the edge." Worried, Margaret looked at Silas. "What do you think?"

"I think we'll need to be careful. We don't want to contribute to the erosion, and we certainly don't want to get too near the brink."

Priscilla chuckled. "I've always wondered what it would be like to practice brinkmanship—and here we are, on the verge of danger."

Margaret smiled. "Well, I guess we just choose our spot to stand carefully and dig in."

"Yes." Silas stepped forward with the spade. "Right here?"

"A little to the right, I think." Margaret moved the detector back and forth over the area. "*Hmm.*"

Beverly eyed her keenly. "I'm no expert, but that almost sounds like two separate finds."

"You may be right." Margaret lowered the head of the detector to earth. "Try here first, if you don't mind."

Silas placed the tip of the spade where she indicated. "There?"

She nodded.

Diane raised her video camera and began shooting. The other four women watched as Silas cautiously sank the blade and turned over the sod only a foot out from the fence and a yard to the side of one of the leaning posts.

Diane held the camera out to Beverly. "Do you mind?"

"Sure."

Shelley borrowed Beverly's trowel, and she and Diane knelt to chop apart the clod of dirt and grass while Beverly resumed recording the dig.

"I'm not finding anything," Shelley said after she'd chopped, pounded, and sifted her clod to bits.

Margaret put the metal detector over the spot where they were working, then swept it back over the hole. "I think you need to go deeper, Silas."

He chopped out another piece of sod and scooped two spadefuls of dirt beside it. Diane and Shelley went to work again.

"Nothing," Shelley said after a minute's work.

Silas dug out a couple more scoops. As Diane crumbled the clods with her trowel, it pinged on metal, and she let out a whoop. They all crowded close as she scrubbed the chunks of soil away.

"What is it?" Diane stood and held out a rusty, oddly-shaped piece of metal to Silas.

"Here, use this." Priscilla handed him a rag.

Silas rubbed away more dirt. "Some sort of hardware."

Shelley still crouched by the hole and was poking at the bottom of the depression with her trowel. "This looks like rotted old wood." She held up a sliver.

"And this..." Silas's jaw dropped as he stared down at the object in his hand, and he looked around at the five women. "I can't really believe this, but it's an old lockset."

He held it out toward Beverly so she could record the find. They leaned in to look, and Shelley jumped up to have her turn peering at the crumbly bit of old steel.

"A lock," Diane said reverently. "As in a lock from a chest?"

"Perhaps," Silas said, still staring at it. The rust had reduced it to a flaky lump, but they all could see the remains of an opening, shaped distinctively like a keyhole, though the edges were uneven and crumbly.

"It must have been," Margaret said softly.

Diane eyed her keenly. "Run your metal detector again, Margaret. You thought there were two objects."

Silas leaned on his spade and took out a handkerchief to wipe his brow.

"I can dig," Shelley offered.

Margaret switched on the metal detector and let it hover over the hole. The signal for metal was there, but it was faint. As she slowly moved the detector in a widening circle around the hole, the beeping grew louder, then faded. She zeroed in on the place where it put out the strongest signal.

"Over here, I think, but it's very close to the fence."

Shelley stepped up beside her. "Let me at it."

"Oh, be careful." Margaret stood back. They all watched as Shelley carved the hole into an ellipse, leading toward the edge of the cliff. "I don't like you getting so close and taking dirt away," Margaret admitted. She could imagine the edge of the bluff crumbling and Shelley slipping over the old fence and falling a hundred feet onto the rocks below.

"I'm okay." Shelley swiveled after each bite of the blade and emptied the dirt carefully to one side. Beverly gave the camera to Reverend Locke and crouched with Diane. Trowels in hand, they sorted through the debris.

"Not finding anything," Beverly said.

"Let me go deeper." Shelley raised the spade.

"No, wait. Let me check the hole first." Margaret gingerly stepped up and turned on her detector. After a moment's listening, she said, "Okay, but go a little to the left too. And be careful!"

"I thought it was all rock under here," Silas murmured, aiming the camera at the spot where Shelley was working.

Shelley dug out three more spadefuls and stepped back. "There you go, ladies."

"Perhaps we should have brought a screen," Priscilla said. "You know, like they use at archaeological digs."

"Hindsight is twenty-twenty," Silas said.

They stood in silence while Diane and Beverly chopped and stirred and rubbed away at the dirt.

Diane sat back on her heels. "How about another dig, Shelley?"

"Okay."

"May I help?" Priscilla sounded timid but hopeful.

Diane jumped up. "Of course you may. I'm sorry I didn't ask before if you wanted to do this. Take my trowel."

"If you're sure."

"Absolutely."

Priscilla knelt in the grass beside Beverly. Shelley turned over two more clumps of earth, and they attacked it with their trowels. The hole was now quite large.

"I'd say that's about eighteen inches deep," Shelley said. "How deep do we want to go?"

Margaret turned on the detector again and the two of them considered the sounds it emitted.

"I think you're in the right spot," Margaret said.

"Nothing in this pile except a few more wood fragments," Beverly reported.

Shelley's next scoop brought up another piece of hardware.

"I think it's a hinge!" Priscilla sounded as excited as Shelley. She carefully brushed dirt off the item and handed it to Margaret.

Margaret set down the metal detector, with the handle leaning against her leg, and peered at it. "That's what it is, all right. Maybe we'll find another to match it." She couldn't keep a quiver from her voice as she handed it to Diane.

"It's really looking like there was some sort of box here at one time," Diane said, extending the hinge for Silas and the camera.

"That's what I was thinking." Margaret smiled at her. "Wouldn't it be fantastic if we really did find Thorpe's treasure? Old First could be restored back to the way it was at its peak."

"Hey," Shelley said, "do you think that old key we found might fit this lock?"

Diane, who now held the rusted lock, said, "I don't think any key would go in it now. It's too far gone. But it might have once—a couple of hundred years ago."

"The size of the keyhole looks about right," Beverly said. "Of course, a lot of trunks and boxes had the same type of lock back in the old days."

"We can take the lock home and compare it to the key," Margaret said. "It wouldn't be conclusive, but if the size is a lot different, it would at least rule it out." She ran her detector over a fresh pile Shelley had overturned and was rewarded with strong, quick beeps.

"Sounds like we've got something here. Ladies..."

Beverly and Priscilla moved in, and in a few seconds, Beverly triumphantly held up the second hinge.

Shelley let out a little crow. "We are smokin' now!"

Beverly held it beside the first one. "Looks like a match to me—as near as we can tell, anyway. They've been in the ground a long time."

"You know," Priscilla said, looking up at her brother, "you could display the hardware and some of the wood fragments at the church. People would come to see them, and you could put a box out for donations."

"There may be something to that," Margaret said. "The Founders Day events were canceled, but we could still plan and set up a historical exhibit. If we can make the connection to Old First, these things would be a wonderful addition."

Diane frowned. "Yes, but what I'm wondering is . . . "

Everyone looked at her expectantly, and she gave a sheepish shrug.

"I just want to know what was in the box. If it's all rotted away, and there's nothing here but the remains of the box . . . "

"Maybe we just haven't gone deep enough," Shelley said.

Margaret looked at Diane. "I hate to say it, but maybe the contents were ephemeral—documents, for instance."

"Or banknotes?" Priscilla asked.

"Oh, that would be awful, if the money rotted away," Shelley said.

Silas squared his shoulders. "I don't see any evidence of that. I think we should continue. If the bottom of the box rotted, there could be something under the debris we've uncovered."

"That's true," Diane said.

Margaret was more than willing to continue the search. Shelley rose and got the second metal detector and began working it over the ground on the side of the hole opposite Margaret. Hers emitted a strong stream of blips.

"There's still something there. Diane, give me the spade!"

Margaret gritted her teeth. "I don't want to sound like a broken record, but please be careful, Shelley."

"You are near the edge," Diane said. "How about if I hold onto your belt, just to make sure you don't go over?"

Shelley laughed. "I'm fine, but if it makes you feel better, go ahead." As if to prove her security, she stepped down into the hole.

Margaret held her breath and sent up a quick prayer. *Lord, her heart is pure, even if she is a little reckless. Please protect her!*

Shelley cut into the small patch of sod left between the hole and the edge of the cliff. She chopped through the grass roots and gingerly scooped the clod back toward her. After tossing that up beside Beverly's feet, she scraped dirt from beneath it away from the edge. A few pebbles and clumps of earth tumbled over the brink, but the sound of the waves breaking below drowned out any noise they made when they hit bottom. Margaret had to force herself not to call out another warning. Diane held steadily onto the back of Shelley's belt while the digging continued.

"Hey!"

"What?" Diane asked.

Shelley thrust the handle of the spade behind her and crouched low. She reached forward and pulled something from the dirt at the very edge of the cliff.

"Is it just me, or does this look like a gold coin?"

CHAPTER TWENTY-THREE

B everly stared at the flat disc in Shelley's hand. Still covered with grime, it looked about the size of an old half dollar—or one of the heavy silver dollars from the last century.

"Here." Shelley gave it to her and climbed out of the hole.

Beverly tried to clean off the coin with her gloved fingers, and Reverend Locke offered her the rag his sister had brought.

"Thanks." Beverly took off her gloves and wiped several layers of dirt from the coin, and then rubbed gently with the cloth. "It's certainly a coin." The more she rubbed it, the more promising it looked. Her adrenaline began to flow. "I...I can hardly believe it, but I think it *is* a gold piece."

She handed it to Reverend Locke.

He held it close and squinted at it. "We should take this to a coin dealer. I don't think it's American."

"If it belonged to Jeremiah Thorpe, then it could be pre-American Revolution," Beverly said. "Maybe a Spanish dollar?"

"I'm not well versed in such things." Reverend Locke looked around at them. "However, it does seem to confirm those old stories."

Beverly smiled as it sank in. "We really found it."

"Well...part of it." Diane arched her eyebrows. "Doesn't it seem like there should be a whole pile of coins? Wouldn't the metal detectors be going crazy if there were?"

"They'd certainly be making more of a fuss than they are," Margaret said. "Shelley, get yours. Let's see if we find any more treasure."

Reverend Locke took the spade and sank it into the hole again, producing a loud thud.

"What was that?" Priscilla asked.

"The treasure?" Shelley leaned eagerly over the hole.

"Afraid not. I think the shovel struck rock that time." Reverend Locke poked about in the hole for another minute or two, but soon it was obvious that he was scraping stone. "I guess they buried it shallowly because that's all the dirt they had. Remember, we're on top of a rock outcropping."

"There could have been more dirt here in colonial times," Margaret said. "Wind and rain might have eroded it quite a bit."

"That's true," he said. "But if there's more treasure here, I don't think it's more than two feet deep."

They ran both detectors back and forth, over the hole, around it, along the bottom of the fence, with no further results. Shelley even poked hers out through the hole, under the fence, and down the cliff a few inches, but the reading showed nothing abnormal.

"I don't get it," she said.

"Maybe someone found it before we did," Beverly said slowly. "The box was already rotten, so they left it there and took the coins out. And they dropped one and missed it."

"That's possible," Reverend Locke said.

Diane went to her knees and crept toward the railing.

"Diane Spencer, what are you doing?" Margaret demanded sharply.

"I want to look over the edge. I have a theory."

"You'll fall."

"Somebody hold my feet, then," Diane said calmly.

Beverly chuckled and hunkered down. She grasped Diane's ankles. "Okay, Sherlock, do your thing."

Diane went flat on her belly and pulled herself forward. She stuck her head and shoulders under the bottom rail of the fence. Beverly could almost hear Margaret sucking in a breath, but she refused to think about it. Diane was one smart cookie, and whatever she had in mind probably made sense. Silas Locke turned on the video camera again, and Beverly gritted her teeth. How would Diane like that little twist? Of course, she wouldn't tell her until this was over and Diane was safely away from the cliff.

"Can you give me a few more inches?" Diane yelled.

"I'll help," Shelley said. She knelt and grabbed one ankle, while Beverly held the other. Diane inched forward another half foot, hanging down over the edge.

"I admit, ladies, Margaret isn't the only one watching who is nervous," Priscilla said.

"Okay! Bring me up."

Beverly and Shelley pulled Diane back, and she rolled over and sat up in the grass.

"What did you find?" Priscilla asked.

"Well, I think Reverend Locke is correct—the soil on top of this hill isn't very deep. Whoever put that box there probably dug as deep as they could and hit bedrock. But I also think that this rim of the cliff may have stuck out farther at one time. When this railing was put up, for instance. A couple of the fence posts are so close to the edge that they're exposed on the outer side for several inches below the surface here on this side. No one would put a fence that close to the edge."

Reverend Locke cautiously stepped closer to the railing and studied the bottom of the post nearest him, where it met the turf.

Diane glanced around at the others. "I'm thinking that when this thing was buried, it was close to the edge, but not this close. Maybe a couple of feet back from the brink. But over time, the soil has eroded, and after a hundred years—or two hundred, or whatever—one face of that rotting chest was right at the edge. Exposed to the weather, it probably deteriorated even quicker."

"What are you saying?" Margaret asked. "You think the coins fell out and down the cliff?"

Diane shrugged. "I think it's possible."

Margaret frowned. "But someone would have found it."

"Maybe someone did," Beverly said.

"You know," Reverend Locke said slowly, "Clyde Tanner told me once that someone found a gold coin on the beach when he was a child. I always thought he meant down on the part where people swim, but maybe not. What if he meant down there?" He pointed out beyond the railing. "What if somebody found one down among the rocks at the bottom of this cliff?"

"Not many people go there," Margaret said uneasily. "It's a mess of big rocks."

"Wait a minute," Beverly said. "Who is Clyde Tanner? Maybe we could ask him about that."

The Reverend Locke shook his head. "He passed away about a year after I came. He was in his nineties when I met him—a former deacon of the church. That man had a sweet spirit, and he told a lot of interesting stories. I've often wondered about that gold coin he mentioned. But I suppose it happened a hundred years ago. He didn't give me any details."

"But where are the rest of the gold pieces?" Shelley asked. "Would they be down there in the rocks?"

"I doubt it," the reverend said.

"Wouldn't the tide carry them out?" Diane asked.

Margaret shook her head. "Seems to me they'd settle in the sand or between the rocks. But we've had so many hurricanes over the years, and the outgoing tide is a strong force…"

"So there might be a few down there in the rocks," Shelley insisted.

"Don't you think people have searched down there before?" Beverly asked.

Shelley scowled. "Maybe they have, but they obviously didn't find all of the treasure. Can we go down there?"

"The tide is in now," Diane told her. "Most of the rocks are underwater. It would be pretty dangerous at any time, though."

"The water comes right up to the cliff most of the time there," Margaret said. "Diane's right. I don't think it would be safe to go there, even at low tide."

"There's another thing to consider," Reverend Locke added. "If it gets out that we found this up here, and what we think might have happened to the rest of it, lots of foolhardy people would try to find it."

"We don't want anyone getting hurt," Margaret said with a shudder.

Beverly nodded. Margaret had nearly drowned in these waters once, and she was no doubt thinking of that. No sense in starting a treasure-hunting frenzy that could lead to tragedy.

"They'd probably dig all the soil off this hill too," Diane said. "We're replacing our divots, so to speak, but if a hundred people came up here, it would be chaos."

Shelley raised her chin. "Listen!"

They all stood still. Over the sound of the breeze and waves pounding the rocks below, a faint strain of a deep, sonorous bell wafted to them.

"What is that?" Reverend Locke asked.

His sister frowned. "Isn't that the church bells?"

"No. It's...different. Deeper, for one thing."

Beverly and Diane stared at each other.

"It's the old bell," Beverly said.

Diane broke into a grin. "It sure is. I wonder if it means something."

"Maybe." Margaret smiled at them over the empty hole. "Maybe it means this isn't the end our quest. Maybe we still have a chance to save Old First."

ABOUT THE AUTHOR

Susan Page Davis is the author of more than forty published novels. A Maine native, she now lives in western Kentucky with her husband Jim. They have six children and eight grandchildren. Susan is a past winner of the Carol Award and the Inspirational Readers' Choice Award, as well as Heartsong Presents Favorite Author of the Year. Her novel *Captive Trail* won the 2012 Will Rogers Medallion for Western fiction.

A Conversation with Susan Page Davis

Q. How did you start writing fiction?

A. I've always loved reading fiction, and I wrote complicated stories even as a child. But I never thought I could actually sell my stories until I was well into adulthood. I worked for several years as a news correspondent and also wrote some magazine articles. It wasn't until I was forty-five years old that I decided to pursue a career in fiction. It was about two years before I sold my first short story to *Woman's World* magazine, and my first book was published when I was fifty years old.

Q. Many people dream of writing a novel one day. What advice would you give to a budding author?

A. Read a lot, write something every day, and connect with other writers. I didn't have much of a support group in my early writing days. I never joined a writers' group until after my first book was bought. Don't wait that long! There are wonderful online groups that you can access, no matter where you live. My favorite is

American Christian Fiction Writers (www.acfw.com). I would also advise attending at least one fairly large writers' conference if possible.

Q. Why is fiction such an effective tool for communicating truth?

A. Fiction lets the reader explore difficult issues in a safe place. We can see characters destroy their lives or build them up, without any danger to ourselves. The author can present options that the reader may not have considered, and in a form that is pleasant to ingest.

Q. The title of this book is Hopes and Dreams. *Do you have a short "bucket list" of yet unfulfilled hopes and dreams you'd like to share with your readers?*

A. Of course. I'd like to spend more time with all of my children and grandchildren. I would like to do more traveling, maybe with some of them. I've been to the U.K. once, but that was in college. I'd especially like to return there and visit my daughter Megan, who lives there now. I'd also like to see more of Europe and perhaps Australia and some other locations in the Pacific. I'd love to explore ruins in Mexico, Central America, and Peru. I'd like to take drawing lessons. And I'd like to make bread as good as my mother's.

Baking with Shelley

Banana-Chocolate Chip Muffins

¼ cup sour cream
1 teaspoon baking soda
½ cup butter, softened
¾ cup sugar
1 egg
1½ cups flour
¼ cup wheat germ (optional)
Pinch of salt
1 cup mashed bananas
1 cup semisweet chocolate chips
1 teaspoon vanilla

Preheat oven to 350 degrees. Stir sour cream and baking soda together. Set aside. Cream butter with sugar until light and fluffy. Add egg, beating well. Beat in sour cream mixture. Stir in remaining ingredients. Don't overmix. Spoon into greased muffin pans and bake for about eighteen minutes. Let cool before removing from pan.

FROM THE
GUIDEPOSTS ARCHIVES

This story by Hilary Hemingway of
Cape Coral, Florida, originally appeared in
the September 2002 issue of *Guideposts*.

My father was a commercial fisherman when I was
young and he had to spend long weeks at sea. One
day shortly after I'd turned ten, he was scheduled to be off
the coast of Jamaica. We were at our home in Miami. Mom
was washing the dinner dishes when her face drained of
color. "Mayday," she whispered.

Without even wiping her hands, Mom grabbed the phone.
She called the Coast Guard and told the man on duty that
she was concerned about her husband.

"Yes, ma'am, we know your husband sure did run into
some trouble," he replied. "They're having a heavy storm
and he radioed in for help when his boat started taking in
water. We flew out there about an hour ago and dropped
him a heavy-duty bilge pump."

"I don't believe that the pump is working," Mom insisted.
"You need to do another flyover."

The man tried to placate Mom. "He must be all right, Mrs. Hemingway, or we would've heard from him."

"You haven't gotten a Mayday?"

"No, but we'll let you know if we hear anything." Mom hung up. Without saying a word, she went into her bedroom and knelt by her bed. An hour passed. Mom came out, looking even more anxious. She called the Coast Guard again. This time she had steel in her voice. "You had better send a plane out right now or you'll be retrieving the bodies of Leicester Hemingway and his crew."

They said they would send out a rescue plane as soon as possible.

Mom was awake that whole night praying. Early in the morning the phone rang. It was the Coast Guard. They had found my father and his crew floating in debris fifteen miles off Jamaica. Dad's boat had sunk, but all were safe.

Dad arrived home that same afternoon, weary and sunburnt. "The bilge pump they dropped didn't work fast enough," he said. "Too much water was coming in. It started pouring over our transom. I radioed in a Mayday, but my call never got through."

But it had—to Mom.

Read on for a sneak peek of the next exciting book in
Miracles of Marble Cove!

Ringing True
by Patti Berg

The first hint of Tuesday's early morning light slipped through the window of Beverly Wheeland's office and streaked across her computer screen, highlighting the list of campaign slogans she'd been working on since long before dawn. Running for mayor of Marble Cove had seemed to be such a manageable endeavor when she'd entered the race. Now she was faced with the most daunting task: searching for a slogan. The words to describe her cause—her campaign platform—could make or break her efforts to win the election.

With the mayoral race on her mind, and the sound of the surf drifting in through the open window, she quickly saved her file and swallowed her last few drops of now cold coffee. Slipping her feet into her running shoes, she tied the laces, did a few routine stretches, and jogged down the stairs.

The scent of sausage frying on the stove drew her to the kitchen. She hadn't expected her father to be up already, but he was standing at the counter, slicing a Red Delicious apple, still dressed in his pajamas, the robe her mother had given him the Christmas before she'd passed away, and his favorite, well-worn slippers.

"Good morning." She pecked him on the cheek and he greeted her with a smile.

"Want some turkey sausage and make-believe eggs, with one of Shelley's sugar-free oatmeal cookies on the side?"

"Thanks, but I had a yogurt earlier."

"You don't eat enough to keep a bird alive," her father said, shaking his head.

Beverly ignored the comment, which was one of her father's favorite refrains, and plucked a wedge of apple from her mother's pink Depression glass fruit bowl. "This'll tide me over until I get back from my run."

A moment later, she slipped out the front door, standing in the midst of her father's beautifully landscaped garden. Earlier in the year, she'd helped him nurture the hydrangeas he and her mother had planted years before, and their blooms were once again amazingly large and a deep, dramatic blue. A hummingbird darted among the rosy mauve blossoms of the clematis climbing up and around the porch, and the flowers cast off a light, sweet scent that mingled with the salty sea air. She took a long, refreshing breath, realizing—not for the first time—just how much she had come to love living in Marble Cove.

Beverly did some more stretches, and then began her run. She started out slowly, warming up, then gained speed as she made her way to the boardwalk. She had the place all to herself this morning. It seemed ages since that had happened. Vacationers had flocked to Marble Cove over the summer, but the past three days—Labor Day weekend—had, she hoped, seen the last of the summer rush.

She'd recently managed to thwart a land developer's efforts to build a major resort complex in Marble Cove, and she'd won. Now she had to fight that same developer—Dennis Calder—for the job of mayor. She was determined to win, not just for herself, but for her community.

A cool breeze blew in off the Atlantic, whipping up and around the lighthouse. As she had many times in the last ten days, she wished Jeff Mackenzie was in town. She missed talking with him. Bouncing ideas off him. Feeling his hand in hers. The warmth of his smile. His kiss.

Russia was such a long way away, but that's where he'd gone this time. A photographic tour along a portion of the Trans-Siberian Railway. It was a good contract and nice money. He couldn't have turned it down. Still, she wished he were here.

She stopped running and sat down for a moment on one of the benches that had been installed for sightseers, so they could look out over the rocky coast and the Atlantic. Pulling out her cell phone, she hoped to find a message from Jeff, but she hadn't had one in days. Nothing said she couldn't send him a text message, though.

Her fingers started to punch in letters on the very small keyboard.

Any new pictures of St. Petersburg? The Kremlin? The contrasting faces of young and old? Something that will win you a Pulitzer Prize?

The ring tone announcing she had a text message sounded light and airy. Suddenly a photo of the golden domes of St. Petersburg's St. Isaac's Cathedral, with the purple and red glow of sunset as its backdrop, popped up on the screen, followed by Jeff's message: *Heading home tomorrow. See you soon.*

She closed her eyes and thought about their past, their present, and...and whatever the future might hold in store for them. Smiling, she stood and tucked her phone back into her pocket, twirled around, not caring if anyone was watching, and came to a stop with the view of Marble Cove stretching out before her. Its quaint houses. Its church spires. Its cobbled Main Street, planned and built well over a hundred years ago.

As Beverly began to run again, she spotted Silas Locke, the pastor of her church—Old First—walking in the opposite direction along the water. She slowed down, but he hadn't seen her, and she didn't call out. The almost always staid middle-aged man, with a nearly bald head, wore a windbreaker over a dark shirt and his clerical collar, and the bottoms of his black slacks were rolled up until they came close to showing off his knees. He looked deep in thought, with his shoulders slumped, as he had since the fire had destroyed Old First's roof and the town authorities insisted the church be closed until repairs could be made.

If only she and her friends could find the treasure they'd been hunting the past few months.

She slowed again to a walk and took in a deep breath, watching Reverend Locke walk up the beach, at last looking up from the sand toward high cliffs and a rugged stretch of coastline, where not all that long ago he, his sister, plus Beverly, Margaret, Shelley, and Diane, had taken metal detectors and found little more than rusty hinges, a lock, shards of what could have once been a box—and one intriguing gold piece.

The treasure they'd sought the past few months seemed to have disappeared over the centuries. Whether it had been found years ago by someone strolling the cliffs, they might never know. Maybe the box had rotted and the rest of the gold coins had simply worked their way down to the rocks below, then washed out to sea. Or maybe Reverend Thorpe—the eighteenth-century minister and founder of Old First Church, as well as the town of Marble Cove—had truly absconded with the money, as some centuries-old legends seemed to imply.

Beverly sighed. It would be so easy to think that they'd wasted their time looking for the treasure. But they'd heard the old church bells ringing as they searched the cliffs; softly, miraculously. The ringing was a sign; they'd been sure of it. A sign that the church was calling them back, letting them know that they needed to continue their search.

Beverly looked toward town, off in the distance spotting Old First's bell tower, a stoic sentry above the town. It was silent now. The congregation had been meeting at Diane's church since the fire. People were no longer allowed inside the sanctuary, yet she and her friends sensed—no, *knew*— that *something* of value had to be there in the church.

Running faster now along the beach, she turned her attention back to her campaign. Slogans again paraded through her head. She'd been told to keep them snappy and succinct, to tap into the core of human values—the community's values. She'd skimmed every book and Web site on how to run a campaign, but all her slogans felt lifeless and drab.

She was all alone on the stairs leading up to the lighthouse, and as she climbed each step, she recited the slogans, thinking they might sound better out loud. *"Beverly Wheeland—For You; for Marble Cove; for the Dream."* Definitely too cheesy, she decided, mounting the last step and running toward the lighthouse. Another slogan came to mind. *"Looking out for everyone, not just Number One!"*

Beverly shook her head. That was awful. Definitely not right for her campaign.

"Talking to yourself?"

Beverly recognized the familiar voice and whipped around to face Dennis Calder. Observing his attire—a business suit, tie, and shiny black tasseled loafers—she assumed he wasn't out for a morning jog.

"Hello, Dennis." She ignored his comment. "Beautiful day, isn't it?"

Dennis nodded. "Perfect for capturing a few good photos of the sunrise. My campaign Web site's about to go online, and I want to include a few pictures of our community, you know, what we have to offer…what we could offer."

Beverly's eyes narrowed. "Still trying to overdevelop Marble Cove, I see."

He sighed. "Look, Beverly. You might have succeeded in destroying my plan to build a resort complex here in Marble Cove," he said, "but I assure you, that's only temporary. Once we have a new mayor and like-minded town council members, I'm sure the complex will find its way back on the drawing board."

"But I'm going to be the new mayor, Dennis." She gave him what she hoped was a confident smile. "I'll have veto power, and I will not let the quaintness of Marble Cove be destroyed. I don't want that; neither do our citizens."

He'd chuckled throughout her argument. "Sorry to disappoint you, Beverly, but there is no way you can beat me in the mayoral race."

"You're mistaken. But on the off chance you do win—and that would take a miracle—you'd have a serious conflict of interest on your hands, if you try to get the resort approved."

He frowned, deep in thought. Hadn't the conflict-of-interest issue even crossed his mind?

She looked at her watch as she began to jog in place. "I'd best get going," she said. "I've a telephone conference in an hour, and—"

"Here. Take this along with you." Dennis thrust a colorful red, white, and blue tri-fold campaign flyer at her. She could see his name in big print, followed by the words "Prosperity and Progress." Though she didn't like the sentiment, she had to admit that, as campaign slogans went, it was pretty catchy. It spelled out Dennis' platform in three short, succinct words. No doubt it would make a lot of citizens of Marble Cove take notice. Could hers do the same?

Dennis turned away from Beverly and snapped another photo, just one more iconic shot of the Orlean Point lighthouse, before offering her a hasty salute and disappearing.

It seemed useless to argue with Dennis Calder. He had his ideas for Marble Cove and she had hers, and apparently the twain would never meet. Suddenly she had a deplorable vision of a Marble Cove of the future if Dennis had his way, awash in gaudy neon signs and her beloved Newport Avenue plowed under to make room for a casino.

She couldn't let that happen. She had to win.

Suddenly her slogan—her platform—came to her. It was perfect!

Beverly Wheeland: Embracing Marble Cove's Heritage.

A Note from the Editors

We hope you enjoyed Miracles of Marble Cove, published by the Books and Inspirational Media Division of Guideposts, a nonprofit organization that touches millions of lives every day through products and services that inspire, encourage, help you grow in your faith, and celebrate God's love.

Thank you for making a difference with your purchase of this book, which helps fund our many outreach programs to military personnel, prisons, hospitals, nursing homes, and educational institutions.

We also create many useful and uplifting online resources. Visit Guideposts.org to read true stories of hope and inspiration, access OurPrayer network, sign up for free newsletters, download free e-books, join our Facebook community, and follow our stimulating blogs.

To learn about other Guideposts publications, including the best-selling devotional *Daily Guideposts*, go to Guideposts .org/Shop, call (800) 932-2145, or write to Guideposts, PO Box 5815, Harlan, Iowa 51593.